Today, yet again, I sit back and consider the Friends with which the Lord saw fit to place me in my hour of need, and I am struck with awe at His goodness and mercies. For not only did He give me a family, not only did He give me companions, He prepared me to join a mighty force, fighting for His justice. I am but one of many Friends helping in this, my cause. And I am honored and humbled to be numbered among their ranks.

Prudence Willard
Marietta, Ohio
November 1858

SECRETS OF WAYFARERS INN

Family Secrets
River of Life
All that Remains
Greater than Gold
A Flame in the Night
Never the Twain Shall Meet
The Innkeepers' Conundrum
At Face Value
Moonlit Shadows
Picture This
Forget-Me-Nots
All the Inn's a Stage
Stolen Goodbyes
Red, White, and True
The Secret Ingredient
Submerged Surprises
Hushed October
Before It's Too Late
Mercy's Song
There's No Place Like Holmes

SECRETS OF
WAYFARERS INN

There's No Place Like Holmes

ROSEANNA M. WHITE

Guideposts

New York

Cover and interior design by Müllerhaus
Cover illustration by Greg Copeland, represented by Deborah Wolfe, LTD.
Typeset by Aptara, Inc.

Printed and bound in the United States of America
10 9 8 7 6 5 4 3 2 1

CHAPTER ONE

Tess Wallace slid the awkward box into the back seat of her car and then debated for a moment. She ought to just hurry back to the inn with it. That was the logical thing to do, and it was going to be a weekend of logic.

But it was also going to be a weekend of fun, and she just couldn't resist an early peek. Brandishing her most jagged key as a small knife, she sliced open the tape, folded back the flaps, and grinned in pure delight at the assortment of items Emma at Antoinette's Closet had been helping her find used and cheap.

A gust of wind tore down the street, slicing right through Tess's heaviest winter coat, but she ignored the shiver and reached inside the box. Emma, as always, had come through. Tess pulled out a deerstalker hat in red and tan tweed and put it on.

She felt Sherlockian already. And the assortment of fabric in the box proved that Emma had found other hats in a variety of colors. Browns, grays, a black, even one in pink-and-gray check. Chuckling a bit, she reached for a cherrywood pipe. Now, there also ought to be…yes! There on the bottom, the glint of old-fashioned magnifying glasses.

"Tess!"

She spun around, pipe still in her hand, unable to place the voice that shouted her way. Her brows drew down a bit when she spotted Sylvia Weber jogging toward her, hand waving. Her fingers were enveloped in purple gloves, and a matching ear-warmer headband held her waist-length blond hair back.

Tess waved with the hand not holding a pipe. Oh, heavens, she must look ridiculous. Her fingers fell to the hat covering her hair—though when another icy blast of wind whipped down the street, she was tempted to simply untie the flaps so they could protect her ears rather than take the thing off.

"I'm so glad I saw you! I was going to give you guys a call as soon as I got inside." Sylvia, all smiles, came to a halt a few feet away. "We just got the coolest donation in at the museum, and I knew you and LuAnn and Janice would want to see it right away." Then, of course, she narrowed her eyes, and her smile twitched. "Um…have I interrupted you on your way to a Sherlock Holmes convention or something?"

Tess laughed and swiped the hat from her head, wind or no wind. "Actually, yes. Well, sort of. We're hosting a little event at the inn this weekend. My uncle's club. The Sherlock Society."

Sylvia raised her eyebrows. "Your uncle runs a Sherlock Holmes club?"

"His lifelong passion." Tess nestled the hat and pipe back into the box and closed the flaps. Then she checked her watch and pressed her lips together. She'd be lucky to make it back to the inn before the society pulled in, but she shouldn't be rude to Sylvia. Though the Inn Crowd hadn't exactly gotten off on the right foot with this woman and her husband, Sylvia had been making a real effort to prove them worthy of the trust Maybelline had placed in them, handing over the reins of the Underground Railroad Museum this month while she was away on her honeymoon.

Tess fastened a smile in place. "He's a professor of English Lit at Oberlin. He started this club…oh, heavens, I don't even know when. A long time ago. Thirty or forty years, maybe."

"No kidding." A glint—interest?—lit Sylvia's eyes. "I've always been a bit of a Sherlock fan myself. Is this event at the inn open to the public?"

"I'm afraid not, no." Tess closed the rear door of her car but kept her smile in place. "Uncle Harold and his crew have booked the whole place, even though they only need six of the rooms, to guarantee quiet and privacy."

And frankly, Tess and her friends were looking forward to the quiet weekend too. Oh, there would be some heated debates going on in the parlor, no doubt. And an endless supply of hot water for tea and coffee would be required. But with only eight guests who probably wouldn't even leave the inn until they checked out on Sunday, it might be their easiest weekend all year.

And she'd get to see Uncle Harold. A pang of guilt struck her square in the stomach when she counted back and realized it had been a full two years since she'd hugged her favorite uncle. Her *only* uncle left, now, after Uncle Charlie passed away three years ago. The last of her father's generation, of the five

Westerfield brothers, and the one she'd always most enjoyed spending time with, other than her own father. Harold was a special one. An odd one, but a special one.

"Well, I shouldn't keep you then, if you have to get back to the inn to get ready for him." Sylvia backed up a step. A gust of wind snagged a strand of her long hair and deposited it directly into her mouth. She peeled it away with a comical glare. "Hope they make it in before the snow comes."

"Oh." Tess waved that away. "I really doubt we're going to get much of anything. It seems the meteorologists have become sensationalists lately—every storm's the biggest one of the century, according to them."

Sylvia chuckled. "Too true. Well, I'll get in touch later about that donation you guys will want to see, all right?"

Donation? Tess had to blink twice before she remembered that Sylvia hadn't just hailed her to say hello. She'd begun with something about a donation to the museum. "Sure, that sounds great. Anytime, really. You have our number?"

"Yep. Have a great weekend with your uncle, Tess."

"I will. Thanks." Lifting her hand in a wave as Sylvia turned, Tess pulled open the driver's door and climbed in. There *were* a few snowflakes in the air, already drifting down, swirling here and there when another gust of wind went by, but they didn't look particularly ominous.

Even so, she whispered a prayer that any weather would hold off while her eighty-four-year-old uncle was driving the three hours from Oberlin. Because they all knew he wouldn't turn the wheel of his ridiculous van—painted with the famous

Sherlock silhouette and the titles of each and every one of Sir Arthur Conan Doyle's popular stories—over to anyone else.

Man, she missed him. After checking traffic, she pulled out onto the street and pointed her car toward home. The inn had made it a bit hard to get away for a weekend lately. And she didn't exactly encourage Uncle Harold to drive this far very often. Frankly, she'd feel a whole lot better if he limited his driving to around his own town, during daylight hours.

But there was no convincing him of such things. Good grief, the man still taught two classes a semester! Retirement, he'd claimed twenty years ago, just didn't suit him. And since he remained one of the most popular professors at Oberlin, apparently the college hadn't argued with him.

At any rate, she was so glad he'd had this idea for a getaway for his club. They had a lot of catching up to do. And she'd planned a big family lunch for Sunday—Lizzie and Michael and the kids were coming over, and Jeff Jr. They hadn't seen their great-uncle in even longer than it had been for Tess.

A few minutes later she was pulling into the inn's parking lot, noting a distinct absence of Sherlock-themed vehicles in the lot. Good—she'd beaten him here. Claiming her box of goodies from the back seat, she hustled into the inn's kitchen entrance.

Winnie looked up with a smile from her place at the counter. "Success?"

"Emma, as usual, outdid herself. I have no idea how she found all this stuff for next to nothing, but I'm grateful." She smiled at the rows of unbaked Cornish pasties on cookie sheets. "I see you've outdone yourself too."

"You know me—I love an excuse to try something new." Winnie grinned as she crimped the edge of a meat pie with a smooth maneuver. "The fridge is packed with classic British foods for the weekend for the society. I've left instructions on heating them, in case I don't make it in with the snow."

"I seriously doubt it's going to snow that much. But thanks." Tess aimed herself toward the café, and from there toward the front desk.

She found Janice behind it, the phone clamped between shoulder and ear as she clicked the computer's mouse. She wore a tight smile and a frown in her eyes. "Uh-huh. Yes, I totally understand, Mrs. Kelly. We do extend our cancellation policy in such cases, I assure you. Just give us a call on Sunday morning, and we'll be happy to let you know how the weather's looking." Janice typed something in then shifted so she held the phone in her hand. "Uh-huh. You too. Goodbye now."

She ended the call with a loud exhale and looked to Tess. "Yet another Sunday guest concerned about whether they can cancel if we get a blizzard."

"All this hype—we'll probably be lucky to get an inch." Tess shook her head and deposited the box behind the front desk. "But as long as Uncle Harold doesn't cancel."

Laughter sounded, not just from Janice, but from the parlor, and LuAnn joined them at the desk a moment later. "You know very well that nothing as mundane as a snowstorm could keep the professor from a weekend of mystery-solving." She motioned toward the sitting area. "I've got the corkboards and whiteboards set up for them, as requested."

"And I've been dusting off my violin skills." Janice made a face. "Goodness gracious goat, but they're rusty! I need to practice my other instruments more often instead of always turning to the piano."

Tess slid the box onto the desk and grinned. It was true that they always took care to make sure their guests were comfortable, but this was more than that. This was her friends going above and beyond for *her*, and for the uncle they knew she'd missed. "Thanks, guys. Guess I'd better take care of all this stuff." She patted the box.

Her friends chatted while she unloaded the hats and pipes and magnifying glasses, making predictions about the weather, the state of the rooms after the last guest checked out this morning, the lunch crowd at the café. And then Janice asked, with a teasing note in her voice, "So where's Brad taking you for dinner tomorrow?"

Tess glanced up from her arranging of pipes just in time to see the pretty pink flush in LuAnn's cheeks. "Spagna's, I think. We're both in the mood for Italian."

Tess was tempted to add a bit of teasing of her own—she couldn't be happier that LuAnn and Brad were finally exploring the possibilities of something more than friendship—but when she glanced up, her gaze snagged on the giant Sherlock silhouette slowing in front of the inn, turn signal flashing. "They're here!" It came out a little squealing, a little girlish. But her friends clapped, looking nearly as giddy as she felt. "I'm going to go help them in."

"I'll cover the door," Janice said.

LuAnn picked up the empty cardboard box. "And I'll get rid of this."

The cold wind bit again the moment Tess stepped outside, but she ignored it and zipped up the coat she'd not yet gotten around to taking off. She hurried toward the lot, getting there just as the van stopped, snug in one of the many parking spaces.

Her beeline for the driver's door hitched when the passenger door opened first, and her uncle's lined face emerged, wreathed in a grin. "Tessie!"

A pang followed the hitch. He *hadn't* been driving? Confusion warred her relief, both of which she covered with a grin as she rushed into his open arms. "Uncle Harold!"

He gave her his signature hug—both arms squeezing tight until she gasped, a chuckle in her ear—and then he set her back, hands on her shoulders, as he'd done as long as she could remember. "Well, my girl, I'm sad to report that you've not grown an inch since last I saw you."

She laughed—as she'd been doing every time he said that since she was fourteen. "As long as I'm not shrinking."

"Did you get the gift I sent you for Christmas?"

In answer, she lifted her foot and tugged up her pant leg a few inches to show off the socks he'd sent—tan, with dark brown Sherlock silhouettes, complete with deerstalker and pipe.

"I couldn't resist when I saw them," he said with another chuckle. "And who better to send them to than my sleuth of a niece? Graham, did I tell you how this young lady and her friends have actually solved a few mysteries lately? Does a heart proud."

The sliding door of the van had of course opened by now, and Tess turned to see which of the collection of literature lovers within answered to Graham. She'd met quite a few of her uncle's club members over the years, but they came and went as their lives took them to and from the college. She'd never met Graham.

He was a thirty-something fellow with curly hair and glasses. Brown eyes twinkled behind them. "You may have mentioned it a time or ten on the drive here, Professor."

"When you weren't shouting at me to turn the wheel." This came from a feminine voice that sounded a bit testy. A moment later, the owner of said testy voice rounded the van.

"Matti!" Tess held out her arms for the woman she knew was one of Uncle Harold's best friends—a professor of Classic Languages at Oberlin, a few years younger than Tess. They'd met quite a few times over the last thirty years and had always gotten along like cousins. Appropriate, given that Matti had claimed Harold as a father.

Matti's smile was stiff though, as was her hug. "Hey, Tess. Good to see you. I hope you have a medal ready for me, for actually convincing this lug to let me drive."

Tess grinned. Maybe Matti was just stiff from what could have been a stressful drive. "How about a cup of something hot?"

"Even better. Come on, crew. Bud, can you get our bags?"

"Already got 'em, honey." Bud—Matti's husband—had opened the back doors and was handing out luggage to the half-dozen other Sherlockians who had climbed down from the van.

"I've got yours, Professor," another unfamiliar man proclaimed.

"My gratitude, Tom." He hooked an arm around Tess's shoulders. "Lead the way, Tessie."

She did, and Janice held the door open for them as they neared, the group of eight—nine, counting Tess—entering with banter enough to prove them all good friends, despite the sixty-year age range between Harold and the youngest member, who was a student at Oberlin.

Once inside, Uncle Harold let go of Tess so he could hold out his arms toward LuAnn, who was covering the desk. "CC!"

LuAnn laughed and came around to hug him.

Matti, just behind Tess, sighed. "I thought her name was LuAnn."

"It is. CC is for—"

"Carbon Copy," Uncle Harold said, tweaking LuAnn's nose. "This one is just like me, aren't you, my girl? An English teacher, a lover of mysteries and stories of all varieties, and even a confirmed bachelor."

"Actually," Janice put in from the door she was just closing, "she's seeing someone."

Uncle Harold splayed a hand over his heart. "Ah, she cuts me to the quick! Abandoning our brotherhood!"

LuAnn rolled her eyes and returned to the desk. "Let's get you all checked in, shall we?"

There was a bit of chaos as they checked everyone in, let them all pick hats and pipes, much to their delight, and then got them settled in their rooms. Tess and her friends turned to the café while the visitors were upstairs, prepping the tea and coffee and a few snacks that Winnie brought out.

The crew was tromping down the stairs again en masse when the front desk phone rang. Being closest, Tess picked it up. "Hello, Wayfarers Inn, how may I help you?"

"Hey, Tess. It's Sylvia, from the museum. I just wanted to check and make sure Jim got there okay."

"Jim?" Tess turned to survey the group of mystery lovers. There was a Tom and a Hiram and an Ollie, but no Jim that she could recall. "I'm sorry, Jim who?"

"Jim Sutherland. I sent him over with the chair."

Her brows drew together. "With the *what?*"

"The chair—that donation I started to tell you about on the street? I wanted to make sure he got it unloaded okay before the snow hit."

Tess looked up, out the windows, and gasped. Those few little flakes swirling around had invited their friends. The world outside was now a blur of racing snowflakes, and the ground and trees and shrubs were covered. "Oh goodness! When did that start?"

"About fifteen minutes ago. But Jim should have had time to get there and get it unloaded. I was expecting him back by now."

Tess turned to LuAnn and Janice, who had apparently been drawn her way by the incredulity in her tone. She lifted her brows. "Has anyone seen a delivery man with a chair?" she asked the room. After receiving nothing but blank looks and shaking heads, she turned back to the phone. "Did you send him to the rear door, Sylvia?"

"That's where I told him to go, yes. You have a loading dock there, right?"

Janice hurried off to check with Winnie, who would have seen anyone coming toward the loading dock, but soon reported that no one had arrived at the inn save the Sherlock Society.

"Weird," Sylvia said in reply. "I wonder where he could have gone. He was in a truck, so he shouldn't have had any problem in the snow. Man, I hope he's not out in it with that chair in the back!"

Tess switched the phone to speaker mode so LuAnn and Janice could hear. "What exactly is this chair, Sylvia?"

"An antique. A local bought it from an estate sale and was going to have it reupholstered but donated it to us instead. As they dismantled it, they saw a stamp on the bottom for Quaker Inn Station. Do you know of it? An inn out in Chester Hill during the Underground Railroad days—they were very active in the UR. Anyway, there was also a bullet lodged in the thing, and a rolled-up photograph in a hollowed-out leg that had Prudence Willard in it. I knew you guys would want to see it."

Tess looked up to meet the gleam in her friends' eyes. "We definitely would, yes. But why did you send the whole chair instead of just the photograph?"

"Because it's a chair with a bullet in it! How cool is that?" Then Sylvia's tone grew serious. "What in the world could have happened to Jim though? He's not answering his phone."

And the roads, despite being treated, were covering fast. "He has to be somewhere between the museum and the inn—it's not that far. Want us to help you look for him?" Not how she'd planned to spend her evening, but there were worse things than a twenty-minute walk in falling snow.

"You'd do that? Oh, that would be great. I'll start at this end. Jim's about thirty, fair hair, gray eyes, and he was in a 1980s Chevy truck. Gold. Hideous thing, but it goes great in the snow."

"Okay. We'll head out now from our end and see if we spot him." She disconnected and spun, intending to reach for her coat and hat.

She found her uncle holding both—and wearing his own, along with a grin of pure mischief.

Tess sighed and took her coat from him. "Thanks. Now you go get your club started. You've got a lot to talk about, don't you?"

"Don't be ridiculous. You know how I love walking in the snow. And this?" He motioned toward the phone and pulled the wool hat Janice had knit for Tess onto her head for her. "You're not going off sleuthing without *me*, young lady. If you three are out on another adventure, the Sherlock Society is coming along."

This Jim fellow being late was surely no great mystery—but that wouldn't stop Uncle Harold from turning it into one. Tess zipped up her coat and surveyed the all-too-eager collection of society members poised behind him.

So much for a quiet weekend.

CHAPTER TWO

They turned the last corner, and somehow Tess wasn't surprised when she saw that the only cars parked along the street were a few snow-covered sedans. No trucks, "hideous gold" or otherwise. And no moving vehicles passed them at all. It seemed most of Marietta had already hunkered down on this Friday night to wait out the storm. The only life to be seen was a man walking his dog at the other end of the street, the exhaust billowing out of one of those parked cars—evidence that someone would *soon* pass them, she supposed—and their own group.

Tess pulled her hat a little lower over her ears. "Maybe he didn't head to the inn at all. He could have put the wrong address in his GPS or something. Gone the other way entirely."

"Or decided it was a crazy errand on a snowy night and just headed home." LuAnn was barely identifiable, between her hat pulled low and scarf tugged high. Tess had to grin at her.

Uncle Harold planted his hands on his hips and surveyed the scene before them. "Well, take notes, my detectives. One never knows when something might be just the clue we need. Ollie, Kim, any tracks of interest?"

Tess exchanged an amused glance with LuAnn and Janice before glancing over to the young married couple that had walked the entire way with their eyes glued to the road...and their arms charmingly entwined, laughing their way along the streets.

Ollie shook his head. "There were no tracks at all that led from the inn, and the others we picked up along the way all made different turns. None seem to have originated here—assuming the snow and other cars didn't obliterate any, that is."

"Really hard to say with the snow still coming down though." Kim offered a cheerful grin. She'd claimed the pink and gray deerstalker and looked adorable in it, which her husband had been quick to point out as they'd left the inn.

"Well, excellent attention to detail." Uncle Harold grinned at them and then leaned close to Tess. "They met at a club meeting four years ago, you know. Brought together by Sherlock."

Tess nodded. "I remember you mentioning something about that when they got married. So sweet."

A *click* came from just ahead and then a whir. A sound that Tess had all but forgotten existed until twenty minutes ago, when Hiram first got out his new Polaroid camera—she hadn't even realized there *were* new models, but he had one complete with a rain cover to protect it from the snow—and started documenting their walk.

The idling car eased out, so slowly it would have been funny were it not so wise.

"That's the museum?" Hiram pointed at the brick building across the street, whose sign was partially obscured by snow.

Janice nodded. "That's it."

He took another photo of it. "No lights on."

He had a point, and Tess frowned. "Let's go over and see if Sylvia's still there." If not, if this Jim guy had shown up, Sylvia would have called again, right? That would have been polite.

The car puttered by at a snail's pace, the young woman in the driver's seat gripping the wheel and leaning forward, obviously nervous at driving in the snow. Tess couldn't blame her. If given her druthers, she stayed off the roads in weather like this too.

Once the car had ambled by, their group crossed the street, a few of the society members slipping a bit and laughing over it. Tess cast a glance over at Uncle Harold—a slip was the last thing he needed—but he looked as sure-footed as a mountain goat. Just like she remembered him being in the snow. She recalled countless snowy weekends as a girl when he'd shown up to take her sledding or ice skating. He was a decade younger than her father—the youngest of the five brothers, where Dad had been the oldest—and had always been the fun-loving one.

He'd have made such a great father. She'd waited for years to hear he'd found someone and was settling down, but it had never happened. Maybe the right woman had never come along. Or maybe he was just too set on being like his fictional hero, a confirmed bachelor.

Heavens, she sure hoped that had nothing to do with it. What an empty reason for making life choices.

Janice, on Tess's left, lifted a hand to shield her eyes from the snow and squinted. "Is that a note on the door?"

"Looks like it," LuAnn said. "Or some sort of paper, anyway."

Tess stepped up on the curb in front of the museum, though she hung back a moment as Hiram wielded his camera yet again. Another of the members—Tom, the youngest of the crew—took a few photos as well, but with his phone.

Hiram elbowed him with a teasing smirk. "You know that's useless, right? We can't exactly all look at the ones you take on there. Or tack them to the bulletin board."

Tom elbowed him right back. "Yeah, well those tiny little prints that pop out of there aren't exactly useful either. At least with mine we can zoom in and project them onto a screen if we need to. I'm telling you, I should have brought my flat-screen and—"

"Blasphemy!" Hiram laughed and pulled the photo free of his camera. He opened his coat and, shielding the photo from the snow, he waved it back and forth for a moment and then tucked it into the camera case with the others he'd taken. "Sherlock would be horrified."

"Nonsense." Uncle Harold clapped Hiram on the shoulder and winked at Tom. "He all but invented criminology—I daresay he'd be using any technological advances that could aid him in it."

"Dollars to donuts he'd have had the first camera phone on the market." Tom tucked his phone into his pocket and flipped the finger flap back down on his convertible gloves.

Janice was squinting with interest at the gloves rather than either of the cameras. "I bet I could knit those."

LuAnn laughed and stepped up to the door. "Okay, let's see what this says, shall we?"

It was definitely a note, Tess verified as she drew nearer too. And it was addressed to "The Wayfarers Crew." Her eyes flew over the lines as LuAnn read it out loud.

I tried to call you at the inn but was directed to voice mail, and I don't have your cell numbers. We decided we'd better get home before the snow gets worse. Still don't know what Jim has done with the chair, but he just posted a photo of himself on Facebook, so he's obviously fine. We'll figure out the rest tomorrow. Thanks for your help!

"Interesting." Uncle Harold leaned closer to study the paper.

Tess lifted her brows. "What's so interesting? It's a rather reasonable explanation. On Sylvia's part, anyway. I hadn't thought to give her my cell number, and we did tell Winnie to head home. We usually set the inn phones to forward to one of our cells if no one is working the desk, but I guess we forgot."

"No, I did it." Janice patted her pockets. And then pursed her lips. "But then I guess I forgot my phone."

Uncle Harold waved his fingers. "No, no, that's not what I find interesting. Not the message. The paper itself. Have you documented it, chaps?"

Hiram and Tom both leaned in for another photograph.

"Ooh, let me guess. The paper could be a clue. Is there a watermark? It's probably made from some rare cotton rag whose fibers originate in a remote African village where, if we were to trace it, we'd find there's also a manufacturer of hideous gold paint." LuAnn raised her brows. "Am I right or am I right?"

Uncle Harold chuckled and carefully pulled the paper from the door. It came easily, the tape obviously not willing to fight the elements. "I was more interested in the writing. Seems a bit odd that your friend would type a note rather than writing it by hand, doesn't it?"

"Well, now that you mention it…" Janice tilted her head to the side. "Maybe she has terrible handwriting?"

"Possibly. Matti? What do you think?"

They all turned around to see what Uncle Harold's right-hand woman might have to say, but Matti wasn't even looking at the door or the note. She was leaning against the side of the building, staring out at the snow. At the speaking of her name, she heaved a sigh and nodded toward her husband. "Bud will put it in the backpack to keep it dry on the walk back to the inn."

"Sure thing." Bud obligingly slid the pack he was carrying off his back and unzipped the largest pouch. Tess blinked at what she could see of the contents. An empty folder, into which he tucked the damp paper, but also a collection of baggies, rubber gloves, tweezers, small vials…

"Evidence collection kit." Bud grinned up at her, LuAnn, and Janice—the only ones who probably looked surprised at what he was dragging around Marietta with him. "The professor won't let us go anywhere without it."

"What kind of detectives would we be if we didn't have those things?" Uncle Harold handed over the paper and then struck a pose, arm extended as if waving a banner. "Sally forth! Tallyho! Back to the inn!" He winked at them. "Methinks we could best sort through the evidence over a nice dinner. Whatever your lovely cook had going smelled divine."

"I could eat." Tom tucked his phone in his pocket again.

Graham started back to the sidewalk, snorting a laugh. "You can *always* eat."

"I'm a growing boy."

Tess smiled and linked her arm with her uncle's again. Partly to make sure he didn't slip on the transition from protected doorstep to snowy sidewalk. Mostly just because she'd missed him. "It's a good group you have here," she said once they were walking again, the society half leading the way and half bringing up the rear. They'd formed little clusters of twos and threes and were bantering in much the way Tess and her friends did, seeming to enjoy the snow.

Uncle Harold surveyed them with a proud eye. "It is. It's always a good group, but this particular membership is among the best we've had. We always have a wonderful time together. Now"—he shot her a smile and patted her glove-covered hand on his arm—"give me the latest on those great-great-niece and nephews of mine."

She regaled him with stories of the triplets as they walked back, their conversation frequently interrupted by exclamations from either the Sherlock Society or Tess's friends. As they stomped the snow off their boots and entered the inn again, Tess had to grant that her dismissal of the storm may have been premature. They'd been out there maybe an hour, and there were already several inches.

"We'll get dinner set out for everyone while you put your things away," LuAnn announced to the crowd.

Tess took care of her snow-covered gear, grabbing LuAnn's and Janice's stuff too, while they hurried to the kitchen. Within a few minutes, the café area was filled with the laughing, chattering society, and Tess was helping carry out the soup and bread that had been warming in the kitchen.

One of the guests must have fetched the whiteboard LuAnn had set up in the parlor too, because Kim stood at it, marker in hand. She'd neatly written three things and was even enumerating them. "Okay, so for our short story, we've got 'A Case of Identity.' Novel this time is *The Valley of Fear.*"

"Long live Moriarty!" Graham waved a napkin in the air like a flag.

"How many times do I have to tell you, Graham—he is *not* Sherlock's archnemesis. He's only in two stories!" This from Bud, who added a sad shake of his head, as if Graham's opinion were a cause of great despair.

Kim smirked and pointed to the last item on her list. "And in an interesting turn, our *real* mystery, which the professor has dubbed 'The Adventure of the Gold Truck.'"

Tess unloaded her baskets of bread onto the two tables the club had taken up. She helped Janice deliver the bowls of soup and then stood with her friends at the back of the room, out of the way.

"I doubt the disappearing truck is really that mysterious," LuAnn said quietly, as the guests continued their banter. "But I *am* curious about this chair Sylvia was sending over. Where did she say it was from? Quaker...?"

"Quaker Hill? Or Station? Or..." Tess pursed her lips. "Quaker something."

"Chester Hill—that's where she said it had been, I think." Janice started out of the café, toward the office. "Let's see what we can find."

After telling Uncle Harold where they'd be if anyone needed anything, Tess followed LuAnn and Janice toward the office and its computer. Janice was already typing by the time Tess pulled up a chair, but she didn't bother sitting down when she saw that the list of hits was rather generic. Gas stations, Ohio Quaker gatherings in general. But one was a reference to a book. "Wait, I think we have that, don't we? The Washington County Underground Railroad one?"

"We do." LuAnn sprang to her feet and raced out the door before Tess could even wonder which shelf it would be on.

Chuckling, she sat down. "We'll just leave finding it to Librarian Lu. Can you click on that, Janice?"

"Sure." A moment later, a scan of a page in the book popped up.

Tess leaned close enough to read it on the screen. No photos of the place had ever been found, apparently, but Quaker Inn Station of Chester Hill had been an active part of the Underground Railroad.

"Interesting," she muttered, hooking an arm on Janice's chair. "Chester Hill—I assume that's modern Chesterhill, just two words instead of one. So only, what, twenty miles from Marietta? Maybe thirty? Not very far."

"Considerably farther in the nineteenth century than it seems to us. That would be about a day's travel from here, right?"

Tess nodded. "Prudence probably knew someone from there, since they worked toward the same goals."

"Got it." LuAnn bustled back in, the thin, glossy book in hand.

"Page thirty-five," Janice said, pointing at the number visible on the bottom of the scan.

LuAnn read the page aloud to them as she took her seat again, though the information was pretty sparse. According to the book, the inn was run by Quakers who often helped escaping slaves along...but as they were also open to the public, they frequently hosted the slave hunters seeking them too.

"Interesting." Janice leaned back in the cushy executive chair.

Tess sat back in her harder version too. "Hmm. We've certainly learned that the Quakers in the area did a lot to help with the Underground Railroad through the years, so that's no surprise. My question is...what does a chair with a bullet in it have to do with the Underground Railroad?"

CHAPTER THREE

Duck Creek,
Marietta, Ohio,
September 1858

Prudence tucked her scarf more securely into her coat and dug the knitted gloves out of her pockets. Though the day had been warm, a chill had come upon the area with the setting of the sun, and it was doing its best to gnaw through her clothes. She wouldn't be surprised if there was a frost tonight. When she'd set out from the farm, the temperature had already dropped to forty. Patience had honked her disapproval and retreated into her nest of hay in the barn, obviously wanting nothing to do with Prudence's jaunt into the cool night.

Jason's lips had thinned as well, but he'd only handed her the scarf she now wore and said, "The air will be cold this night. Be warm—and stay dry."

She'd smiled up at him and assured him she would be. Warm, dry…and careful. Hunkering down behind the foliage that would be fiery reds and oranges in the daylight, she prepared to wait for the fugitives she'd be helping tonight. Two of them, the message had said. Her job was to rendezvous with them here and lead them silently to the hotel and its secret room.

When exactly they would arrive from the Virginia side of the river, she couldn't be entirely certain.

Her stomach rolled, objecting to the dinner she'd made herself eat an hour earlier. She'd forced it down, knowing she'd need the energy tonight. But she hadn't much wanted to.

Her hand splayed over her churning middle. Another month of disappointment. No child.

Her eyes stung. Perhaps it was a mercy. The Lord's way of sparing her another loss. Maybe it was better not to hope than to suffer the pain each time she lost a babe.

A twig snapped, jarring Prudence from her thoughts and the prayer that had formed on its heels. She peeked out from the cover of the autumnal leaves, eyes willing the darkness to give up its secrets. It could be nothing but an animal, she knew. It could be the couple she was meeting. Or it could be an enemy. She wouldn't budge until she knew for sure.

Seconds later, a dark shadow stepped into view, the moonlight shining upon a frightened face. Her contact—his wife must be behind him, still hiding. Jason certainly would have insisted upon going first, if he and Prudence were the ones running north toward freedom.

"Over here," she said in a whisper, raising up just enough that he'd be able to see her head.

The man turned toward her and picked his way through the undergrowth, his chest heaving. "You the conductor?" His voice was the quietest of whispers. Even so, she could make out the raw pain in it.

His way must have been harrowing. Prudence nodded, her gaze searching the space behind him. "Thy wife?"

He stood before her, his hands tightly clenched. "She was captured—just this afternoon. I'm going back for her. Figured I'd best find safety for the night, and a meal if you can spare it. But first light, I'm going back for her."

At the word *captured*, Prudence's heart squeezed, all discomfort in her stomach forgotten. She rose to her full height and held out a hand. "Captured where? Nearby?"

"'Bout five miles away, to the south, I reckon." His hand shook as he put it in hers. "I'd gone ahead to scout it out. Thought she'd be safe in the cave we found."

His control was slipping. She could hear it in the wavering of his voice as surely as she could feel it in his trembling fingers. She clasped his hand tightly between hers. They couldn't stay here long, exposed as they were.

But one thing must take priority. "Let us pray for her, here and now. What is her name?"

"Shandy." The name emerged from his lips with love and aching.

She didn't close her eyes—she didn't dare just now. But she lowered her head a few degrees. "Dear Lord, we beseech Thee now on behalf of Shandy. Please wrap her in Thy hands and afford her Thy protection. Give Thy peace to her as well as to her husband here, who needs it so acutely. Give us Thy wisdom in searching for her. Amen."

"Amen." The man squeezed her fingers. "Thank you."

She released his hand and turned to lead him along the path toward Marietta. "What is thy name?"

"Billy."

She led him onto the path she'd followed to get there. Away from the water. Away from his wife. She knew he must be feeling the growing distance between them. "I will get thee to safety, and then if thee would tell me all that happened, I will do anything in my power to help thee."

"I ought to go back. Oughtn't to have come without her." The mumble seemed to be aimed at himself more than her.

Even so, Prudence felt it necessary to whisper in return, "Thee did the right thing. Alone, thee can do little to help her. But with God, anything is possible. We will help however we can, Billy. I promise thee."

After that, only night noises surrounded them. The familiar landscape of Duck Creek gave way to the dirt track that would lead them to safety, bypassing any late-night boatmen on the Ohio River, as well as the more regularly populated areas of Marietta. She followed it as far as she could—always ready, at any moment, to abandon the track in favor of the dense forest growing at its edge. But they saw no one as they walked ever closer to town.

They reached the familiar path she'd led countless fugitives on before. Along the river, using as cover both the night and the wisps of fog curling up from the water, toward the tunnel that had its entrance at the riverbank. She opened the concealed door and waved him in. She followed him into the space, closed the entrance behind her, and groped for the candle and flint she always kept here.

A moment later, light flared, and she got her first good look at the man's face.

It was a mask of worry and regret, but he made no vocal objection. He wouldn't. She didn't know how long he'd been on the run, but slaves learned quickly that silence was their best friend on the Underground Railroad.

Prudence crept forward, knowing he'd fall in behind. It didn't take long for them to emerge into the small room among the other servants' quarters that was kept empty for this purpose. "Here." She put the candle on the stand and reached to help him unfold from the space. "I will show thee how to access the tunnel from in here—if ever thee hears anyone coming, just duck back into it." She demonstrated how to work the hidden door.

He nodded, but his jaw remained set, his lips grim.

Prudence motioned toward the narrow cot. "Rest, my friend. I will bring thee something to eat and some water, and then thee can tell me all thee knows of thy wife's whereabouts."

After his next nod, she slipped out into the corridor and quietly made her way upstairs to the kitchen. She was a familiar figure in the Riverfront House—no one would think twice about her being here, even at such an hour.

And the cook knew not to question a few provisions gone missing. Prudence liberated some bread and ham and cheese from the pantry, along with a pitcher of water, and moved on silent feet back downstairs.

Her stomach pains had eased, at least. One small comfort.

Oh, Father God… After praying the same prayer so many times, she didn't even know what to say now. Whether to pray for the child she so longed for or to pray that, if it were to end badly, it never even began? How much heartache could they really endure?

But she and Jason had each other, at least. Her chest ached as she knocked on the door. That was more than this poor man currently had. And his wife! In the hands of a slave hunter, no doubt. Not only alone, but possibly injured, and certainly fearful of what fate awaited her.

When he opened the door, she slid back inside the room and set the provisions down. "Have all thee likes," she whispered. "There will be more tomorrow."

He fell on the meal like one starved—as refugees usually did. She waited a few minutes as he ate, cautioning him to go slowly and pouring him a glass of cool water to rinse down the bread. Only after he paused for a long breath, his eating slower, did she say, "Now. What can thee tell me?"

Billy leaned back against the wall, half a sandwich still in hand. "The last conductor got us past a town and told us how to make our way here. Said he'd send the message on that we were coming and that someone—you, I s'pose—would be waiting."

Prudence nodded. That much was exactly as she'd expected. "Thee had Shandy waiting in a cave somewhere?"

He nodded, looked at the food in his hand again, but didn't take another bite. "We'd just filled our canteen, and she was powerful tired. I told her to sit for a few minutes. I'd make sure the way was clear. It was daytime, but it was so forested, we figured we could make our way undetected." The way his eyes glazed over, she knew he was seeing it again. The cave, his wife. "We had a lot of distance to cover today. But Shandy, she's strong. Don't think she ain't. She can walk circles round me most the time. It's just we been traveling so long, and we didn't get much sleep the night before, hidden beneath the floorboards of a house."

Prudence offered a small, encouraging smile. Though she wasn't sure he really focused on her enough to see it. "I can well imagine."

"So I just went a bit ahead, to get the lay of the land and make sure the way was clear. Then I heard her screaming." His nostrils flared. "I run back, quick as I could—but quiet too. We had a plan for this sort of thing. That if one was caught and the other not, the free one had to *stay* free, so's to help."

"Wise."

"Tormenting. To see her being dragged away by that lout and not *do* anything." He squeezed his free hand into a fist. "I wanted to try. But he was a big fella—and had a gun on him, plain as day. I knowed if I made a move, he'd just shoot her. So instead, I watched. Watched him drag her toward a horse. Watched him take her away, where he met up with another fella."

Prudence let out the breath pent up in her chest. "I know how difficult that must have been. Does thee have any idea where they took her?"

His head jerked in a nod. "They was traveling near the river. I followed for about a mile or so, till a rain come up and they pitched a tent. I debated trying to overpower 'em, but they was both armed, and I heard 'em talking about taking turns on watch. Figured I'd as likely get us both killed as her saved, so I hightailed it here. If you can help me, ma'am—you or anyone else—I gotta get her back. I ain't going on without her."

"Thee did the right thing," she said again, mustering a smile that she prayed held the light of encouragement in it. "Now, tell me all thee can about Shandy. What she looks like, what she was wearing. I will send word to the Friends, and they will keep an eye out for her and let me know the moment she is spotted. We will make a plan to recover her."

He nibbled at his bread, his eyes shifting from pained to incredulous. "I don't know who these friends of yours are, but I don't reckon there's much they can do to get her back. Probably some hunters old man Marsh hired to find her."

"Never underestimate what the servants of the Lord can achieve with His help." She lifted her brows. "And who is Marsh?"

"Mr. Marsh—her owner." His lip curled as he said it. "Me, I was from a neighboring plantation, and old Mrs. Houdershelt ain't likely to spare the coin or the effort to get me back. But Marsh's a different story."

She made note of the names. "And Shandy herself?"

His face softened again. "She was wearing a cotton dress—green, 'cause Mrs. Marsh liked that color, and Shandy, she was a house slave. Too pretty to be a field hand. Had her hair in a braid, and I imagine she'll keep it that away. She always do. Gray eyes. And she got a mole right here." He touched his right cheek, a sad smile on his lips. "Looks like a dimple's always winking at me, even when she's not smiling."

Prudence took inventory of the room—there was a blanket, wash water in the pitcher, plus the drinking water and a few scraps of food still on the plate. Enough to see him through until tomorrow. "All right. I will go home now and speak with my husband and the Friends. Stay in this room at all times. I or another employee here will bring thee supplies in the morning. If thee hears anything suspicious, remember to get thee quickly into the tunnel."

At his nod, she indicated the clothing stacked neatly beside the bed. "I recommend thee changes into those as soon as possible—so thee blends in with the other servants here. Just in case. But again, thy best hope is to remain quiet and unseen in this room." She paused and summoned a smile. "I know waiting is the most difficult thing we are asked to do. But trust me and be still. Rest up. Thee will need thy strength after we've recovered thy wife and thee both are once more en route to freedom."

The poor sandwich looked as though it would be squished to nothing in his clenched fist. But he whispered his agreement.

Prudence slipped out of the room, out of the hotel, and hurried toward the farm, praying as she went. She kept her pace quick enough to fend off the early autumn chill, checking the position of the moon to gauge the time.

Not terribly late yet. She could talk to Jason and still pay a quick visit to Arnold Morris. He would be able to get a message out to other Friends in the area first thing in the morning, and he would forgive the late hour, given the nature of the visit.

Warm light glowed from the windows of the house as she drew near, lighting the fog in a halo of beauty. She let her silent prayer drift to a pause, sure to be taken up again soon, and hurried through the kitchen door.

Her feet came to an abrupt halt the moment she clicked the door shut behind her, her brows lifting when she saw not just Jason at the table with a steaming mug of coffee, but Arnold as well.

Their neighbor greeted her with a smile. "Good evening, Prudence Willard." He lifted his mug in salute. "I had the strangest feeling tonight that I had better come by for a visit. And when thee was not here, I had a feeling I knew why."

Thank Thee, Father God. He was already making provision.

It was the greatest sign of hope she could have asked for that they would find Shandy and return her to her husband, safe and sound.

The day was stretching into evening, and Prudence's stomach was fierce in its cramping, her head aching with it too. Continual reminders of arms still empty of a child. Or was it perhaps anxiety over the fact that she'd had to leave the hotel this afternoon without any new word for her secret guest?

The clop of hooves on the lane drew her gaze to the window, though it was a moment before she could make out the identity of the rider. When she recognized Arnold Morris, her breath escaped with a whoosh. Likely, he would have nothing definitive to tell her, but he would at least report on how far the word about Shandy was spreading. That would surely be encouragement for Billy.

Wiping her hands on a towel—and not at all minding her escape from the smell of onions caramelizing on the stove—she hurried out onto the porch. Jason straightened from the pump outside the barn and started her way, still dripping from his cleanup. He reached the porch and her side just as the Friend dismounted.

"The Lord was surely at work today," Arnold said by way of greeting, holding the reins still in his hand and making no move to come into the house. "I talked to three Friends who came into town from across the river. They saw the young woman and her captors—in fact, they gave them directions."

Prudence knotted her apron in her hands. "God be praised. What information did they have?"

Arnold's gray brows drew together. "Her captors asked the quickest way to Boaz."

Prudence frowned as well, the disquiet in her stomach intensifying. "That's right along the Ohio River, is it not? On the Virginia side?"

Their neighbor nodded. Jason let out a breath. "More than that—it is where they have regular slave auctions."

Auctions? Prudence settled a hand on the porch railing. "These men…they may not be hunters hired by her owners, then."

"It seems not."

Her stomach refused to settle. She wasn't sure if this was good news…or the worst news possible. On the one hand, it meant the captors wouldn't be heading directly south, back to her owners.

On the other, it meant that they might have only days before Shandy was in the hands of *another* owner.

Arnold put one foot on the step, leaning closer to them both. "I've already spoken with the other Friends in Marietta, and we've sent word to those in the surrounding areas as well. We have a plan—but we'll have to act quickly. And we'll be limited by the funds we can raise."

She knew, even before he laid it out, what they would do— what Quakers along the Ohio River had done many times before. They would put up their own money and try to buy her at the auction, for the sole purpose of freeing her. But rarely did they go to an auction with a particular person in mind to bid on.

And a strong, pretty young woman could fetch quite a price. Sickened by that thought as much as the smell of onions, Prudence let her eyes slide shut and prayed.

CHAPTER FOUR

Tess poured more coffee into her mug and followed the sounds of laughter from the sitting room. The Sherlock Society had all come down for breakfast within a few minutes of each other, and they were now ready to get down to the day's business. She had to admit to a certain curiosity about how they worked, so she was glad to hurry through breakfast cleanup with Janice—Winnie hadn't made it in—while LuAnn helped the crew move their props.

She glanced out the front windows as she walked by, shaking her head in wonder at the six inches of snow that had blanketed the world. It had tapered off overnight, but she figured maybe she ought to believe the forecasters now when they said it was going to start up again midmorning and that up to twelve inches by tomorrow was likely.

"There comes the snowplow, finally," Janice said behind her, her fingers curled around a steaming mug as well.

"I have a feeling the café isn't going to see much traffic for lunch." There certainly hadn't been anyone other than the guests there for breakfast. Tess paused by the window to watch the plow scrape by on the street, the familiar noise filtering in through the walls.

"That's good, considering Winnie and the servers have already called in saying they can't get out. It would all be on us. Not that we couldn't handle whatever small bit of traffic did come." Janice shrugged. Then she grinned. "Though I suppose you never know. Maybe a snowstorm makes everyone within walking distance want soup."

Tess chuckled and turned away from the cold radiating off the glass. "I'd say maybe we should close, but feeding the society lunch and supper as well as breakfast is part of their package anyway. I don't imagine we'll mind if a few others make their way in for lunch."

Another guffaw of laughter came from the sitting room, drawing them that direction. When Tess stepped inside, she saw the boards set up again. Kim was once more stationed with the marker at the whiteboard, though at the moment that post seemed to involve more laughing than writing.

Graham sat on the floor with a hardback book, a stack of white index cards, and a fast-moving pen. Tom looked to be doing the same thing—whatever it was—but was sprawled in a chair, using a book as a writing desk.

Tess moved to where Uncle Harold sat in an armchair and dropped a hand onto his shoulder. "So what are you solving this morning? An actual Holmes story, or are you still trying to find our missing delivery?"

"Both." He flashed a grin up at her. "This morning's schedule was only a short story anyway, so we decided we could easily work on your mystery as well. I've assigned the boys with making the clue cards for each."

"Clue cards." Tess's gaze found LuAnn, who never went anywhere without a notebook and pen and an ever-growing collection of lists. She couldn't help but grin at her friend. "Are you in heaven, Lu?"

LuAnn, sheaf of papers in hand, stood behind Tom's chair. She grinned right back. "It's a special sort of paradise."

Tom angled a look up at her. "What was that last bit again?"

LuAnn consulted the papers. "Five foot ten, about one-eighty."

"Perfectly average," Tom muttered, going back to his cards. "This description could apply to about half the men in town, I suspect."

Tess and Janice both made their way over to LuAnn and Tom. "What's all that?" Tess asked.

LuAnn held up the papers with a flourish. "Sylvia emailed more information on this Jim fellow."

Janice frowned. "He still hasn't turned up?"

A shake of LuAnn's head matched the glint in her eyes. "And she sounded none too happy about it. I think she's beginning to suspect he took off with the chair."

"He stole a chair?" Tess knew her doubt saturated her tone. "Why in the world would someone do that?"

"Because it had a bullet hole in it?" Janice shrugged. "I hear that makes it super cool."

Tess snorted a laugh.

"Or maybe this wife of his has a dastardly redecorating scheme that requires antiques she can't actually afford."

Tom jabbed a period onto whatever sentence he'd just written.

Tess was about to ask about "this wife" but didn't get her mouth open before Hiram turned from the corkboard. "I've got the photos from our walk up in chronological order for now. Does that work, Professor?"

"It's a fine starting point." Uncle Harold motioned toward the collection of small, white-bordered photographs. "What do we have? Anything of interest?"

Hiram shrugged. "I'm not sure yet. Looking back through, I certainly didn't see any gold pickup trucks in the background. I kinda hoped I would. But maybe there's a clue around the museum, if we look harder. He did start from there, obviously."

"There. I think that's the last of these for now." Tom stood from his chair. "Who has the thumbtacks?"

"Me." Graham stood from his sprawl on the floor, his scattered cards swept into a haphazard stack he held in one hand, a plastic pack of multicolored tacks in the other. "Coming."

The two young men converged on the large corkboard, saying something about one of them taking the left and the other the right.

"Here." Graham held out the tacks. "Open this, will you?"

Tom attempted it one-handed for a moment before rolling his eyes and trading Graham cards for tacks. "I swear these packages are meant to remain closed for all eternity. How do they expect anyone to actually get a tack out?" He pried at the plastic, bending and twisting it. Apparently it fought back with valiant effort. And won.

Tess bit back a smile at Tom's frustrated growl. "Do you need scissors?"

"Never! I can manhandle a stupid little plastic case."

Graham set all the cards down on an end table. "Here, try prying the little circular bits apart."

"What do you think I'm trying to do?"

"Got me."

"How many detectives does it take…?" LuAnn grinned as she watched the two men wrestle the tiny plastic case.

Janice pressed her fingers to her mouth, looking every bit as amused but with a touch more concern. "Oh, this isn't going to end well."

Right on cue, the plastic gave way, sending an explosion of thumbtacks raining over the guys. Graham staggered back a step to avoid the shower and bumped the table. The cards went to the floor in an avalanche of white.

Tom surveyed the mess with mouth agape as Uncle Harold laughed from the safety of his chair. "Um. Oops."

"Well, you got them open." Kim bit her lip, but if she was trying to hold back her grin, she failed. "Good job."

Her husband snorted a laugh.

Tom shot them a look that somehow crossed pleading with accusation. "You gonna help here?"

"Nope. I'm going to let you clear that minefield before I take another step." Kim turned back to her whiteboard. "What were you saying, honey?"

Tess moved forward, though she was careful to examine every place she set a foot. "Here, I'll help. We'll have them picked up in no time."

"I would recommend counting them—assuming it was a new box, you know how many you're looking for." LuAnn lifted her brows. "Last thing we want is a tack surprising a guest in the rug or on a chair cushion."

Graham winced. "True that. Here." He used his foot, clad in a thick-soled shoe that would be impervious to the little tacks, to scoot all the brightly colored projectiles near him toward Tom. "I'll clear this area and then pick up the cards." A wrinkle of his nose broadcast his opinion on that chore as he took in the new carpeting of white paper. He must have hit the table hard to send them scattering so wide. "So much for our careful order."

Crouching down, Tess plucked up the tacks nearest her, using the opposite palm to cup them. At least it hadn't been a pack of straight-pins—these were much easier to spot and pick up. A few minutes of work and she had a considerable collection in her hand, matching the one in Tom's.

"Shall we count?" Tom offered her a smile and reached for the mangled plastic that had once been a container.

"Goodness gracious goat, don't try to use that thing again. Here." Janice had apparently run upstairs to her sewing room, because she approached now and held out a small container with an easy-open lid.

"Hey, now, that's easier. Why couldn't these things have come in one like that to begin with? Thanks, Janice." Tom took the offered box as if it were the best thing he'd seen all day and started counting the tacks into it.

Once he'd run out of his, Tess added hers to the mix and sighed as she said, "Ninety-four, ninety-five, ninety-six. We're missing four."

"Time to look in and under and around, I suppose." Tom nudged Graham, who'd plopped himself onto the floor in the middle of a sea of white notecards, with his foot. "Hey, any tacks under there?"

Graham breathed a laugh. "I think I'd notice if there were." He rubbed his temples. "Ever notice how alike our handwriting looks, Tom?" He held up two cards. Both written in black ink, both written all in caps with blocky letters. Tess had to study them for a moment to see the slight differences in the hand.

"Boy, that'll make sorting those about as fun as searching for tacks. Almost." Tom dropped down to all fours and crawled half-under a chair.

"It shouldn't be too difficult to tell them apart, Graham." Uncle Harold's words came out a bit garbled. Tess looked up and over and saw that he had one of the pipes clamped between his teeth and a deerstalker on his head. She had to smile at the sight. "Once you read them, I mean."

"You'd think. And it's certainly clear on the ones that say 'four-wheeled carriage' and 'pickup truck.' But this is kinda weird." Graham held up two cards, though Tess couldn't imagine that anyone farther away than she was could possibly read them. "This one's mine, I'm pretty sure. I wrote *Sutherland describes Windibank.* But then we have this one that Tom wrote. *Sutherland description.*"

Uncle Harold stood. "Two Sutherlands—I hadn't noticed that."

Tess frowned and ran her fingers along the edge of the rug in search of tacks. "Who?"

"In the story. The young lady who came to Sherlock with the mystery was a Miss Sutherland." Graham set the two cards into different stacks. "What's even weirder is that her stepfather's name is James Windibank. We have a James and a Sutherland in the story, and then Jim—presumably short for James—Sutherland in real life."

"Aha! Ninety-seven!" Tom scooted out from under the chair, brandishing a green thumbtack as if it were Excalibur.

Uncle Harold padded toward Graham, though he paused a few steps away. "I believe I just found ninety-eight."

"You okay?" Tom spun toward him, still on his knees.

Harold lifted his foot. "Fine. Though from the crunch, the tack may not have been so fortunate."

"Nah, it looks fine." Tom snatched it and looked up with a grin. "Thanks, Professor."

"My dubious pleasure." Uncle Harold pointed toward the cards with his pipe. "May I see those, Graham?"

"Sure."

Tess's fingers brushed something hard, drawing her gaze down just before she jammed her fingertip up against the point of a yellow tack. "Ninety-nine." She got up so she could add it to the container.

The pipe was again hooked in Uncle Harold's mouth, and he was waving the two cards in the air in seeming triumph. "Do you know what this means?"

Everyone looked at him, expressions of either expectation or question on their faces. Tess, tack container still in hand, turned to give him her full attention.

Her uncle strode toward the Polaroids tacked up already. "Where's that note that was tacked to the museum door? That's our main clue."

"Uh..." Graham scrunched up his nose and nudged his glasses back into place. "Why?"

"Didn't you read the story, my boy? The note was the key."

"Well, yeah, but...that note isn't from the story."

Rather than address that rather valid point, Uncle Harold tacked the two white cards beside one of the photos. "Bud, where did we file that letter?"

"I think it should be right here somewhere." Bud, stationed beside another end table strewn with folders, went digging.

Hiram tapped another of the photos. "What about this, Professor? That car that was idling outside the museum. Think that could be related?"

"Bah. Ignore the distractions. This is our focus." Uncle Harold tapped the image of the note on the door.

Tess took a step back, knowing her uncle wouldn't like the frown on her face one bit if he turned around to look at it. But he didn't. He was muttering something about typewriters and squinting at the tiny Polaroid photo.

She looked down, trying to catch Graham's eye. He was still looking at her uncle, though, and his bafflement seemed colored more with curiosity than concern.

If only she could feel so cheerful about it. Instead, a shadow seemed to settle over her heart. Why was her uncle focusing on this coincidence? The two mysteries had nothing to do with one another.

"Pass me the rest of the Sherlock clues as you sort them out, Graham. We'll find this missing chair in no time." Uncle Harold pulled his hat down a little more and grinned at the bulletin board.

Tess backed up a step, gripping the container of tacks. This made absolutely no sense. And usually, her uncle would have been the first to point out a lack of reason, not the first to fall into it.

Her breakfast went sour in her stomach. He was eighty-four. It was to be expected that things would start slipping. His health, his sight, his hearing…his mind. But she'd yet to see any evidence of it. He didn't wear glasses, he didn't need a hearing aid, he'd outpaced her on their walk yesterday.

So why *this*? Of all things to fail first, how could it be his mind? His mental acumen had always been his pride and joy. What he'd based his whole life on. If that failed, if this small confusion was symptomatic of a bigger problem, then where would that leave him? He would hate that far more than a physical limitation.

She drew in a sharp breath and told herself to stop fretting. So he made one weird mental leap—that was no big deal.

But even if not, it had still made the thought, the fear, crystallize.

She wasn't ready to lose him. He was the last of her father's generation. The only uncle she still had. She didn't want to think about the end of his life drawing ever nearer—and it all happening three hours away, where he lived alone.

Pivoting on her heel, she scanned the room for Matti. She'd come down, hadn't she? But Tess didn't see her now, just Bud.

"Tess?" Janice moved to her side, lines etched between her brows. "What's wrong?"

Tess shook her head, not quite ready to vocalize the nebulous fears. "Not quite following Uncle Harold's train of thought, I guess. And I was wondering where Matti's run off to."

"That I can answer." Janice pointed toward the café. "I saw her head that way with her coffee cup a minute ago, while you were hunting tacks."

Tess summoned a smile and handed over the colorful, troublesome things. "Thanks. I'm going to go talk to her for a few."

"I'll take over the hunt for number one hundred." Her own smile bright and unaffected, Janice turned back to the group.

Tess slipped out the door, crossed the lobby with another amazed glance at the white world outside, and entered the café.

Matti stood at a window, her arms crossed over her middle and a steaming mug clutched in one hand. She seemed lost in the snowy world outside.

Or maybe in a world inside her own mind. She made no move to indicate that she was aware she had company, so Tess made it a point to clear her throat while she was still a few steps away. She didn't want to startle her and send hot coffee flying.

Matti jumped, but only a little, and turned her head a bit. Shadows ringed her eyes, and tension lined her face. It relaxed a few degrees when she spotted Tess. "Oh. Hey."

"Hey. Didn't sleep well last night?" Tess slid up beside her at the window. How to broach the questions suddenly swarming her mind? Should she just come right out and ask if Uncle Harold's mind was slipping? If there'd been other occasions like the one a minute ago? Other health concerns he hadn't seen fit to tell her about? She wouldn't put it past him to "protect" her from reality.

Matti shrugged and raised her cup for a sip. "Not great— not the fault of the bed or room, I assure you. It was really comfortable."

Tess chuckled just a bit, since she figured Matti expected it. "But not *your* bed or room. Sometimes that's all that matters."

"Yeah. I guess that's it."

It didn't sound like that was it. Tess eased a step closer. "Are you okay, Matti? You don't seem—"

"I'm fine." As if to prove it, she turned to face Tess fully, a smile on her lips that was obviously more force than feeling. "Did you need something?"

"Um." The direct question left her uncertain. She rubbed a hand up her arm and studied the woman before her. Tess had always considered them friends but the distant type. They never exchanged letters or emails or phone calls, except for rare occasions when one or the other of them wanted to surprise Harold with something and needed some help. But whenever they'd been in the same place, they'd always gotten along well.

And she knew, deep in her heart, in that same place that had gone cold with fear a few minutes ago, that something was wrong. Something was upsetting the woman before her. Maybe Matti was worried for Harold too. Tess drew in a bolstering breath. "Yeah. I just wanted to chat with you about Uncle Harold. You see him so much more often than I do, and I'm never sure if he's being completely honest with me about his health. I know he's…he's getting up there. I want to stay abreast of anything going on with him."

Matti looked at her, obviously surprised by the question. "He's fine. Fit as the proverbial fiddle."

Tess wanted to feel relief, but that was a bit hard to do when he was in the other room talking about how a typewriter could help them find Jim Sutherland. "You're sure? Physically and mentally? No memory lapses or anything?"

Matti's brows lifted. "Well, he does misplace his car keys regularly. But he's been doing that for twenty years." She reached out and put a hand on Tess's shoulder. Her smile still looked strained but not quite as forced as before. "I'd tell you if I had any concerns. I know how much he means to you."

"Thanks. I know you would." But if it wasn't Uncle Harold that had Matti upset…what was it? "Is there anything I can do for you, Mat?"

A shutter fell across Matti's eyes again, and she pulled away. All the way away, a full step. "No. I'm good. Thanks."

Without another word, she hurried past Tess toward the sitting room and nearly collided with Kim, who'd bounced to the doorway and was calling out, "We're heading back out into the snow! The professor says he can lead us right to this Jim guy, but we need to start at the museum again."

Dread knotted Tess's stomach. Her uncle was obviously confused. And clearly, no one else was going to call him on it. They'd just follow him blissfully into the storm.

CHAPTER FIVE

"Tell me what those grandchildren of yours have been up to, Tessie."

Tess frowned at her uncle, though he didn't look over at her to see it. His gaze was fixed on the snow-covered path before them. "Uh...well, I told you all the most interesting things last night." Not that she couldn't pull out some more stories—there were certainly plenty of them. But he'd asked almost the exact same question on their walk home the evening before. "Was there something in particular you wanted to hear more about?"

"Hmm?" He blinked at her, and it seemed to take his eyes a second to clear before he grinned. "Oh, pay no attention to me, my girl. You know how I am—I'm just thinking this through. I'm not really paying attention to what I'm saying."

Something he had always done, it was true—but it seemed different now. Less endearing, more troubling. Did he even remember what she'd told him about the triplets last night? "I can tell you again, if you want. So you have some background noise while you think." That's what he'd always claimed he needed. Like Sherlock's violin music—something to engage one part of his mind while another worked.

Uncle Harold chuckled, patted her arm, and stepped away from her. "No need, my girl. I'll just talk to my Sherlockians about the mysteries afoot."

Should she feel dismissed? Tess let out a long breath and fell back a step, even with her friends. They'd been chatting as they walked too. It only took her a moment to tune her mind to what they were saying, rather than to her uncle.

"Now for the important question." Janice, only a strip of her face visible between scarf and hat, turned twinkling eyes on LuAnn. "What are you going to wear on your date tonight?"

LuAnn laughed and swept her gaze across the winter wonderland they were trudging through. "Ski pants and a parka?"

"Well I was going to recommend that red dress with some stilettos, but..." Tess arched her brows at the snow. "Might be a bit impractical today."

"At this rate, I can't imagine we'll even *have* our date." LuAnn pursed her lips as she surveyed the slush-filled street. The plow may have come by, but it hadn't exactly cleared things well.

"Oh, don't say that. If it doesn't start snowing again, another swipe of the plow will have things manageable," Janice—ever the optimist—said.

LuAnn shrugged. "If not, we'll just do it tomorrow or Monday instead."

Oh, how Tess loved seeing that smile on her friend's face. The kind that said particulars didn't matter, because she knew the want-to was there. The kind that basked in the knowledge of affection felt and returned. That rested in the realization that after all these years, romance had found her again.

Tess let a happy sigh fog the air. She knew LuAnn had been satisfied with the life God had given her...but she also knew her friend had always wondered what might be different if her fiancé hadn't died before their wedding all those years ago. She knew she still felt the occasional pang over the family she didn't have, especially when the rest of them were with their kids and grandkids. She didn't have *regrets*, but she'd confessed to having sorrow over it.

But now she had another chance at romance, and Tess couldn't be happier for the woman she loved like a sister.

"CC!" Uncle Harold turned around with an impish grin and waved a gloved hand. "Come walk with me, my dear. Perhaps you can help me explain it to these pups."

"*It*? What's *it*?" Despite the question, LuAnn lengthened her stride so she could move up into the space between Uncle Harold and Kim and Ollie.

Tess and Janice closed up the hole she left, exchanging a smile. It was always entertaining when Uncle Harold and his "carbon copy" got started on something—and usually involved "schooling" the rest of them.

"You read 'A Case of Identity' last night, did you not?"

LuAnn nodded. "I needed the refresher. It's been years since I'd read it."

Uncle Harold shot a look over his shoulder at Tess and Janice. "And what about you young ladies?"

Tess felt her cheeks warm. "Um..."

Janice chuckled and patted her arm. "I didn't either. Was it assigned as homework, Professor? If so, I didn't get the memo, and formally request an extension."

Uncle Harold gave them a chiding look, which he ruined with another grin. "Perhaps CC should give you the summary."

"All right." LuAnn held up for a step so she was walking between them and Uncle Harold, easily heard by all. "It's really a pretty simple one, as Sherlock stories go. A young woman comes to hire Sherlock to solve the disappearance of her fiancé. She experiences a bit of indecision about even seeking help, which Sherlock of course notices. But eventually she comes in and tells them about how she inherited a decent amount from her father but works in a typing pool and lets her mother and stepfather use the inheritance to run the household. Her stepfather is a lot younger than her mother, barely older than her, and is very much against her going out and meeting people. But she went to a ball while he was out of the country and fell for a fellow by the name of Hosmer Angel."

Tess laughed. "Now that's a name."

"Memorable, isn't it?" LuAnn angled a smile back at her. "So anyway, they had a whirlwind romance, with the full approval of the mother of Miss Sutherland—that's the girl—while the stepfather was away. They decided to get married. She felt bad about doing it behind the back of the stepdad—James Windibank. So she sends him a message letting him know. Meanwhile, the wedding day arrives, and in a fit of passion, Hosmer makes her swear that she'll be faithful to him forever, no matter what. They head to the church in two separate carriages, but when they arrive, they find that he's not in the second carriage. He's *vanished*." LuAnn delivered that final word with a flourish.

As if the heavens had been waiting for her to cue them, snowflakes began drifting down again.

Tess adjusted the band of her hat. "So obviously the suspects are the mother and stepfather. They don't want to lose the money she's giving them. Right?"

"That is, of course, Sherlock's first thought too. He asks some questions—"

"Shocking." Janice chuckled.

"Isn't it?" LuAnn paused as they reached the intersection where they needed to cross the street. There was no traffic, so after a moment, they all stepped down into the slush and hurried across.

Once safely on the unshoveled sidewalk on the opposite side, LuAnn turned back to them. "So the clues, which you may have seen on the cards being pinned to the board at the inn, were as follows. First, the description of Hosmer. He spoke in a whisper all the time."

"Very shy," Kim put in from up ahead.

Ollie nodded. "With eyes so delicate that he had to hide them behind shaded glasses at all times."

"It's also worth noting that Miss Sutherland didn't have the best eyesight either." This Uncle Harold delivered with a dry inflection and a twitch of his mouth that told Tess he was amused by something.

Tess drew in a breath that tasted of love as much as snow. That little twitch was just so Uncle Harold. Something she remembered noting him do all her life. How many times had his mouth moved just like that as he was debating her father or pulling a prank on one of her other uncles?

"Right." LuAnn nodded. "So she knew only the street on which he worked and lived, no particular address. And what Sherlock found decidedly telling was that all the letters he wrote to Miss Sutherland were typed, not handwritten."

"Hence," Harold put in, "why this typed note your friend left is so important."

Even LuAnn sent him a strange look this time, not just Tess. "So anyway, Sherlock naturally requests an interview with the stepfather, and the stepfather sends a note back accepting—a typed note. Sherlock is able to compare this note to the letters from Hosmer and finds that the unique fingerprint of the typewriter is the same—the way the *E* key is worn in a particular fashion. Thereby proving that indeed Windibank and his wife came up with the scheme to convince Miss Sutherland not to marry for a long time to come, thereby leaving them with access to her money."

"James Windibank thought himself quite clever—and as he committed no real crime, there was nothing Holmes and Watson could do." Uncle Harold sent a grin over his shoulder at them. "Let's see how clever this modern James is, shall we? We know he began at the museum. Your friend and her husband helped load this chair into his truck. Correct?"

"That's what Sylvia said." Tess glanced down at the sleeves of her coat, covered already in this fresh snow. It was coming down fast—at this rate it wouldn't take much to cover the roads again. "I didn't actually see the email she sent this morning. What did it say?"

Janice opened her mouth but then waited while an SUV lumbered by at a reasonable snail's pace. The driver waved a hello, though Tess couldn't make out who it was through the snow and the glare on the window. Someone she knew, probably, given that at least two people she knew from church had that particular model.

After the engine noises had disappeared into the snow, Janice tried again. "She gave us a general physical description of Jim, as well as a list of places he frequents and the people she knows are his friends. Said she didn't really expect us to follow up too much, since this is her problem and not ours, but in case we were bored or curious—"

"Or mystery connoisseurs," one of the society men said behind Tess. Hiram? Graham?

Janice laughed. "Right. She sent it along in case we were interested. She and Stan planned to call some folks from home this morning and see what they can find. They didn't want to come out in all this."

"Well, wherever he went with the chair, I certainly hope he didn't leave it out in this snow." Tess squinted down the street through the fast-falling flakes. The museum was just ahead. "So what exactly do we hope to find here today that we didn't find yesterday?"

Uncle Harold said, "Perhaps our Jim returned to the scene of the crime."

"Yeah, he could have returned to steal some matching curtains." That was from Tom, she thought, and he sniggered at his own joke.

Tess did too. "No doubt."

They turned the final corner, putting the snow-frosted museum in sight. A quick sigh escaped Tess's lips in a foggy puff when she saw that no pickup waited outside. She hadn't expected one to be there, really. But some part of her must have hoped they'd round that bend and see the gold truck with this Jim guy, abashed and apologetic, and this little mystery would be solved. Then her uncle could turn back to his fictional mystery and forget he ever thought the two were connected.

"All right." Uncle Harold clapped his gloved hands together as they neared the building, his eyes scanning the facade. "This is surely not the door where everything is brought in and out. There's likely a back door with a loading area, correct?"

"Probably, though I'm really not sure." LuAnn paused at the front steps, which hadn't been cleared of last night's snow. No prints marred the pristine white. "Shall we head around to check?"

"Let's." Uncle Harold turned to wave an arm at the rest of the crew. "Around back, lads and lasses."

A corner of Tess's mouth pulled up. Her uncle was the only one she'd ever met who called her a *lass*. Sometimes he seemed to forget that he was a native of Ohio and not some part of the British Isles whose literature he spent so much time reading.

The sidewalk circling the museum hadn't been cleared either, making it a bit of a trudge as they followed Ollie and Kim around to the little alley that came up alongside the back. There was indeed a back door that seemed better suited for loading and unloading than the front.

"Whoa. Hold up." Ollie brought the entourage to a halt with a lifted hand. "We have tire tracks back here. They start about halfway down the alley—or probably stop there, I guess—and continue to the opposite end. Looks like they turn left there, back onto the plowed road."

"Excellent." After giving LuAnn a pat on the arm, Uncle Harold waded through the snow to pass the couple, heading for the tracks. "They look large."

"Hold on. I have a measuring tape," Bud said as he plowed his way forward too, his pack once again slung over his shoulder.

Tess looked toward the back of the group, where he'd been walking with Matti. It seemed odd that she wasn't coming forward with him. Whenever Tess had seen her before, she was always at the head of things.

Today, she stood alone at the back of the group, her gaze unfocused and her shoulders hunched against the cold. As Tess watched, Graham shifted back to say something to Matti, but it earned only the fleeting touch of a smile before her solemn expression returned. Graham frowned a bit and then shook his head and moved to join the rest of the group.

A prayer whispered through Tess's soul. She didn't know what was bothering Matti, but clearly something was. She prayed that the Lord would help Matti feel His arms around her. She knew Matti and Bud were people of faith—they went to the same church as Uncle Harold—but that sure didn't mean that emotions didn't overcome the peace of His Spirit sometimes.

"Someone ready to take this down?"

Tess looked forward again and saw that Bud was crouching down, a measuring tape extended along the ground. He'd moved to where the tire tracks stopped in front of the door, presumably to keep from stomping on them.

Tess crunched her way through the snow, closer to where Uncle Harold, Tom, and Bud had all stopped.

Tom had his phone out of his pocket. "Go."

"Tire is...looks like three hundred fifteen millimeters wide."

"Got it. Want to measure the space between them?"

"Yep." The sound of the metal tape sliding farther out of its case joined with the continual murmur of snow crystals falling onto the ground and roofs and tree limbs.

For a moment, while the talking stopped, Tess closed her eyes and just listened. She always found it amazing how loud snow really was. It looked so quiet and peaceful, but it had a definite noise to it.

"Width of the vehicle has to be at least seventy-four inches." Bud stood, his boots crunching through snow again.

Tess shifted a bit, wondering what he saw with his gaze glued to the ground like that.

LuAnn and Janice must have been wondering the same, because they eased forward. Tess joined them.

Bud pursed his lips. "Do you think this deeper track might be where the tires were when he was parked? We could get an idea of wheelbase, if so."

Uncle Harold grinned and slapped a hand to Bud's shoulder. "Excellent thought. It seems likely. Even with four-wheel drive, a truck is likely to spin its tires a bit when first starting out, leaving a deeper indentation in the snow. Here, give me the dumb end of the tape." Taking the front end, he walked it away, toward the deeper print Bud had indicated, while Bud returned to the backmost part of the track.

"What have we got?"

Bud brushed snow from the yellow tape. "Nearly eleven feet. Looks like one hundred thirty-one inches or so."

"Long." Tom was still tapping information into his phone. "Give me a minute."

While he presumably looked up what vehicles matched that data, Tess meandered toward her uncle, her eyes following the tracks. She pointed ahead, toward the mouth of the alley. "Looks like he slid a bit, probably as he came to a stop. And are those footprints?"

"Good eyes, my girl." Uncle Harold straightened. "Ready for me to let go of this, Bud?"

"Let 'er rip."

The *whsk* of the tape retracting filled the air. Tess crunched her way down the alley, her gaze on the tire tracks. They definitely slid a bit there at the end, and some other odd marks marred the snow. Footprints, along with another deep gouge. She couldn't imagine what made the gouge at first, but as she drew near, she saw it led directly to an old metal trash can, its top largely without snow.

"Interesting." Uncle Harold paused at the mouth of the alley, hands planted on his hips. "Looks like the can must have been in his way. Tracks are turning left, the can was dragged from left to right."

"Not just in his way." Tess waded toward the metal cylinder, looking from the can to where it had been. "Those tire tracks look like he may have slid into it before he got out to move it."

"Do you think...?"

She was already at the can, bending down to look for any evidence to support her theory. She turned it a bit, then a bit more, smiling when she saw a scuff that looked more gold than silver. "Aha! Looks like a bit of paint transfer."

"Someone take a photograph, if you please!"

Tess stood again and backed out of the way as Hiram stepped forward with his Polaroid. Her gaze narrowed on the lid. Much of the snow had either been brushed or fallen off it, but some of it was packed down around the handle, as if someone had grabbed it.

Someone probably had—no doubt whoever had bumped the thing had put one hand on the lid and used the can's side handles to drag it across the alley. Still. Would that have been enough to dislodge all the snow from the top? Maybe it slid out of his hands and fell to the ground, knocking the snow off.

Or maybe... She pointed to another dent in the snow. "Is it just me, or does that look like where the lid could have been, leaning against the building here?"

"One way to find out." Uncle Harold, after waiting a moment for Hiram—and Tom with his phone's camera too—to finish photographing the can, yanked the metal lid off and eased it into the hole in the snow. "Perfect fit."

"Here, guys, snap a few shots of this too. We've got a pretty clear boot print." Janice was guarding said print with her own feet, smiling when Bud handed her a ruler. Not needing to be told what to do, she bent down and put the ruler alongside the print so the pictures the guys turned to take would include the measurement.

After Tom snapped a few, he tapped another command into his phone. "Yeah, so all those numbers from the tire tracks seem to indicate a pickup truck of some kind. Tires are definitely wider than your average car, and that wheelbase is long enough to indicate a full-size bed. I might be able to narrow down a model year if I had my computer rather than a phone."

"Given the gold paint, it seems reasonable to infer that it's Jim's truck." LuAnn spun from the tracks to the can. "When we get back to the inn, start by looking at the numbers for 1980s Chevy trucks and see if they match."

Tom nodded his agreement.

"What day is trash pickup around here?"

"Huh?" Tess turned back to find her uncle peering into the can. "If they're on the same schedule as the inn on this street, then Friday. Why?"

Uncle Harold leaned into the can, fishing around in the bottom.

Visions of him falling in like some character from a sitcom had Tess reaching to steady him. "For heaven's sake, Uncle Harold, you're too old for dumpster diving!"

His laugh reverberated in the can. "Never!" He straightened, emerging again with something in his hands. "And this is *hardly* a dumpster, my girl."

Tom stepped closer, frowning at the two items in Uncle Harold's hands. "What did you find, Professor?"

First, Uncle Harold brandished a crumpled brochure that Tess recognized immediately as being from the Underground Railroad Museum—though this one was soggy and soiled by a muddy boot print.

Hiram snapped a photograph, as did Tom.

"And the pièce de résistance." Eyes twinkling, Uncle Harold opened his other hand, revealing...a jar?

Tess frowned. "What's so special about that?"

"Ah, Tessie, look at the label."

It looked like a pretty standard, uninspired thing. She'd spent enough time working on the inn's website in recent months to feel a bit critical about the total lack of design quality put into the label. Just a plain black border framing a few simple words written in an old-fashioned-looking typewriter font. *Westhouse and Marbank Jams & Jellies.*

A bit of sticky purple stuff still coated the inside of the jar.

Tess lifted her gaze to her uncle. "Okay. So...what does that have to do with anything?"

He held the jar aloft. "Isn't it obvious? That's the name of the company that James Westibank worked for!"

Tess slanted a glance at LuAnn, praying her friend could read the question in her eyes.

LuAnn probably had no trouble interpreting the *Is it?* But she shrugged, her own brows drawn into a frown.

They all just stood there, staring at him. Uncle Harold rolled his eyes and brandished the jar. "Look it up on those contraptions of yours, lads. See if anything gives us an address. The street was a key in the story too, you know—that Westibank worked near where Angel supposedly did."

"Yeah, but…" Tom frowned at the jar. "Do you really think London and Marietta share many street names?"

Harold's sigh was exasperated. "We won't know that until we look it up."

Tess frowned. It made absolutely no sense that the details from the Sherlock story would be found in the here-and-now. None. But the coincidence was too great to ignore. Even so…how was it possible that Uncle Harold could remember a short story so well but not recall the real-life stories she'd told him last night?

Tom was shaking his head. "I'm not getting any hits on that anywhere in Ohio, much less Marietta."

"May I see the jar for a moment?" Janice had abandoned the boot print and held out a hand, a look on her face that said she recognized something.

Tess refocused on the glass. Now that she took a second look…it wasn't just your average jelly jar, that was for sure. It was a unique shape. Beautiful. She hadn't really noticed before, focused as she'd been on the label, but that white rectangle actually really detracted from the elegance of the glass itself.

Uncle Harold handed it off, and Janice immediately flipped it over. "I thought so. I have a few very similar to this that I bought from a local artisan a year or so ago to hold my buttons." She held it up, bottom out so they could all see...something.

Tess leaned forward, squinting at the stylized *V* stamped in. "Maker's mark?"

"Maker's mark," Janice agreed. "It's from Verre Studio."

Uncle Harold was grinning at Janice as if she were his prized pupil. "And where is Verre Studio?"

"A few blocks over."

"Well then. Onward we go!"

CHAPTER SIX

The glassblower's studio may have been only a few blocks away, but it was a difficult few blocks with the snow gusting down on them with renewed fury. Another inch had fallen just in the short time they'd been out, covering the streets that had been half-heartedly plowed.

Janice was at the head of the pack this time, since she knew the way to the shop without the need for GPS, and Tess had ended up beside LuAnn, toward the rear. Each step felt more like a trudge, but at least from back here she couldn't hear her uncle chattering about Marbank and Windibank and Westhouse and how this would lead them to Jim Sutherland.

Tess really had no idea how these names were all related, though it was certainly too odd to be coincidence. Maybe whoever made the jam and jelly was a Doyle fan too.

"This is weird," she muttered to her friend. "And my uncle..." She waved a hand at where Uncle Harold strode, his physical stamina certainly seeming unhindered by either age or weather. "He can pull up every detail of a Sherlock Holmes story but not remember the stories about the triplets I just told him? I'm worried, Lu. What if he's losing touch with reality?"

LuAnn wove their arms together. "He's just preoccupied. Focused on the mystery."

They were the right words to bring comfort. But somehow they didn't. "I just… He's the last one. And I'm not ready to think about losing him too. The thought of his mind failing, when that's what's always been most important to him—it breaks my heart, Lu."

"Oh, Tess." LuAnn gripped her hand. A rather squishy gesture, given the layers of insulated gloves between them. "I get it. I do. I don't think this is really anything to worry about, and I pray you've got years left with him. But at the same time… it's inevitable. He's, what, mideighties?"

Tess nodded and blinked until the sudden urge to cry passed. The last thing she needed was frozen eyelashes. "I know. But he's otherwise healthy. There's no reason he couldn't have another decade."

But there were never any guarantees. She knew that all too well. It was why she'd always believed in making each moment count.

LuAnn's phone vibrated in the pocket pressed to Tess's side, its ring singing out a second later. They separated enough that LuAnn could reach into her pocket, pulling a glove off with her teeth so she could swipe the screen. Though she still had a mouth full of fabric when she said, "Hello, hold on."

Tess took the opportunity to chuckle. At least until she heard the male voice coming through the speaker. It sounded like Brad, though she couldn't make out words so much as tones.

LuAnn's smile was certainly confirmation of the caller's identity though. Even before her, "Hey, yourself. We're out playing in the snow with Tess's uncle and his crew. Want to join us?"

Another indistinguishable something, then LuAnn laughed. "That does sound warmer than this. But I have a feeling you were calling about dinner."

Though LuAnn didn't sigh, Tess sighed for her. It was no big deal to have a date rescheduled in the grand scheme of things. Maybe Brad would even walk over to the inn for the evening. Still, it was no fun to have to change one's plans because of snow.

Instead of a romantic Italian meal, LuAnn would have to stay home with them and listen to Tess trying not to fret over her uncle.

She pressed her lips together as LuAnn said something about the roads probably being clear by Monday. Tess couldn't control the weather. But she *could* control the amount of worry she shoveled onto someone else's shoulders.

They seemed to have reached their destination, given the way the group stopped up ahead. Janice pointed at a sign partially obscured by snow, and she and Uncle Harold moved toward the door. Tess shifted enough to make out a stylized *V* on the sign. She had serious doubts they'd be open on a day like today, so she wasn't sure what they could possibly gain from coming here.

Despite her doubts, Janice and Uncle Harold disappeared into the building.

Well. It looked like she was wrong.

The line of amateur sleuths surged forward through the door. Tess moved along with them, though LuAnn stepped under the protective awning and waved her on, smiling into the phone. Tess smiled back and did her best to stomp the snow from her boots before she crossed the threshold into the shop.

Heat radiated out, enveloping her so suddenly that a happy little gasp escaped before she could think to stifle it. Of course, everyone else seemed just as pleased by it, so she didn't feel too self-conscious.

Dusting snow from her hat, she stepped out of the way so Bud and Matti could come in too and then looked around.

How had she never been in here before? It was a charming little shop, the shelves full of gorgeous glass items in every color imaginable. Some were functional—vases, bowls, sets of goblets—but others were more art or sculpture. There was a blue formation that put her in mind of angry ocean waves. A yellow one that hinted at a feminine form dancing.

"Beautiful," she said to no one in particular.

"Dude." To Tess's left, Kim smacked Ollie in the arm, her wide eyes glued to the shelf before her, which displayed a set of truly breathtaking drinkware. "I hope you brought your credit card, because I just found what you're getting me for my birthday. And possibly our anniversary. And depending on the price tags, next Christmas too."

As Ollie laughed, Tess skirted around them so she could get closer to Uncle Harold and Janice, though a gorgeous bowl stopped her in her tracks. That would look amazing on the reception desk. They could put decorative little doodads in it, seasonal things...

"Good morning! Wow, what a crowd." A woman emerged from a room in the back, her eyes just as wide at seeing their number as Kim's had been over the drinkware. She smiled, tucking a lock of salt-and-pepper hair behind her ear. "I knew we needed to open the shop today. Can I help you guys with anything?"

Janice stepped forward, the jar from the trash can still cradled in her gloves. "Hello! Cara, isn't it?"

The woman nodded, eyes narrowing as she clearly tried to place Janice. "That's right—Cara Fuller. My husband's the glassblower. You're one of the ladies from the inn, aren't you? I'm not great with names."

Janice grinned. "I am. I'm Janice. That's Tess, one of the other inn ladies, and LuAnn..." Janice stood on tiptoe, looking out over their group.

Tess stepped up beside her. "She's outside on the phone." She held out a hand toward Cara. "So good to meet you. Your husband's work is amazing—I can't believe I've never been in here before."

Cara beamed. "Isn't it? We just opened about a year ago. We've had a studio in Indianapolis for years, but when our son got a professorship at Marietta College, we decided to move to be closer to the grandkids." She grinned and waved a hand at the shelves. "Most of our business comes from custom orders online anyway, so the shop's location doesn't matter all that much."

Janice set the jar down on the counter, beside the cash register. "Well, it sounds as though you'll be getting some in-person business today." She grinned over at where Kim was inspecting price stickers. "But we actually came in to ask you a question about this." She patted the metal lid of the jar.

"Ah." Cara's brow furrowed as she lifted the jar to inspect it, turning it over to check the maker's mark before flipping it this way and that. "Sure. Ronan—that's my husband—made a few dozen of these a month or so ago for the Sutherlands." She wrinkled her nose as she studied the label, though she quickly smoothed it back out. "Paula makes the best jam—her specialty is this amazing Concord grape. Which you know, huh?"

"Actually, no." Janice motioned toward the outdoors at large. "We found the jar in a trash can, and I recognized the mark on the bottom."

"In a trash can?" Cara lowered the jar, her eyes wide with outrage. "You have got to be kidding me! Paula was only doing a limited run with these jars—the whole deal was that if the customer brought them back, they'd get a few free refills. She was giving out brochures for Verre with them, making it clear these are collectible, not just random mason jars. Not that you should even throw those away—almost all of what Ronan does here is with recycled glass. But to throw these away?" She looked back at the beautiful jar and huffed. "I'm glad you rescued it and returned it. I'll let Paula know."

"Well, um…" Janice looked from Tess to Harold and then back to their hostess. "We found it somewhere we suspected a *Jim* Sutherland had been—do you know if he's related to this Paula?"

Cara snorted and set the jar down again. "Unfortunately, yeah. Her husband. And it would just figure that he'd do something like this."

"Oh?" Though Uncle Harold's tone was measured, Tess recognized the gleam in his eye.

Cara drew in a deep breath. "Not that I usually speak ill of anyone—but *usually* people don't throw my husband's work away." She took another deep breath and shook her head a bit too, as if to clear it. "Sorry. Jim is just…supremely self-centered. He and Paula live just down the street from us, so we met them when we moved here. She's a generally sweet woman—and an amazing cook. But Jim…"

"What's he like?" Uncle Harold prodded.

Cara wrinkled her nose again. "Not what I'd expect for her, let's say. Maybe he's just too young and hasn't learned responsibility yet, I don't know. But it seems like every time he bats those 'dreamy' eyes of his—her word—she just loses all gumption."

"His *eyes.*" Harold sent a knowing look at those closest to him—Tess, Janice, Tom, Graham.

But what was she supposed to know? The Doyle character had something noteworthy about his eyes, right? They were weak or something. He wore shaded glasses, LuAnn had said.

Graham let out a long "Oh," as if he'd just had an epiphany. His lips slowly tilted up. "I see where you're going, Professor. Windibank's eyes were his best feature. Clear gray, very noteworthy. Which is why, when he disguised himself as Angel, he wore the shaded glasses."

Tess shook her head. "What does that have to do with Jim Sutherland?"

Her uncle ignored her and turned back to Cara. "What else can you tell us about this fellow? Or better still, do you know where we can find him?"

"Find who?" A tall, broad man emerged from the back. He wore a leather apron over jeans and a button-down shirt in a burnt-orange color that brought out the red in hair otherwise starting to gray. He had a pleasant look to his face, and he smiled at his wife even before he directed his smile to them, the potential customers. Always a sign of good character in Tess's book.

Cara greeted him with a smile too. "Jim Sutherland. He apparently threw away one of your jars."

The man who must be Ronan breathed a laugh and leaned into the counter. "Guess that's why he came in yesterday needing more."

"He did?" Cara frowned. "When was that?"

"Right as I was closing—you'd already left, to beat the snow." Ronan lifted his chin toward the door. "Came in as I was sweeping up, saying Paula had sold out of the collectible jars and wanted to place an order for a dozen more."

"So he was your last customer in here last night?" This came from Hiram, who was still over by the door, though he seemed to be listening.

"That's right."

"And has anyone else been in here this morning?"

Ronan laughed. "Uh, no. Frankly, I thought Cara was a little silly to insist we open today." He winked at his wife. "But she always knows best."

Cara shrugged. "You needed to get that order packed up anyway. So if you were coming in, I might as well too, and if we're here, we might as well turn on the sign."

"And if the sign's on, you might as well make a few bucks." Kim strode toward the counter with a victorious smile and hands full of the gorgeous blue glasses she'd been eyeing. Ollie followed a step behind, a human packing crate. "You have just made my empty china cabinet very, very happy." She slid the items in her hands onto the counter and then started unburdening her husband.

Hiram came closer, holding something in his hand. "So...I found this by the door. Business card." He lifted his brows and held it out toward Ronan and Cara. "Belong to you?"

Cara, being closer, took it and frowned. "Bender Off-Road. An ATV dealership?" She shook her head. "Definitely not ours. Someone must have dropped it."

"Where'd you find it?" Ronan asked.

Hiram, rather than answering aloud, went back over to the door and indicated a spot on the floor beside it with his toe.

"It definitely wasn't there when I was sweeping up yesterday. Jim must have dropped it." Ronan rolled his eyes. "No doubt picking out his next new toy."

"An ATV dealership?" Uncle Harold chuckled, though given the looks the others exchanged, they weren't getting the joke any better than Tess was. "Oh, this is too rich. Where is this Bender Off-Road located?"

Cara glanced at the card again. "Other side of town."

"Can we walk to it?"

She pursed her lips and glanced over at him, no doubt noting that Uncle Harold wasn't exactly a spring chicken. "Well, you probably *can*. But it would take a good forty-five minutes from here, I'd think."

Janice had peeked at the card and nodded her agreement. "It's about half an hour's walk from the inn, in the direction opposite this one. I walked that way with Larry over the summer, when he was on an all-things-with-wheels-and-motors kick."

"But we can't walk there now," Tess put in before Uncle Harold could proclaim it the next stop. "We need to get back to the café to serve lunch, in case anyone comes."

"And they might." Ronan chuckled as he rang up the sales. "Snow isn't enough to keep the customers away."

"You're walking?" Cara surveyed the collection of glass by the register. "Why don't you leave this here today, sweetie, and pick it up tomorrow, or when you have a car? You don't want to risk slipping and falling and breaking all this."

"No, we certainly don't." Ollie settled a hand on Kim's parka-thick waist. "We can just swing by on our way out of town, right, Professor?"

"Or we can drop them off later today. Are you staying at the inn?" At Kim's nod, Cara nodded too. "It's on our way home. It would be no problem at all."

"That's so nice of you," Kim said. "Thanks."

While they finalized the sale, Tess stole a look at the card Hiram had found on the floor. Though what she expected to see beyond the obvious, she really didn't know. It was just a business card, and unlike the jam label, she recognized the business name, as Janice had. Of course, there was no way to know for sure that it had been in the possession of Jim Sutherland.

Uncle Harold chuckled under his breath as he turned toward the door. "ATVs," he muttered. "Brilliant."

Frowning, she followed him to and then through the door. The cold hit her with a mighty whoosh of wind and snow that robbed her of the shop's warmth again. "What's so brilliant about an ATV dealership?"

LuAnn, just sliding her phone back into her pocket, grinned over at them. "What's that? Are we all going for four-wheeler rides or something?"

Uncle Harold laughed. "No, CC. But you've hit on it. You have *hit* on it."

"What?" Tess asked.

He waved her question off as the rest of the crew came out the door. "Oh, I won't be ruining it for the others, my girl. That would be no fun at all. Everyone must figure it out for themselves."

Tess looked at LuAnn—maybe his carbon copy could follow him. But her friend didn't seem to have a clue what, exactly, she'd "hit on" either. She shrugged.

Tess sighed and shook it away. "Did you reschedule your dinner?"

Maybe the flush in LuAnn's cheeks was just from the cold, but Tess didn't think so. Not given the soft smile that stole over her lips at the mere suggestion of Brad. "We're going to play it by ear. If it happens to be clear by tonight, awesome. If everything's clear by tomorrow, we'll do it then, either in the evening or right after church. I didn't figure you'd mind if I vanished while you were having your family lunch with Harold before he leaves."

"Family lunch?" Uncle Harold turned back to her with lifted brows.

Tess didn't like the surprise in his eyes. Not one bit. "Yes— you remember, don't you? I mentioned that I'd have the kids and grandkids over tomorrow after church."

He pulled his hat back on, having apparently taken it off at some point while they were inside. "I don't recall, but that sounds lovely. I haven't seen the triplets since they were babies."

He didn't recall the thing she'd been most looking forward to? Tess forced a smile. "I mentioned it in that email I sent you last week, when you asked about the times for check-in and checkout. Remember? I said checkout was at eleven, but we'd extend it so you could join me and the family for a meal."

Uncle Harold's head swung back and forth in a slow pen-dulum of a shake. "No, Tessie. You said we could check out late and have lunch here, but that was it."

What was the point in arguing with him? She drew in a breath and prayed her smile would show him only how much she loved him, and not her growing worry. "Well. The lunch will include the family, if that's all right."

"As I said—lovely." He took her hand and tucked it into the crook of his arm. But he also shot LuAnn an arched brow and stage-whispered, "Is she always so forgetful?"

LuAnn did a very bad job of trying to hold back a smile.

Tess tugged on her uncle's arm. "Come on. Let's get back to the inn so we can open the café."

"Excellent. And while we walk, LuAnn can tell me all about this book she mentioned she was writing."

Perfect. She was ready for a break from Doyle's fictional characters...and trying to figure out what they had to do with a disappearing delivery man who'd made off with a photograph of Prudence Willard.

Chapter Seven

Riverfront House
September 1858

Prudence didn't look over her shoulder as she headed down the stairs at the hotel, food for Billy in hand. Carrying a plate wouldn't look suspicious to anyone who saw her—but such paranoid actions might, and she'd long ago squelched any desire to indulge in them. Nay, instead she hummed a hymn of praise as she navigated the stairs and slipped through the dim basement toward the servant quarters. Her meetinghouse didn't incorporate music into their meetings, but she still liked to sing a few hymns when going about her day.

"Morning, Mrs. Willard."

Prudence smiled at one of the footmen, in his livery and on his way up the stairs. "Morning, Rutherford. How does thee fare this morning?"

"Just fine, ma'am." He tipped his cap and slid by her, never looking over his shoulder at the room to which he'd know she was heading. "Have a pleasant day. Give my regards to Mr. Willard."

"I certainly shall. Thank thee." She smiled and continued on her path. Her voice would have been loud enough to alert Billy that she was the one coming, but still she shifted the tray of food to one hand and knocked on the door in the agreed-upon way.

It opened with a nearly silent squeak, giving her just enough room to slip inside before closing it again behind her. "Got any news, ma'am?"

Prudence offered a smile that she prayed would bolster him as she handed over his breakfast. "A bit, yes." She pitched her voice low and shared all that Arnold had told her the evening before about where his Shandy was and their supposition that it was not a hired slave hunter who had captured her after all. "It seems they are bound for the auction at Boaz."

Billy sank down onto the cot, eyes vacant with despair. "What can we do then? Waylay 'em? Get to her before they get her there?"

"It is too late for that. They will already be there—the auctions are held every Thursday."

"Ain't that today?"

Prudence nodded and motioned to the food. "Go ahead."

But Billy shook his head and then lowered it into his hands with a groan. "What am I s'pposed to do, then? Can I even get there in time?"

"That would be foolhardy. Thee has no papers that claim thee is free, and if a slave shows up unaccompanied at an auction…"

He looked up, his face a mask of pain. "What can we do then?"

"Thee must trust the Friends. They will do everything in their power to claim thy wife on thy behalf." She sat on the wooden chair so she could lean down and speak even more quietly. "They have done such things before with great success. They are en route even now to the auction, dressed as prosperous farmers rather than in our traditional Quaker garb. They have gathered money from a collection among the Friends, and they will bid on her. They will win her, Billy. We must trust the gracious Father for this. They will secure her freedom and bring her here to thee." The smile she gave him now was bright with hope. "Soon thee will be reunited with thy wife."

Hope warred with disbelief in his eyes for a long, tortuous minute. "You really think they'll get her?"

Prudence nodded. "I believe it. With all my heart. The Lord has made a way, my friend. We have only to trust in it."

The sagging of his shoulders spoke not of defeat but of relief. He nodded. "Thank you. And them."

"Thee can thank them when they come with Shandy." Smiling, Prudence stood again and turned to the door. "I must be about my other duties. Does thee need anything?"

"No. No, if Shandy's all right, then I don't need nothing at all."

"Very well then. Elizabeth or I will check in on thee later." She motioned to the food. "Eat. Thee will need thy strength for the journey yet ahead."

She left him leaning toward the tray. Her normal daily tasks spun out before her in a list, each item ready to be checked off. She reviewed them as she climbed the stairs and turned toward the kitchen, but they all emptied again from her mind when she saw the boy standing in the middle of the hotel's kitchen, his distinctive Quaker hat clasped respectfully in his hands.

Prudence came to a quick halt, brows furrowing. "Hello."

The boy eyed her simple garb and smiled. "Prudence Willard?"

She nodded, trying to place the boy. She'd seen him before, she knew. But where?

He stepped forward, a hand outstretched. "My name is Levi. My parents run the Quaker Inn Station in Chester Hill."

Ah yes, that was it. She smiled. The inn in Chester Hill was quite often the next stop for travelers on the Underground Railroad. It was, in fact, where she'd been charged with sending Billy and Shandy—farther from the Ohio River, farther from the slave states. "Indeed, I know them well. But it has been quite a while since I have seen thee, Levi. Thee has grown!"

The boy grinned and shuffled a foot against the floor, suddenly bashful. "I've sprouted up a good deal this past year."

She chuckled. "Thee must be taller than thy mother now."

"Nearly." His eyes gleamed, but then he sobered. "It is not my parents who sent me today, though. I was visiting family in Virginia, and they asked me to bring thee this message. After talking with a mutual friend yesterday."

A mutual friend? Prudence reached for the envelope he held out, her chest tightening. He must be referring to the word Arnold had put out, asking for information about Shandy. "It is always good to hear from our Friends in Virginia. And kind of thee to stop here to share news of them. Is thee on thy way home?" She kept her smile easy and free of worry.

He nodded.

"Well, I thank thee for pausing here." She slid the envelope into her apron pocket, striving to look normal, just in case anyone was listening or peeking. "Does thee need to await a response?"

The boy shook his head. "I daren't. My mother expects me home today, and there are still many miles to travel."

Prudence smiled. "Lunch then?"

"No, though I thank thee. My aunt sent me with food enough to last the trip home and feed me for a week once there." He grinned again, boyish and innocent, despite the fact that he likely knew very well what news he'd carried to her, and that his parents wouldn't be expecting only *him* home but hidden guests as well.

She spun for the counter. "Allow me to at least send thee with a few cookies, as my thanks for playing postman."

"Well...I'm too smart to ever turn down a cookie."

Prudence laughed and pulled the cookie tin forward. She wrapped up a few in a square of wax paper they kept on hand for just such occasions—though usually it was guests requesting food to take with them either on a day's excursion or the next leg of their journey.

She handed them to Levi with a smile. "Give thy parents my best."

The boy thanked her with a grin and was soon gone. Prudence slipped the letter back out of her pocket and opened it. Her gaze ate up the words as soon as she unfolded the page to reveal them, her breath catching.

Yesterday evening a visitor arrived at our hotel looking for a missing package. I assured him I would help his search by asking other establishments like ours if they received any misdirected packages. He said he will travel to Boaz on Thursday to make inquiries there.

What? Prudence lowered the letter, her breath a fist in her chest. Someone else looking for Shandy? Asking about her? Planning to be at the auction?

"No. No, no, no." A hundred questions, fears, possibilities chased through her mind. It must be an actual slave hunter, unlike the men who were planning to sell Shandy at auction. And if so, he would come armed with letters giving him the authority to take her by force in the name of her owners. There would be no bidding on Shandy at all.

But she'd met men like the ones who had captured and now held Shandy. Men who cared about nothing but a profit. Men who would steal for it. Kill for it.

A shiver coursed through her, and she spun for the door. Men like that had been known to turn on the duly commissioned slave hunters when their legal claim got in the way of a quick profit. And the last thing any of them needed was for Shandy—not to mention the Friends—to be caught in the crossfire.

She had to warn them. Warn the Friends en route even now to the auction that danger could be awaiting them.

"Prudence?"

She whisked her light cloak from the peg by the door, not even turning to face Elizabeth. "I am ill." It wasn't a lie—her stomach was in knots again, her head pounding. "I will return when I can."

"Take your time, honey. I'll cover for you, you know that."

With a grateful nod for her friend, Prudence rushed out the door and away from the hotel. Down the street, out of town, toward the farm. The short distance seemed to stretch onward forever, given that she didn't dare run, lest it draw undue attention. She could only walk at her usual brisk pace, willing the road to pass more quickly beneath her feet.

Finally, the familiar lines of fencing that Jason had split by hand gave way to their yard, their house. Patience honked a greeting, waddling toward her with a flutter of wings. Prudence spared a quick smile and a pat for the goose but didn't slow much. Nay, now she broke into a run, aimed for the barn.

"Prudence! What is it?" Jason straightened from where he'd been bent over a piece of broken equipment inside the barn.

She explained in as few words as possible, shoving the letter at him. She ended with, "I must go. Catch the Friends, warn them. Does thee know who went?"

Jason's eyes flashed. Worry, both for them and, as always, for her. "Isaiah Brown and Johnmark Smith. But they left two hours ago. Thee will never catch them, my love."

She raised her chin. "The Lord will have to grant me wings. I cannot let them walk into danger. And that poor girl—if a hunter with a legal claim is there...escape will once more be her only hope. Our efforts to purchase her will come to naught in that case."

She could see the familiar war in his eyes. The desire to protect her pitted against the desire to help others in need. After an infinite moment, he nodded and abandoned his tools, handing the letter back to her. "I will saddle Charity."

A pleasant hum of chatter filled the café—more than Tess had honestly expected on this snowy day. Though no one had braved the roads that were yet again covered, a few neighbors had come in for a hot bowl of soup when they saw the OPEN sign aglow. With the Sherlock Society factored in, they were nearly full. For now—she suspected the room would be empty long before they usually closed.

LuAnn exited the kitchen with a few baskets of fresh bread in her hands and a smile on her face. "Here." She held out one of the baskets. "Deliver this for me, will you? I noticed that some of the tables were low."

"Sure."

"Then I think we're good, if you wanted to grab a bowl and sit with your uncle."

Tess nodded, smiling at her friend. She delivered the bread, refilled a few cups while she was up, and then had to chuckle when she turned to her uncle's table and saw that the seats weren't just filled—a few extras had even been pulled up around him.

He was, as he always liked to be, the center of attention. And he seemed to be in the middle of a lecture, brandishing his spoon like a pointer. Tess caught something about "a basic misunderstanding of Victorian society on the part of modern Americans" and decided that she'd leave him to his rapt pupils and find somewhere else to sit.

Soup in hand a minute later, she spotted an empty chair at Matti and Bud's table and headed that direction. She may have hesitated to intrude on the couple, but Bud was talking over his shoulder to Hiram at Uncle Harold's table, so she didn't think she'd really be interrupting anything. Still, she felt a moment's hesitation, given Matti's mood that morning. The last thing she wanted to do was make her guest uncomfortable.

Matti, however, looked up with a faint smile and motioned to the chair. "Want to join us, Tess?"

"Thanks. I'd love to." She sat with a happy exhalation. "I'm so glad you guys made it in before this storm struck. It would have been an awfully quiet weekend otherwise."

"To be perfectly honest, I advised against it." Matti swirled her spoon through her soup. From the looks of her nearly full bowl, that's all she'd been doing for the last twenty minutes.

Bud turned back to face them. The look he settled on his wife's face was...deep. Tess couldn't quite pinpoint it. Part worry, maybe. Part determination. And a big part love. "But aren't you glad Harold prevailed, sweetheart? This is way better than being stuck at home."

Matti patted Bud's hand and gave him a smile. "Yeah. You're right."

Tess motioned to Matti's bowl. "Would you like a different kind of soup, Matti?"

"Hm?" She looked down at her cheddar broccoli, seeming a bit surprised that her bowl was still full. "Oh, no. It's delicious. I guess I'm just not very hungry."

Tess said a silent prayer. She didn't know what had Matti so distracted and upset this weekend, but she knew the best thing she could do was lift her up before the Father. And show her love. Right now, she had a feeling the best way to show that was not to press. She summoned up a smile. "So, Bud. Tell me about this evidence collection kit. Do you seriously carry it around all the time?"

At Bud's robust laugh, even Matti's lips tugged up. He nodded. "I do, actually. I leave it in my car all the time. At first I'd only bring it on official Sherlock Society outings—we occasionally stage mysteries for each other, you know. But eventually those mysteries crept into other days of the week too, and we just never knew when we might stumble across something we needed to investigate."

Tess's brows had climbed upward. "You stage mysteries for each other? How did I not know this?"

"Sherlock-inspired ones, of course." Bud nudged Matti's arm with his. "Mat's the one who started it."

For the first time since she arrived, Matti's eyes twinkled. "Well, me and a few of the other early members. We were tired of the professor's know-it-all-ism," she said loudly, teasing, "and thought we'd see if he was really as clever as he thought he was."

From his table, Uncle Harold laughed. "And what did you find, Matilda?"

Matti chuckled. "That it's wiser to let you stage them, otherwise you have it all figured out in about five minutes."

"You see, Tessie, you come by your sleuthing skills honestly."

Tess chuckled and shook her head. "It seems you outdo me by a long shot. We never have everything figured out in five minutes."

"It's a bit different, I suppose, when the mysteries are real. And not based upon stories one has all but memorized." Uncle Harold leaned back in his chair, thoroughly relaxed. The twinkle in his eyes certainly *looked* as sharp as ever. No haze of confusion. No vague expression. "But back to your pack, Bud." He waved a hand.

Bud smiled at Tess. "It's evolved over the years. It started out not much more than a notebook and pen. Then we added a measuring tape, a stiff ruler."

"Magnifying glass," Matti added. She motioned toward the glass, pipe, and hat sitting in the middle of the table like a centerpiece. "Because, you know. Sherlock."

"And it's come in quite handy. Binoculars too. Plastic baggies, tweezers, rubber gloves, tape, some basic mold-making supplies. I used to carry a disposable camera in there, but that's become unnecessary with smartphones."

"Basically, any time someone has mentioned wishing they had something while we're having our little adventures, Bud adds it to the pack." Matti spooned some soup into her mouth.

Bud grinned. "Once a scout, always a scout. I must be prepared."

"Wow." Tess glanced around to see where LuAnn and Janice were and if they were listening. She found them one table over, the impressed arch of their brows proving they were. "Taking notes, Lu?"

Her friend laughed. "And which of us is going to start hauling all that around everywhere we go?"

"Why, you, of course," Tess said. Janice nodded her agreement.

LuAnn, with another laugh, shook her head. "No, no. I'm the carbon copy of the professor. He's not the pack mule." She sent a wink toward Bud and Matti.

The shared laughter warmed Tess…and so did the next bite of soup Matti ate with gusto. Apparently she'd found her appetite.

CHAPTER EIGHT

I t's not a problem at all," Janice was saying to someone in the hall when Tess came down the stairs after fetching a thicker pair of socks. They'd just closed the café, after giving any other neighbors a little more time to come in. Time they'd filled with LuAnn reading "A Case of Identity" to them so Tess and Janice weren't totally in the dark about the story Uncle Harold kept referring to.

"You go on down, and I'll just grab that before I forget and put it in your room."

"Thanks, Janice," Tess heard Matti say.

Tess continued on the last few steps, gaining the third-floor hallway just as Matti was disappearing down the stairs. Janice still stood in front of one of the closed doors, her phone in hand. Tess lifted her brows. "Everything good?"

"Sure. She just asked for a spare pillow for tonight. And Stacy texted a picture of Larry in the snow." With a grin, Janice showed Tess her phone, which was displaying an adorable photo of her grandson doing a good imitation of the abominable snowman.

Tess would no doubt be getting some photos of the triplets out enjoying the snow before the day was over too. "So cute." She glanced toward the stairs again and sighed then pitched her voice low. "Would you pray for Matti with me? I feel like she could use it, though I'm not sure why."

Janice nodded. "Of course. She does seem a little down, doesn't she? Not that I know her very well." She pursed her lips, eyes distant with thought. "You know, I have a few Scripture cards I made last week when I was practicing my calligraphy. Maybe I'll get one and deliver it with her extra pillow."

"Oh, that sounds perfect. I'll grab the pillow, if you want to run upstairs for the card."

"Deal."

Tess hurried toward the closet where they stored the linens, extra pillows, and blankets. When she arrived back at Apples and Cinnamon, Janice was just coming back as well, brandishing a pretty handmade card. She held it out for Tess to see.

Look to the Lord and his strength; seek his face always. —1 Chronicles 16:11 was written on it in beautiful lettering.

"Perfect. And gorgeous, Janice. Hopefully that will let her know that she's in our prayers." She fished in her pocket for the ring of room keys and soon had Apples and Cinnamon open. After she set the pillow on the bed, Janice positioned the card against it. They slipped out again with a shared smile.

"Ready to head back into the snow?" Janice asked on their way down.

Tess couldn't hold back a sigh. "I guess so. Though I seriously thought this would be a quiet weekend spent in the parlor with the whiteboard. I guess I should have known better. My uncle has always taken any excuse to play in the snow—I should have known that wouldn't have changed just because he's getting older."

Janice patted her arm. "I think it's wonderful that he's still so active. The longer you keep moving, the longer you're able to, that's what my mom always used to say. And all this mystery-solving no doubt keeps him sharp."

"Yeah." Tess buttoned her lips against the questions that wanted to spill out. She'd already promised herself she wouldn't burden LuAnn with them, and that wasn't permission to shove them onto Janice instead.

No, she needed to hand her concerns over to the Lord. Whatever was or wasn't going on with her uncle, He had him in His hand. She knew that.

Still. She wasn't ready for *in His hand* to mean either taking his mind or taking him. *I know You have this all under control, Lord,* she prayed silently as they regained the ground floor and headed toward their snow gear. *But I need Your strength for whatever lies ahead. I know that sooner or later, things* will *change for him, in some way or another. And it all terrifies me. I've said goodbye to so many already...*

The prayers insulated her a bit from the chatter filling the lobby. Along with the others, Tess pulled on her outerwear, but she felt a step removed as she watched them all bantering and laughing. Matti was adjusting something on Bud's coat. Kim and Ollie were still talking glassware. Graham and Hiram were both razzing Tom on the number of rolls he'd eaten during lunch, while the youngest member of the crew claimed yet again to still be a growing boy.

It was a good group, for sure. But at the moment, as her uncle patted his pockets, clearly looking for something, Tess was keenly aware that the only two permanent members of the society were Bud and Matti. The others came and went as their lives took them to and from Oberlin.

And as Tess and her friends knew from their own years of teaching, despite the best intentions, most students didn't really keep in touch with their former teachers after life took them away from the school. There were the exceptions, of course. But they certainly weren't the rule. Uncle Harold had always claimed that his students, his Society, were his family. But how many were really *there* when he needed them?

Her uncle finally found in which of his many pockets he'd stashed his gloves and pulled them on as he shouted, "Ready?" At the enthusiastic agreement, he opened the door. "Sally forth!"

At least the snow hadn't intensified while they were nestled away inside with their soup and conversation. If the hourly forecast could be trusted, it wasn't due to turn from "light snow" back into "heavy snow" for another three hours. That should give them time enough to walk to the ATV dealership and home again. She hoped. It would surely take longer in the snow than it had when Janice walked it in the summertime.

Though Tess couldn't resist touching a hand to her uncle's down-encased arm and saying, "Are you sure you wouldn't rather just settle in by the fire and talk about the actual Sherlock stories? Wading through a foot of snow—"

"Half a foot, that's all." Uncle Harold took her hand and tugged her down to the sidewalk. "It's good exercise."

LuAnn fell into position on Uncle Harold's other side. Her mouth was open, ready to speak, but she didn't bother trying when the sound of rumbling and scraping sliced through the air. The snowplow was making another round.

Tess turned and spotted it coming around the corner. "Oh, good."

LuAnn grinned. "If the snow stops and the plow comes through one more time, I might actually be able to make it to dinner tonight after all."

"This is your date?" Uncle Harold sent LuAnn an exaggerated frown. "I'm not sure I've forgiven you yet, CC, for getting starry-eyed over someone who isn't fictional. And at your age! I thought you were immune."

LuAnn gave him the expected elbow to the side. "My age! Are you calling me old?"

"Unabashedly." His mouth twitched in that way of his again.

LuAnn narrowed her eyes. "And what does that make *you*?"

He chuckled. "I believe the technical phrase may be 'older than dirt.'"

"I think it's lovely." Janice looped her arm through LuAnn's. "A second chance at love after all these years of dedicating herself so fully to her students and God's work. She deserves it."

"She certainly does." Nothing had made Tess happier than those years with Jeffrey. Raising a family with him. Just knowing that no matter what life brought, there would be someone at her side to weather it with her. She still missed him so much.

And she praised God for that gleam in LuAnn's eyes now. Her friend's life had been full and beautiful without a husband, Tess knew. But God was full of surprises. And she was having such fun watching the budding romance between Brad and LuAnn.

"You know, Professor..." LuAnn shot him a teasing grin. "It isn't too late for you either. Brad has two eligible aunts."

Tess and Janice both hooted with laughter at the thought of either of the sisters—the younger of whom was almost ninety—paired with her uncle. And their laughter was apparently reason enough for him to shudder.

"No thank you, my girls. I am quite content with my lot. Like Holmes himself, I have my mysteries, my music, and my friends—a fellow needs no more than that. Now"—with a flourish, he motioned them closer—"let me regale you with the tale of how one of our former members, Jack, and I staged a recreation of *The Hound of the Baskervilles* a few years ago."

The story kept them entertained through the snowy walk—some parts of which were relatively easy, where industrious townspeople had come out to clear off their sidewalks already. Other parts, they were trudging through the inches, though Graham and Tom had taken the lead so they could break the path for the rest of them. Janice provided the directions whenever they reached an intersection.

Just as Uncle Harold was wrapping up his tale, the familiar sign of the dealership came into view. "Jack devised quite a clever setting for the adaptation. But I have to say, this one's proving even more interesting. ATVs!"

"Wait." LuAnn turned a frown on him. "Is that what you think is going on here? A restaging of 'A Case of Identity'?"

Uncle Harold chuckled. "My prize pupil. Of course it is. What else could it be?"

"But..." LuAnn darted a look at Tess that said, *Well, at least you know there's nothing to worry about* and then around the group. "But you obviously didn't do it. And they all got here when you did. How could any of you have set all this up?"

"That *is* a bit of a mystery." Uncle Harold surveyed his club members too, craning around to accomplish it. "Someone has really done their homework."

But they all looked at him blankly. And Tess for one didn't detect any trace of deception in their postures or faces. The two guys up ahead even craned around to send them curious looks, obviously trying to figure out who had done it as well.

Matti shook her head. "Professor, you know none of us were that on top of things this time. Kim and Ollie have been closing on their house, Tom's been overwhelmed with his new classes, Graham and Hiram have both been working fifty-hour weeks. And we..." She trailed off and stiffened. "Well, you know Bud and I haven't had the time for this."

Uncle Harold merely turned his arched brows on Tess and her friends. "Then perhaps one of you has been recruited to assist. I don't know who is responsible, but clearly someone is. Because this, my friends, is a brilliant interpretation of our chosen story."

For a minute, Tess did actually wonder if maybe LuAnn or Janice could have put something like this together. But they would have told her—and they wouldn't have looked so confused at her uncle's strange logical leaps, if that were the case. They certainly wouldn't have just let her blather on about concerns for his mind.

No, the Inn Crowd was certainly not responsible. But neither, it seemed, was the Sherlock Society. It would have been quite a process for any of them to set something up in Marietta without help, and who would they have contacted for assistance other than the inn? They'd have been their logical contact.

Tess shook her head. "It wasn't us, Uncle Harold. And I daresay we would have been in on it were it any of the others. Sorry to say, I don't think this has anything to do with your story of the weekend—it's just a weird coincidence."

But LuAnn's silent message to her a minute ago did have a point. If he thought that's what this was—whether he was right or not—it did explain his thinking. He might be misguided, but he wasn't downright confused. That eased the tension in her chest quite a bit.

The gleam in Harold's eyes didn't dim any. "Let's just see if your Mr. Sutherland was here, shall we?"

"Let's see if *anyone* is here." Janice took the lead, high-stepping through the snow in the unplowed lot. The various all-terrain vehicles they had on display were under an overhang, but still some snow had blown in to cover them. Inside the building that housed the business proper, lights were on, but the OPEN sign wasn't lit. Janice tried the door, but it didn't budge. "Hmm."

Uncle Harold stepped up beside her and knocked on the glass door.

Tess stayed a few steps away rather than crowding in, surveying the situation. There was a truck parked by the side of the building—late model, black—with very little snow on it, proving it hadn't been there overnight. And tire tracks leading from it to the road, partially covered over again. Clearly someone *was* here.

"There's a second set of tracks too." Hiram pointed to what he'd seen. And indeed, a second set mostly followed the first into the lot and then stopped in a parking spot a few stalls down. Hiram directed lifted brows at Bud. "Wanna measure? See if it's the same as the one from the alley?"

"I'm on it." His handy-dandy pack in hand, Bud hustled in that direction.

Tess turned back to the door when she heard the *snick* of a lock. A smiling man was even then pushing it open. "Well now, I didn't expect to see anyone else today. I was just locking up. Can I help you folks?"

Was it just her, or did his voice sound a little too bright?

"Anyone else?" Her uncle flashed the salesman a winning smile. "Have you had other customers today, Mr....?"

"Bender. But just call me Andy." Andy held out a hand and shook Uncle Harold's gloved one. "You folks want to come in?"

Janice looked down at their snow-encrusted boots and then at the tile floor polished to a shine. "No, no. We'd make a mess of your showroom. But if we could have just a minute of your time to ask you a couple of questions, that would be wonderful."

"Sure. Let me grab my coat, and I'll be right out."

Hiram came over, waving a Polaroid snapshot in the air once he was safely under the awning, out of the snow. "Same measurements as the tracks behind the museum," he said.

"Of course they were." Uncle Harold nodded his approval.

Andy, clad now in a heavy coat over his jeans and button-down shirt, stepped outside again with a big smile fastened in place. "There we go. Now, what I can do for you all?"

Though everyone looked to Uncle Harold, he nodded toward Janice, LuAnn, and Tess. Probably thought he was sharing the fun.

Well, Tess and her friends certainly had plenty of experience with asking questions. She smiled at Andy. "We're trying to find a friend and thought he may have stopped by here recently. Do you happen to know Jim Sutherland?"

"Oh, sure. *Jim* was here this morning." Andy waved a hand toward the side of the building, where they'd noticed the tracks. "He came in to take a look at our most popular four-wheeler model—the 450 HO."

"In this weather?" LuAnn asked.

Andy shrugged. "We do sell plow attachments too. You'd be surprised how many times bad weather inspires a purchase."

Tess was still stuck on the way he'd said *Jim*. Almost as if there were air quotes around the name. Why the emphasis? "Do you know Jim well?"

"He's come in a few times lately. I wouldn't call us friends, but I know him when I see him."

"And is he always looking at the same thing?" Uncle Harold swept his gaze over the vehicles in the parking lot and then through the glass door toward the models in the showroom. There were certainly a variety—four-wheelers, dirt bikes, go-carts, dune buggies.

"Um." Andy's brow wrinkled. "Just...four-wheelers." He sounded none too sure. Then nodded a bit too enthusiastically. "He's checked out the different models, but he's not looking for a dirt bike or anything. Definitely four-wheelers."

"Four-wheelers!" From the back of their crowd, Kim's exclamation was followed by a laugh. When Tess turned, she saw the young woman slapping a hand to her head. "Oh, duh! Of course! Windibank, posing as Angel, made his escape from a *four-wheeler*! The carriage, in the story."

Uncle Harold chuckled. "Well done, Kimberly."

With the Doyle story now fresh in her mind, Tess drew in a sharp breath. The four-wheeled carriage had indeed been a key piece of the puzzle for Sherlock Holmes, though Tess hadn't quite understood why. Apparently they were easy to get out of without the driver knowing, given that Holmes had referred to it as an old trick. Unlike, she supposed, one of the open rigs, like the smaller one Miss Sutherland and her mother had taken to the church in the story.

"Any other questions?" Andy burrowed his hands into his pockets.

"Have you ever met his wife?" Ollie asked.

Andy shook his head. "Nah, it's always just Jim that comes in."

Uncle Harold swept a gaze over the group. "Anyone else have other questions for Andy?" At the collective head shaking, he held a hand out again toward the dealer. "We do thank you for your time on this snowy day."

Andy shook again. "Sure thing. Happy to help." With that, he slipped back inside.

Uncle Harold held out his arms and waved his hands inward, like a sports coach calling a huddle. "All right, everyone, put together what we've discovered thus far."

Bud rejoined them, still zipping his pack. "We know that the vehicle parked here is the same one from behind the museum—or the same model, anyway. Measurements were an exact match."

"And we know that Jim Sutherland was here. So it stands to reason that he was also the one behind the museum," Kim added.

"Which," Tom said, "we could also surmise from the jam jar, was a limited-edition item that his wife purchased. While there are certainly more of those around town, the chances of someone else who had one also having the same model truck are pretty slim. Not to mention the gold paint on the trash can."

"We know that his wife's jam business is called Westhouse and Marbank." Hiram slid his newest photograph into his camera bag.

"Which is the same name as the business in 'A Case of Identity' where James Westibank worked—a wine distributor."

Graham wore a crooked smile. "That man must have handled a lot of bottles."

"Bottles—of grapes. Grape jam is Paula Sutherland's specialty, which we learned at the glassblower's." Janice's eyes had widened. She turned them on Tess. "It does line up rather perfectly."

It did, Tess had to admit. So what did that mean? Had someone among them come up with this, set it all up for the rest of the group? She still didn't know how they could have, but for the moment, she'd just have to table that thought and focus on the rest of it. "Okay. So if we accept that these parallels are purposeful, what does that imply? That Jim Sutherland is...what? Our villain? Our culprit?" She sighed and looked to her uncle. "But there's no monetary interest like in the short story. Westibank's entire motivation was Miss Sutherland's income, which he wanted to keep. Jim Sutherland just has a *chair*. With a photograph. Nothing worth money enough to warrant something like this."

"True." Her uncle tilted his head. "But I daresay it's more about what's important to a person. For some, it's simple money. For others..." He shrugged. "No one has mentioned the key clue yet. The one that allowed Sherlock to solve the case."

There was silence for a beat, then Matti said, sounding nearly exasperated, "Oh, come on, you guys. *The letter.*"

Of course. The thing that had started it all.

CHAPTER NINE

The letter." Tess, her gaze locked on Matti, sighed. "Like the one Sylvia left on the door of the museum. But there's only been one letter. The whole thing for Sherlock was that he had two to compare and could see that the *E* key had the same wear."

"Yeah," Tom said, "but Sherlock had to take some action to acquire that piece of evidence. He had to send a note to Westhouse and Marbank requesting an audience with Windibank." He folded his arms over his chest, his face a mask of consideration. "So do we need to reach out to this Jim guy somehow?"

"How, though?" LuAnn asked. "We don't know where he works, just that he was helping Sylvia and Stan out at the museum. And he's apparently a neighbor of Cara and Ronan." She turned a bit to look back at the light snow drifting down. "The modern-day equivalent would be sending him a text or something, but we don't have his phone number either."

"Wait!" Janice bounced a bit with excitement. "Remember what Sylvia's letter actually said? That they knew Jim was fine because he'd just posted a photo on Facebook."

LuAnn reached into her pocket. "I think I'm friends with Sylvia on Facebook, and she must be friends with him. Bet I can find his profile."

Tess stepped back and watched the group. They were all straining toward LuAnn, trying to see her tiny screen over her shoulder once she freed it from her pocket, while Uncle Harold presided over them from a step away as well, that crooked smile she'd always loved on his face. He was in his element.

Rightly so, apparently. He'd known from the moment they spotted the letter on the museum door that something strange was afoot, and had seen right away this morning that it was no coincidence that their mystery had so much in common with "A Case of Identity."

But while the others seemed to have no trouble accepting that this was another example of a story reenactment, Tess couldn't keep from going back to the *how*. How would one of them have set it up? She'd chatted with pretty much everyone last night, and none of them had ever been to Marietta before.

But maybe someone had reached out online. To...Sylvia. This all originated at the museum, after all. Maybe Sylvia had been recruited into helping.

Tess looked up, back toward the heart of Marietta. Not that she could see the museum from here, of course. Was that possible, though? Could Sylvia be the one behind this?

She hadn't seemed to know that any Sherlockians were coming to town yesterday when they ran into each other on the street—and Sylvia wasn't the greatest actress in the world. When she and Stan had come to town under false pretenses a few months ago, Tess and her friends had been able to tell right away that something wasn't right.

Kind of like… She spun back to the door of the ATV dealership. Kind of like how Andy Bender here had been acting. Like he was reciting lines.

She closed her eyes and tried to think back to the encounter yesterday afternoon. Man, had it only been twenty-four hours ago? They'd tromped through an awful lot of snow since then.

Sylvia had hailed her to tell her about the chair. Had that all been a ruse, part of the game? Was there even a chair? Or was that just part of the story she had come up with to help out whichever of these guys had staged this thing?

Sylvia had been amused at Tess's props. Had asked her if she was attending a Sherlock convention. Proof, perhaps, that she already had Sherlock on the brain? Or was it simply the logical first thought when one saw someone with a deerstalker, pipe, and magnifying glass?

Tess's lips quirked up. Probably the logical first thought. But that didn't rule out the other. She *had* said she was a fan of Sir Arthur Conan Doyle. Maybe she was in some online group and had met someone from the society through it. It wasn't entirely unreasonable.

"What are you thinking?" Janice slid up beside her and spoke in hushed tones.

"Just trying to work through how someone would have set this up for Uncle Harold and his group. I keep coming back to Sylvia."

Janice pursed her lips. "She's certainly at the heart of this whole thing. The one who sent the chair with Jim, the one who taped the letter to the door." She wrinkled her nose. "Not to sound like a nervous Nellie—or maybe like a suspicious Sally—but...what if this is all a red herring? A decoy mystery to distract us from something else?"

A pang struck. Tess wanted to believe the best of Sylvia and Stan, and she knew Janice wanted to as well. But the couple had deceived them all before when they were on the hunt for information, and Stan hadn't seemed exactly repentant. He was definitely the sort who thought the ends justified the means.

"But what would they be trying to cover up with this?" Tess darted a glance back at the rest of the group, who were paying them no attention. "Something about the chair? They didn't have to mention it to us."

"Or something we don't even know about?" Janice shrugged. "Let's hope not. It's more reasonable to think they were just recruited by someone else to help with this staged mystery."

"It is." Tess tapped a finger to her thigh. "Except that in the story, the true villain was the one who orchestrated the letters. That would be Sylvia."

Janice granted the point with lifted brows. "So...what? She's the one who planned for Jim to lead us on a wild-goose chase?"

"Maybe. I really don't know."

"Aha! Found him!" LuAnn's shout spurred Tess and Janice to spin back to face her and the rest of the group. She was smiling down at her phone. "Now that I convinced my app to load properly. Jim Sutherland, with ten mutual friends, from Marietta, Ohio. Looks like many of his posts are public, so we can scroll through without having to friend him first."

"Huh." Tom squinted at the screen. "He even looks like how Windibank is described. Well, I mean, the striking gray eyes and fair hair. Doyle didn't really describe him otherwise, aside from being over-confident."

"Doesn't look like he's been on this site for long. Not much here to see." LuAnn scrolled down, then back up, with a fingertip. "Quite a few reposts, half a dozen photos. That's it."

"Wait, go back." Kim was leaning into LuAnn's shoulder. "That second photo."

LuAnn scrolled, tapped, and widened her eyes.

Tess and Janice edged closer, though they couldn't get anywhere near visual range of the phone. "What is it?" Tess asked.

"Looks like a photo of a typed sheet of paper." LuAnn breathed a laugh. "Good eyes, Kim. I thought it was just a meme on a white background."

Harold leaned closer, squinting. "Can you enlarge that, CC? And Bud, if you would—"

"I'm on it." Bud slung his pack around and unzipped it. After a moment's fishing, he whipped out the white copy paper with the typed message from Sylvia.

"Check the *E*'s first," Harold instructed.

Bud stepped a little more under the cover of the roof when a gust of wind blew errant snowflakes his way. "Nothing odd about them on here. But it looks like there's a bit missing from the lowercase *o*. Top left. Little tiny opening."

"Top left of an *O*..." LuAnn manipulated the image on her phone a bit and grinned. "Here."

When she held the phone out, Tess managed to jockey herself into a position to actually see it. As she'd expected given LuAnn's reaction, the *O* she'd zoomed in on was as Bud had described.

Uncle Harold chuckled. "May I presume that we all know what this means?"

"Back to the museum!" Graham, on the edge of the group, held out an arm and proceeded to follow it out from under the porch area and into the snow.

As the rest of them fell in behind, Tess eased into position beside her uncle again. She'd see if she could maybe solve the mystery of more concern to her—who the architect of this little mystery could be. "So how do you guys pick which stories you're going to study during your weekend?"

"Democratic process, to an extent." Uncle Harold cast a gaze upward when they stepped out into the weather again. The clouds, Tess noted, were still heavy and gray. "Our choices are limited a bit by what we've done recently. The canon, after all, has only so many selections. Though with the turnover in the group, it doesn't get too redundant for anyone."

"Much to my surprise," Bud piped in from behind them. "When Mat roped me into this thirty years ago, I thought for sure it was going to be boring." He chuckled. "Turns out, I can't imagine life without it. It's been really great to get to know the other avid readers. And we always spot something new, every time we read one of the stories."

"So this story? 'A Case of Identity,' I mean. Was it voted on, or just up for its turn?" Tess looked from her uncle's profile to Bud and Matti, over her shoulder.

"Up for its turn—though it was also a last-minute addition," Matti said. "We were planning on only covering *The Valley of Fear* this weekend, but when we saw the forecast and realized we might be snowed in—we'd originally scheduled some downtime for sightseeing—Harold and Bud and I thought we'd better toss in a short story too. So we added the next short story from our list."

Tess felt her brows pull down and had to make a concerted effort to smooth them back out. "You keep a list? Like a schedule?"

"A loose one." Her uncle smiled. "The youngsters even have it online and update it regularly."

So it would have been readily visible to anyone who went looking.

Harold chuckled and wagged a gloved finger at her. "I know what you're thinking, Tessie. That one of us staged it. But we never recreate the stories we're currently reading—that would be far too obvious."

"So the fact that this is 'A Case of Identity' points to someone *outside* the society?"

He nodded. "Exactly so. Which is most intriguing. Who would go to this trouble for us? I hope to figure that out. I honestly didn't expect such a thing this weekend."

"Have you guys ever done a reenactment of this one before?" she asked once they'd crossed the street and were back on a sidewalk.

Harold shook his head. "To be frank, this isn't one of our favorite stories." His lips twitched. "Especially for the ladies among us. One of our first members, Gigi, especially railed against it for its closing observation on women."

Tess snorted her agreement. At the end of the story, Sherlock Holmes didn't reveal his findings to Miss Sutherland because "there is danger for whoso snatches a delusion from a woman." As if the heartsick girl would rather think her beloved mysteriously vanished than to confront the truth about her own mother and stepfather's cruel trick.

Tess could understand this Gigi's opinion. She had shaken her head too.

The flurries were a light but steady snow again by the time the eleven of them tromped back down the alley where they'd found the trash can and tracks. There were more tracks now...but the trash can was nowhere in sight.

Relevant? Tess had no idea, but she wasn't surprised when Hiram and Tom both paused to take some photos. The rest of them, however, hurried toward the museum's back door.

"Do you think anyone is even here?" Janice huddled close to Tess and LuAnn.

The cold was seeping through Tess's winter gear, for sure. She was ready for a heated interior, a blanket, and maybe a cup of cocoa. "I have no idea, but I hope we answer the question soon so we can get home."

LuAnn chuckled. "Yeah, I've had about enough mystery-solving for one day."

"Should we go around front or try back here?" Kim and Ollie were a step away from the back door, Kim looking to Uncle Harold for guidance.

His answer was to step up beside them and bang on the door.

Tess honestly didn't expect the knock to yield a result, so she jumped when, within a few seconds, the door swung open.

Sylvia stood in the doorway, dressed in winter gear of her own, and a cat-ate-the-canary smile. "'It's not actionable, sir. It's not actionable.'"

The words sounded vaguely familiar. "Wasn't that what Windibank said?" Tess murmured to her friends.

LuAnn nodded. "In response to Holmes confronting him."

Uncle Harold's booming laughter echoed through the alley. "'It is quite too transparent, and it was a very bad compliment when you said it was impossible for me to solve so simple a question.'" He held out his arms.

To Tess's utter stupefaction, Sylvia, laughing along with him, stepped outside and into his embrace. "Professor! I can't believe how long it's been!"

Uncle Harold gave her one of his patented squeezes and then held her back at arm's length. "Gigi. I ought to have known it was you. You always did take issue with this story in particular."

"A woman's delusions, indeed." Sylvia grinned and stepped back, taking in the rest of the group with a continued smile. "I hope you had a few hours' entertainment, anyway. When I saw online that this story was next up for you guys, I couldn't resist."

"Wait." Tom was frowning at them, his cell phone still out and poised to take more photos. "I am clearly missing something."

"I think we all are," Janice agreed.

Tess knew she certainly was. Did Sylvia actually know her uncle? Well, clearly she did. But how?

Uncle Harold chuckled again and motioned toward Sylvia. "Allow me to introduce one of the Sherlock Society's earliest members. Gigi was a student at Oberlin when I first conceived the idea."

LuAnn's brows arched. "Wait. Sylvia's name's not Gigi."

Sylvia laughed and flicked the end of her braid. "Not Gigi, the name. Initials—GG. For 'Golden Girl,' which was a play on my hair. Well, and the fact that I joked about being his best student." Her gaze went to Tess. "I can't believe the professor is your uncle! When you mentioned him yesterday afternoon, though, I knew it had to be him. I love that you're still running the society, Professor."

"Well, what else would I be doing?"

Graham lifted a hand, a question dug into his forehead. "Okay, so...you set all this up, clearly."

Sylvia grinned. "In a bit of a whirlwind. I was still recruiting people to help me this morning. Had to really do some badgering with Andy Bender, who claims he's no good at this sort of thing."

"He *did* seem a little uncomfortable," Tess agreed.

"You pulled this all together since yesterday evening?" Uncle Harold whistled. "I'm impressed."

"Seriously." Hiram tucked his camera back into its bag. "Last time I helped with one of these mysteries it took us a whole week to figure out how to stage all the details. You had to type up the notes, plant the trail to lead us to the glass-blower and the ATV place, make the tire tracks and whatnot in the alley—"

"Rather polite of the snow to cooperate." Sylvia grinned and tucked her braid into her coat. "I wasn't sure what I was going to do if it didn't."

"You created a fake social media profile." Kim lifted her brows. "Right? There's not actually a Jim Sutherland, is there?"

"Of course not." Uncle Harold turned to survey the messy alley. "That was clear from the start."

It was? Tess exchanged a glance with her friends that verified they certainly hadn't considered that "from the start" either. But then, they'd thought they were dealing with an actual chair-thief, not a story recreation. But it certainly made sense now. Just as Hosmer Angel had been a fabricated character within the story, so was Jim Sutherland.

"So the jams and jellies?" Janice asked.

"I had just purchased a few of those specialty jars, so I figured jam could play the part of the claret Windibank's company imported. Both need glass containers." Sylvia chuckled. "Of course, it was just Smuckers inside. But Cara and Ronan thought my idea was a hoot and were happy to play along. They called after you guys left." She motioned down the alley. "Stan was swinging by to pick up the stuff you guys bought on his way to the inn."

"To the inn?" Harold cocked his head.

"Well sure. Had to get the chair there before this snow gets any worse. Honestly, I was about to tack another note to the door leading you guys back there—I planned to make sure you saw it and then scurry along and intercept you there."

"So there really is a chair?" LuAnn sounded as surprised as Tess felt.

"There really is a chair." Sylvia pulled the museum door closed and locked it with a set of keys she extracted from her pocket. "I could have shown it to you here, I suppose, but I thought you guys would get a kick out of inspecting it at your leisure."

"Okay, so...there's no Jim Sutherland." Graham stepped into the middle of the alley, directly into the tire tracks they'd so carefully measured that morning. "But what about his gold truck?"

"Stan's truck is the model we described—just not gold. The paint on the can was courtesy of some junk we were tossing out anyway." Sylvia shot a glance upward, her smile dimming. "We'd better hurry. Looks like it could let loose again any minute."

"Excellent. I hear hot chocolate calling my name." Tess turned with her friends toward the alley's exit, not at all sad that they'd solved this "mystery" in record time.

They could finally get back to the weekend's plans. The society could play with their clue cards and bulletin boards, and the Inn Crowd could take a look at this photograph of Prudence Willard.

CHAPTER TEN

September 1858

Prudence clutched her cloak shut with one hand, her other pressed against the letter from Levi's family in Virginia that still rested in her pocket. She'd reread the missive on the road here, finishing it this time—they'd included a description of their visitor, and Prudence now scanned the crowd, in search of a man who matched the words they'd penned.

She felt more than a little out of place here. Most of the people crowding around the auction block were men. The few women were here with husbands, their eyes scanning the lines of slaves as one might the produce at the mercantile. Weighing strengths against obvious weaknesses.

Prudence kept to the back of the crowd, in the shadows of the line of crimson-leaved trees. Her simple dress would make it clear she wasn't here to purchase a slave. But she scanned the people gathered, looking for familiar faces in unfamiliar hats and coats.

There, in the first row of onlookers before the auction block, she spotted the Friends. Isaiah Brown and Johnmark Smith, when dressed in the garb of affluent businessmen, looked no different from anyone else. Nothing to denote them as Quakers—and they would be minding their speech here too, she knew, carefully scrubbing any *thees* and *thys* from their vocabulary.

If anyone discovered they were Quakers, it could turn ugly fast. Everyone knew the Friends were abolitionists. If they were at a slave auction, it was certainly not to uphold the legal right of one human being to purchase another—it was to undermine it however they could.

Lord, direct their gazes my way, she prayed. *Let them see me so I can safely warn them.*

A commotion to the left cut her plea short and drew her gaze that direction.

A line of slaves was being pushed forward, their hands and feet bound. Her stomach knotting, Prudence looked at each one. Each one a soul crying out against this bondage. Each one a son or daughter, likely a sister or brother, a husband, a wife, a mother or father. A friend.

She clenched her hands inside her cloak. Would that she could swoop down and free them all. Cut the ropes binding them and wing them safely north.

Her gaze snagged on a green dress, on hair in a neat braid. Shandy. She was third in line, standing tall enough to prove her spirit wasn't crushed but with a deferential bend to her head to proclaim she wasn't prideful and difficult. She was, as Billy had said, pretty enough to warrant a position in a house rather than working the land—but not so pretty that mistresses would deem her a temptation for their husbands.

How her heart must ache for *her* husband. Hope must be a dull flicker, at best.

The auctioneer stepped forward. His shout was largely unintelligible from where Prudence stood, but she didn't need to hear the exact words to know that he had opened the bidding on the first person in the line, a skeletal older man whose spine was bent from his years of labor. No one was quick to respond, though eventually someone shouted something that earned a roar of laughter from the crowd, and the auctioneer apparently accepted it as a bid. A minute later, the fellow was led off to the jeering buyer.

The second person to be untied and led onto the block was another woman, her stomach swollen with child. Prudence sucked in a breath and pressed a hand to her own stomach. Empty of life—but in some situations, that was surely a blessing. Did that woman wish she could protect her unborn babe from the indignity of their life?

Prudence inched forward, putting herself in a better line of sight for the Friends. She had to get their attention quickly. The bidding on the pregnant woman opened strongly and quickly rose as the auctioneer shouted words like "breeder" and "two for the price of one."

Neither Isaiah Brown nor Johnmark Smith so much as glanced in her direction. Did she dare to weave through the crowd? She must—there was no other recourse. Perhaps if anyone took note of her they would simply think she was the servant of one of them. She'd be sure to greet them as if it were so.

Father God, go with me, I beg Thee. With a deep breath, she tucked her head down and slipped as unobtrusively as she could into the crowd.

Other than an elbow jostling her here and there, no one seemed to pay much attention to her. But the relief of that soon gave way to panic when a bid quite a bit higher than the previous one resulted in a quick sale of the woman with child.

Shandy was next on the block.

Prudence's heart sped. Maybe the man the Friends in Virginia had spotted wasn't even here. Maybe he was no danger. Maybe…

"Four hundred dollars!" The shout from her right made Prudence jump.

"Four and a quarter." Johnmark lifted a hand, seeming perfectly at ease.

Prudence dodged another woman and came within view of the unknown bidder just as he said, "Four-fifty."

"Five hundred." Though he spoke without a tremor, Johnmark couldn't possibly be as peaceful as he sounded. From what Arnold had said last night, they had managed to raise a trifle over six hundred dollars for the purchase of Shandy. Not a large sum for a slave in cities deep in the south, but what they deemed an ample amount here on the shores of the Ohio, in a small town. They'd expected to have to pay no more than five.

But the other bidder, after only a moment's hesitation, said, "Five twenty."

Obviously anticipating a good-sized commission, the auctioneer ordered Shandy to walk around, up and down the stairs, proving herself able of body.

Prudence stole a glance at the man bidding against Johnmark—and barely stifled a gasp. He matched the description of the man the innkeepers at Chester Hill had sent.

Brown hair, longer than average—it brushes his coat collar. He has a birthmark on his right cheek, just below his eye, and a hat with a blue jay feather tucked into the band.

She'd been impressed with the detail of their description. And now she found herself looking at the embodiment of it. The birthmark, faint but unmistakable, the feather, the long hair.

But…that made precious little sense with the theory they'd been operating under. If this man was a slave hunter, sent by her owner, why was he bidding on Shandy? He needed only to present the papers proving her the legal property of someone already, and she'd be removed from the auction.

He wasn't a slave hunter then—at least not one hired by her rightful owner. So who was he? And why was he bidding so fixedly on her, when he hadn't raised a hand for the woman before her—one who, by most accounting, would be the more desirable purchase, given the babe on the way?

She didn't know. But it couldn't be good.

"My bid's at five twenty," the auctioneer shouted, gleaming eyes focused on the Friends. "Do I hear five fifty?"

A third man lifted a hand. "Five fifty."

No. This could easily get out of hand.

The woman standing beside the third bidder slapped him on the arm, scowling something fierce. Prudence couldn't hear the words to accompany the movement of her mouth, but she'd guess they had not come for a maid today. Or perhaps, given the finger the woman pointed at the end of the line, where a few poor children were huddled together, she had a specific age for one in mind.

"Five hundred sixty," Johnmark said.

The woman glared. The man, presumably her husband, buttoned his lips.

But the long-haired fellow lifted his hand again. "Five hundred seventy-five." He too must be reaching his limit, otherwise he likely would have increased the bid by more than fifteen dollars.

Good. That meant the Friends stood a chance, at least if no other bidders entered the fray. And if this man could somehow be taken out of the running.

Prudence edged closer to him. Whoever he was, he was clearly a threat, or Levi wouldn't have been told to detour to Marietta with a message about him.

She had to do something. But with the press of the crowd and the continued shouts of the auctioneer, she could think of only one thing to do.

Weaving through the bodies as the bidding continued to climb, she finally reached the stranger just as Johnmark called out, "Six hundred."

The man opened his mouth.

Prudence lunged, deliberately catching her foot on that of the man beside her target, to make the trip look realistic. With a squawk of dismay, she rammed into her mark hard enough that he staggered back.

"What—?" His exclamation was cut short as he too tripped on someone else's feet. His arms spun out, grappling for something to steady him.

He found her cloak, pulling her down with him. She'd intended to follow him down anyway so she could be sure he didn't shout another bid from the ground. She'd shove a handful of cloak in his mouth if necessary.

"Six hundred going once!"

God bless Anna Barton for her handiwork on this cloak, making it so voluminous that Prudence had no trouble tangling the man up in it.

Those standing nearest them cleared out of the way. A few chuckled, but no one made any move to intervene.

"I'm so sorry!" Prudence all but shouted into the fellow's ear, to cover the auctioneer's announcement that the bid was going twice.

"Get off me!" He pushed, batted at her cloak, and managed to get himself more twisted up in the fabric without any help from her.

"Are you all right?" Proud of herself for remembering not to use *thee*, Prudence pushed herself to her knees.

"Sold!" the auctioneer cried.

The mutter of the fellow on the ground wasn't nearly so polite a declaration. He sat, whipping her cloak back at her and looking as if he'd prefer it to be a blade.

She drew back a few more inches, as much as she could before colliding with another set of legs that were quick to move out of her way.

The Friends had won Shandy. They would waste no time in claiming her, paying the fees, and spiriting her away. But Prudence figured she had better make sure this fellow didn't chase after them.

"Again, I'm so sorry." She pushed to her feet and reached out to help him get to his—though her interference no doubt caused more harm than good, as she intended. "The mistress is always saying how clumsy I am. She sent me with a note for him, that's all. I was just trying to get to him. I didn't hurt you, did I? Jack said I dislocated his shoulder last time I knocked him for a tumble, but he was exaggerating."

Back on his feet, he pulled himself free of her hands. "Will you hush your prattle, girl?" He strained up on his toes, thunder in his eyes. He must have seen the Friends leading Shandy away, because he muttered something, the syllables of which Prudence couldn't make out, but the bite came through loud and clear.

His gaze flashed to her, swept over her from boot to crown, and narrowed. Before she could see his intention in his eyes, he'd circled his hand around her arm and yanked her into step with him as he stormed from the crowd.

"Are you here with them?" he hissed into her ear, the arrow of his gaze toward Isaiah and Johnmark demonstrating who he meant by "them." "Did they task you with making sure no one else won her?"

"What?" Panic clawed at her stomach. Why would he even suspect that? Had she tipped her hand somehow? "No, I promise."

It was the truth. Her words ought to have rung with it.

But her captor didn't even look down at her again. He was too busy tracking Isaiah, Johnmark, and Shandy with his gaze, muttering another something sharp and angry when the trio vanished into the field full of horses and wagons and carriages. *Lord, help them to fly away. Fly away safely home.*

They halted at the edge of the field, his grip on her arm tightening. He spun her to face him. "Where are they taking her?"

Stuttering out an honest *I don't know* wouldn't appease him, she could see that. So she lifted her chin and tugged on her arm, though he didn't free it. "Thee seems mightily concerned over one particular slave girl. Just bid on another if thee is so desperate for—"

"*Thee?*"

Had she…? Oh no. Prudence sucked in a sharp breath.

The man's gaze narrowed on her face. "You're a Quaker."

She tried again to pull her arm free. If she could just put some space between them, she could dart into the carriages, wagons, and horses too, circle around, back to where she'd tied Charity, and get home. Back across the river, into the relative safety of Ohio. Back to Jason. Back to Billy, with the news that the Friends had Shandy with them and would no doubt soon arrive, if they didn't in fact beat her there.

Perhaps she failed to warn Johnmark and Isaiah about this man, but she'd foiled his plans to purchase Shandy. That was surely something.

Though she still didn't understand who he was or what he was doing here, bidding on Shandy. Ought she to try to find those answers, or did wisdom demand she simply hurry home and help Shandy and Billy to their next stop in Chester Hill?

The man didn't seem keen on letting her decide. Perhaps his height gave him a view of something she didn't see—he tightened his grip on her arm and pulled her off toward the right. "Are they Quakers too?"

She had to assume he meant Isaiah and Johnmark. But she couldn't afford to let him know she assumed so. "Who?"

He sliced a hard gaze down at her face, one that said, *Stop playing innocent*, and tugged her onward. "You want to get in the way? Then consider yourself a part of this. Come on."

The little yelp she emitted in protest barely made a dent in the air full of bids and shouts.

CHAPTER ELEVEN

The sidewalks had been shoveled. They were being covered again, but Tess still greeted the mostly cleared walkways with lifted brows, which she directed toward her friends. "I'd completely spaced the clearing. Did one of you call someone?"

Janice motioned toward the parking lot, where a familiar truck resided. "Thorn texted a little while ago, saying he'd swing by so at least the first half of the snow would be cleared. Someone will probably have to do it again in the morning, but it'll make it easier."

"For sure." Tess motioned for the society to follow her around to the back entrance. They wouldn't usually direct guests in this way, but the mudroom made it a much better option for all the snowy boots and hats and coats than the lobby. They probably should have used it earlier too. "This way, guys. Make a pile for anything dryer-safe."

"There's Stan's truck." Syliva nodded toward a truck parked at the loading dock, visible when they rounded the corner of the inn.

The inn's door was open. Tess frowned at that for a moment—until she saw Thorn step into the opening, lift a hand in greeting, and then shut the cold and snow back out.

"Good thing Thorn was here when Stan arrived, to help him in with the chair." Janice bustled ahead of the rest of them to open the door.

"You know what's even better? That we're about to get in out of the cold." LuAnn gave an exaggerated shudder. Or maybe not so exaggerated. Tess's toes were about numb again, and she was beginning to fantasize about hot chocolate and fuzzy slippers.

First, though, the necessities of cleaning up after an eleven-person hike through the snow. "I'll handle the run to the dryer," she said to her friends.

Janice nodded. "I'll get the hot drinks ready."

"And I'll check on Thorn and Stan and this mysterious chair." LuAnn pulled off her hat and ran her fingers through her hair.

Warm air soon embraced Tess as she made her way inside, moving as far out of the way as she could to allow others in behind her, and gathering the stack of gear to be taken downstairs.

Ten minutes later, she'd taken care of her tasks and made her way back upstairs. Happy chatter filled the café and lobby area. Tess wove her way around the tables, aimed at the carafes of hot water and coffee. She grinned when Janice greeted her with a prepared cup of chocolaty goodness.

"Ah, you *do* love me." She took the warm mug, wrapping both hands around it.

Janice laughed. "Like a sister. Cookie?"

"Obviously." She pried five of her fingers off the mug so she could receive the treat and wasted no time in taking a bite.

LuAnn, a mug already in hand, slipped up beside them. "Thorn's heading back out. Stan turned over the box of Kim's glasses to her and has the chair in the kitchen. He said he'd take it apart for us as soon as we're ready to see it." She looked out over the room.

Tess followed her gaze to where Sylvia was laughing with Uncle Harold and Bud. "Funny that she knows him, isn't it?"

LuAnn chuckled. "Well, teachers know a lot of people, as we all well know. I suppose it shouldn't be too surprising that some folks around here were in one of your uncle's classes at some point. Oberlin's not that far away."

"True enough." Tess took another nibble of her cookie and washed it down with a sweet sip.

"Oh, I insist!" Uncle Harold clapped a hand to Sylvia's shoulder, his voice booming over the others. "Once a member, always a member, I always say. We'd love to have you join us. And your husband too."

Sylvia beamed. "It would be just like old times. What are you discussing tonight?"

"Well." Tess let a sigh ease out. "Looks like our guests are back to focusing on their pre-selected activities. Want to check out this chair?"

"I know I do." LuAnn practically leaped away, back toward the kitchen.

"She smells history," Janice stage-whispered.

"And it smells sweet," LuAnn returned over her shoulder.

"Really? All I smell is the soup from lunch." Tess drew in a deep breath of it as they entered the kitchen. She checked her watch. Pretty soon it would be time to load the pasties into the oven. The day, it seemed, had disappeared into the snowy streets. But her uncle and his crew had enjoyed themselves, which was certainly the most important thing.

It took her a moment to spot Stan. He was crouching beside the table, wiping the wooden legs of a chair with a rag, presumably to remove any snow that had found it. "Hey, Stan."

He looked up, greeting the three of them with a nod. "Afternoon, ladies. Thorn said this was the best place to set this up right now, since the professor's crew will be in the café and parlor."

They all murmured their approval of Thorn's direction and rounded the table to survey this mysterious piece of furniture.

It wasn't really anything remarkable. A pretty standard Victorian chair, with a wooden frame, including arms, and a padded back and seat that were in desperate need of reupholstering. Hence, Tess supposed, why the purchasers had been dismantling it and found the photograph.

LuAnn pulled a chair out from the table and sat. "So can you remind us of the chair's story? We've been a bit distracted with Sylvia's game all morning."

A corner of Stan's mouth tugged up. "Yeah, she about went crazy when she realized Professor Westerfield was coming to town. I've never seen her move as fast as she has since she ran into you yesterday, Tess. She's been a blur of energy, setting everything up." He gave the chair one last swipe and stood up.

"She did a fabulous job." Janice pulled up a chair too. "I think the group thoroughly enjoyed the unexpected mystery."

Stan grunted. "Meanwhile, I've been running all over town in the snow leaving clues." But a smile won his lips, despite his moody tone. "Crazy woman. Anyway." He set the rag on the end of the table and wiped his hands on his jeans. "So, the chair."

"The chair." Tess took another sip of her hot cocoa. "Sylvia said it was purchased at an estate sale and donated to the museum when the people found something in the leg?" She eyed the wooden appendages dubiously.

Stan nodded. "We got all the information we could from the people who donated it. They'd found it at one of those big flea markets, so who knows where it really came from before they bought it. Planned to reupholster it and use it as a display piece in their entryway, I think."

Janice wrinkled her nose. "It certainly needs a face-lift. I'm not even sure what color this fabric originally was. Green? Gray?"

"Just imagine the life it's seen." Eyes gleaming, LuAnn set her mug on the table and leaned forward to touch the well-worn wood. "This thing's probably at least a hundred and fifty years old. Maybe older. And if it was from an inn, it probably had hundreds of people sit in it over the years."

"Um, ew." Largely just because she knew it would make her friend object, Tess made a face. "That is a lot of probably-not-so-clean bodies sitting on that thing. Hygiene back then wasn't exactly delightful."

LuAnn, laughing, swatted her logic away. "That is not the way to look at it, Tessa Wallace! Think of the stories those people had to tell. The places they'd come from, the ones they were going to. The family dramas, the romances lived out and maybe even told as the person sat in it."

"I'm more interested in the story of how the thing got this." Stan tilted the chair back onto its rear legs and, balancing it with a foot, pointed at a hole he'd revealed on the underside.

"The bullet hole Sylvia deemed 'so cool'?" Janice asked.

"Not just the hole. The bullet's still in there." Stan poked a finger into the wood—though it was splintered enough that Tess would have advised against it. Presumably he touched metal.

Tess leaned against the table. She was no LuAnn, always weaving a story for every situation, but she had to admit to some curiosity. Why would a chair have a bullet hole in it?

"Kind of gruesome." LuAnn shivered. Definitely exaggerated this time, since the room was snug and warm.

"Not really." Tess set her cup down beside her friends'. "If the bullet's still in there, that means it didn't penetrate through, right? Didn't hit whoever was on the other side of it."

Janice lifted a finger. "True. And the entry hole is on this side, so it clearly hit from the bottom. I would assume the chair was like this, or on its back altogether."

"Like in a genuine Wild West shoot out." LuAnn held her hands like six-shooters and mimicked taking shots at the chair. "Someone dives behind it. I suppose it's that or else someone, what, sliding underneath it to shoot upward?"

"It would be odd for the bullet not to go all the way through, if that were the case," Tess said. "But someone could have shot from a floor below, I suppose. It could have gone through the ceiling and lodged in the chair."

Janice nodded. "Hard to know for sure, but either way, you're right—the chair stopped the bullet, so that's good news for whoever was behind it."

"Did Sylvia say there was a stamp on it?" Tess circled LuAnn's chair and crouched down closer to the chair.

Stan tapped a finger to the inside of the frame, which she hadn't been able to see from standing. There, faint but legible, was a brownish-black stenciled PROPERTY OF QUAKER INN STATION.

"We looked up the inn last night." LuAnn had leaned forward too, elbows on knees. "It's a shame it's no longer standing—I bet they would have loved to get this back."

"We certainly would have, had it been from the Riverfront House." Janice scooted forward for a closer look too.

"We have some anecdotal history of the inn at the museum but not much. Certainly nothing to explain this stuff." Stan lowered the chair all the way onto its back and reached into his pocket. "I imagine if it was just the bullet that the couple who purchased it had found, they would have kept it and had a conversation piece." He pulled a multi-tool out of his pocket and flipped the screwdriver up.

Tess shifted a bit to give him room as he bent down in front of the chair, reaching with his tool into a corner hidden by a wooden piece. He soon had an ancient-looking metal screw backed out of the first hole and had moved to a second.

A minute later, he pulled the leg carefully from its place and handed it over. Janice, being closest, took it and peered inside the hole in the end of the leg. "Hollow. But empty. Is that typical of furniture of this time, to have hollow legs?"

Stan shrugged. "I'm not really a furniture expert."

LuAnn frowned and reached over to touch a finger to the top edge. "It seems odd to me. Like it was deliberately hollowed out after the chair was made. If you look at the edge, you can see where it was stained first, then chipped away."

"Good observation." Tess took the leg when Janice held it out to her. She ran a finger along the edge too, and into the hole. It was well done, smoothly bored. Certainly not something someone had done quickly. "Whoever hollowed it had the proper tools though. This compartment is smooth and even."

Stan was going at the other front leg now. "There are initials in there. Not sure whose."

Not carved in—Tess would have felt it with her finger. She tilted the chair leg toward the overhead light, smiling when she saw a small black *LL* inside. "Cool. Here." She handed it to LuAnn, tapping the place she should look.

Janice leaned in for a glimpse too. "*LL*. Do we know the name of the family who owned the inn?"

"I don't," Stan said.

LuAnn pursed her lips for a moment. "Maybe the book mentioned it. Let me get it real quick. Don't show them that photograph until I get back," she added, leveling a finger and a narrowed gaze at Stan.

He laughed and obligingly lowered his screwdriver.

LuAnn hopped up and scurried away, handing the chair leg to Janice. Tess settled into the chair her friend had vacated so she could look at it again too. "It's not a very large compartment."

"No. Maybe...three or four inches deep." Janice measured it with her finger.

Tess chuckled. "Maybe we should carry measuring tapes around with us at all times, like Bud."

"Ha! Half the time, I do. Alas, not today. But it's big enough to hold some valuables, I should think. Money, jewels."

"Not that the Quakers would have had jewelry." Stan lowered himself to a seat on the floor. "Could have stored it for someone else though, I guess. But knowing they were part of the Underground Railroad...all manner of things they could have needed to hide."

Very true. Items for the fugitives, items for other conductors, anything that hinted at their own involvement...

"Got it!" LuAnn hustled back into the kitchen, brandishing the slender book in her hands. "I still have the page marked from last night."

Tess stood to give LuAnn her seat back, but her friend just set the book on the table and started flipping, not seeming to even notice the chair. Tess skimmed the words along with her, shaking her head when she got through the section. It mentioned a few people involved in the Underground Railroad at Chester Hill, but none that started with an *L*.

LuAnn sighed. "Too easy, I guess. We'll have to look elsewhere."

"In the meantime, the photo." Stan had apparently gone back to work on the other chair leg the moment LuAnn returned, because he was even now easing it out of place. "We put it back in because it seemed safest for the time being. And because Sylvia thought it would be cool for you all to see for yourselves how we found it." He presented the leg with a flourish to the three of them.

Janice took it with her usual bright smile and then turned toward them. "Who wants to do the honors?"

Tess touched a hand to LuAnn's shoulder. "Let the biggest history-lover pull it out." In the meantime, Tess was noting that the hollow was different in this leg. A bit smaller, and a perfect circle, where the other had been more of a square to match the shape of the leg.

"I would be honored." LuAnn accepted the leg from Janice and glanced in the hole too.

Tess could see the white edge of a paper inside, and her pulse kicked up just a bit. She wasn't the history buff LuAnn was, but she'd found herself becoming more interested with each passing month at the inn. The discoveries they'd made lit a fire in her, and it sparked up a bit now.

LuAnn's brows pulled together the moment her fingers dove into the hole.

"What?" Janice had apparently noticed the same thing on their friend's face.

LuAnn shook her head. "Paper doesn't feel like I expected it to, that's all." She pulled out the rolled-up rectangle.

They all gaped. It was copy paper, which was clear at the first glance. Standard, modern copy paper. Most assuredly not a photograph from the 1800s.

"What in the world?" Stan shot to his feet, scowling at the paper along with the rest of them. "That's not right. That's not what was in there before."

LuAnn was already unrolling the paper, revealing not a photo nor writing that named Prudence Willard, but a few lines of text written in what looked like permanent marker.

The handwriting was sloppy, barely legible. It took Tess a minute to decipher it.

Sorry. I'll bring it back as soon as I can.

Whatever the photograph had been ... it was gone.

CHAPTER TWELVE

"O f course, Ms. Macintyre. We totally understand." With the phone sandwiched between her shoulder and ear, Tess tapped the note into the computer, glancing up and out the windows that flanked the front door when movement caught her eye. Sylvia, pacing back and forth in front of the door.

Tess couldn't blame her. The snow hadn't just started again twenty minutes ago—it had descended on them in a fury.

"Thank you so much," their would-be guest said in her ear. "Hopefully the roads will be open again, and we'll get there on Monday. I'll be in touch."

Tess refocused on the computer. "I certainly hope so. Stay safe."

"You too. Thanks for your understanding."

"Of course. Have a great evening." Tess sighed as she disconnected and exited out of the reservation she'd just adjusted.

The phones had started ringing shortly after the snow hit them again. Most of their guests due in tomorrow were coming from wherever this storm was coming from. The Macintyres were the third ones to call and cancel the Sunday night portion of their reservation. They already had ten inches of snow on the ground, Mrs. Macintyre had said, and couldn't have braved the weather even if they wanted to—the interstate between the inn and their home had just shut down.

"Another one?"

Tess smiled at LuAnn, who was just coming out of the parlor. "Yeah. That's three of the four—"

The phone rang again, cutting her off. Tess lifted her brows. "I have a feeling this is number four." She answered with her usual, "Good evening. Wayfarers Inn. How may I help you?"

"Hi, this is Jessica Clark. We have a reservation there beginning tomorrow, but our flight from Atlanta has just been canceled. Y'all are getting some snow?"

Tess laughed. "You could say that."

It only took her a minute to alter the Clarks' reservation too, her mind already whirring ahead when she disconnected. She turned to LuAnn. "It's going to take a day or two to clear all this out, if it keeps up at this rate."

LuAnn nodded, glancing toward the parlor when laughter rang out. "If everyone coming tomorrow has canceled already, we ought to offer the Sherlock Society another night. We don't want them traveling home in this."

"Exactly what I was thinking." Tess would feel much better, not worrying about them driving in this, even if the roads reopened by the time they'd been planning on leaving. Not to mention that she'd enjoy the extra time with Uncle Harold.

Janice's voice came from the stairs. "Thanks for the heads-up, Paige. I appreciate it. Uh-huh. You too. Bye now." Janice herself came around the bar a moment later. "Church has been canceled."

"Gee, why?" Tess looked to the windows again. Darkness was falling, but the porch lights showed that the sidewalks, clear half an hour ago, had two inches covering them again already. "Apparently up until now, the storm was just joking. Now it's serious."

Sylvia came to a halt by one of the windows and rubbed her hands up her arms. "Come on, baby, where are you?"

Tess rounded the bar and moved to join her. "He'll be back any second." The words came easily enough, but inside she was thinking that they ought to have told Stan he didn't need to go back to the museum.

At the time, though, the snow had been lazy. They'd all been relieved to hear that Stan had made a scan of the photograph before putting it back in its hiding place, so no one had objected to his insistence that he run back. He promised he'd print out a copy and return in a few minutes. Now, however, he wasn't answering Sylvia's texts—probably because he was driving and couldn't take his hands off the wheel.

"When he gets here, we'll just leave the photo with you. We'd better not linger out in this." Sylvia leaned into the door, the lines between her brows looking permanent. "I don't know why he didn't tell me he was going. I'd have just gone home with him, and we could have emailed the photo. I don't have to stay for the Sherlock stuff."

"Sorry. We should have suggested that." Tess checked her watch. He really should have been back by now. He'd been gone long enough that the scents from the baking pasties were beginning to waft out. Beef, onions, turnips, pastry...

"Hey, I have an idea." Janice slid up beside them. "We have an empty room. Why don't you guys just stay here tonight? Our treat. That way you don't have to go back out in this, and you can still visit with the other Sherlockians."

Sylvia turned her head, the frown easing a bit. "Oh, that's so sweet."

"I see headlights!" Tess peered out the glass.

"That's him." Relief saturated Sylvia's voice as she watched the truck crawl down the street.

"Well, you greet him and share the offer with him. I'm going to go let my uncle know the group can stay an extra night." Tess watched another moment, though, to be sure the truck got into the lot without any trouble.

When she turned, she saw LuAnn leaning on the front desk, phone in hand, gazing at it. And sighing. "Well, I knew it would be the case."

Tess lifted her brows. "Your date officially canceled?"

"Yeah." LuAnn shrugged and tucked her phone back into her pocket, but she couldn't disguise the disappointment in her eyes.

"Good." Uncle Harold poked his head out of the parlor, sending a wink LuAnn's way. "We get to keep you to ourselves. And preserve your bachelorhood a little longer."

LuAnn laughed.

Tess didn't. She could appreciate that her uncle's jest lightened the mood for LuAnn, sure. But he was always so cavalier about these things. Acting like the life he'd chosen was the best. Making it sound like LuAnn would be abandoning the pursuit of what mattered if she opted for marriage and family.

As if it were preferable to be alone, without family near enough to look out for you.

He motioned Tess closer. "We were debating whether to pause before we begin the next chapter. I thought I'd see when that dinner I'm smelling would be ready."

"About fifteen minutes," Janice answered before Tess could look at her watch again.

"But while you're between chapters..." Tess stepped into the parlor so the others could hear her too. "All our guests for tomorrow have canceled. Roads are bad and not promising to get better any time soon. Interstate 77 is closed between here and Cambridge. I'm sure they'll try to have it open again as soon as they can, but the latest forecast is predicting that this won't stop until tomorrow."

"They're saying eighteen inches now." LuAnn leaned into the doorjamb. "If it keeps up at this rate, it could be even more."

Tess nodded. "So if you guys would like to stay Sunday night as well, you're welcome to do so."

Uncle Harold surveyed his posse. "Well, if it's as bad as all that, I don't imagine we'll argue. Anyone?"

Tom looked up from his notebook. "Think classes will be canceled on Monday?"

Uncle Harold nodded. "They may already be."

"I'll check my email." Tom reached for the phone sitting on the arm of his chair.

Uncle Harold looked to the others. "Those of us at the college probably won't have any trouble. If the rest of you need to check in with bosses..."

"Yeah, give me a minute." Bud pushed himself to his feet and trotted toward them. Or, more accurately, the door. "I'll check in real quick on my laptop."

Ollie, Hiram, and Graham were on their phones, presumably doing the same thing. None of them looked particularly distressed about the thought of a delayed return to business as usual.

When the front door opened, Tess left them to their checking and turned back to the lobby area, where Stan was just shutting the door behind him.

"Getting nasty out there." He held out something in a plastic bag. "We'd better hurry home, babe."

Sylvia took the bag. "Or we could stay. The night, I mean. Our friends have offered us a complimentary room, if we're interested." She smiled up at him in a way that made it pretty clear that she was.

Stan smiled back, directing it first at Sylvia and then up at Tess. "Yeah? Well that's nice of you guys. I think we'd better take you up on it."

"Great. I'll check you in real quick and get you some keys."

"And then we'll show you guys this photo," Sylvia said.

"The museum's printer isn't the greatest, and I didn't have any photo paper." Stan unzipped his heavy coat and handed it to LuAnn when she offered to hang it up for him. "And I couldn't get it to duplex, so I eventually gave up and just printed the back separately. But you'll get the idea."

Eager to see the amazing vanishing photo—or a scan of it anyway—Tess typed Stan and Syliva's information into the computer and handed them the keys to Moonlight and

Snowflakes. Rather appropriate for this weekend. "We'll get you guys a set of toothbrushes and other necessities in a bit," she said.

"No rush." Sylvia unzipped the bag and pulled out the papers. "Well, here we go. The photo."

They gathered around it, all of them studying the image itself first. The people were, of course, the most prominent things to note. Tess recognized Prudence Willard right away, from the other photos they'd seen of her. She was standing on the left, a small fowl of some kind in her hands—a duckling or gosling, probably, though Tess wasn't sure which. Her stomach was large with child, giving a pretty good indication of when this photograph was taken. She'd only had two pregnancies that went beyond the first trimester. One with a baby girl who died at birth in 1855, and the second was with Moses, who was born in May of 1859.

The other people, though, Tess didn't recognize. There were four of them, two couples. One older, one younger. Parents and children? It seemed likely, given the arm the older man had slung around the younger woman. They were dressed simply, their garb not much different from Prudence's. Their skin was darker though. A family she'd helped lead to safety, perhaps? That would explain why the photo was secreted away in a chair leg, though it didn't explain why they'd even risk taking a photo, or why it was at Quaker Inn Station instead of here in Marietta.

Behind them was a farm. Though the photo was black and white, Tess imagined the fields a lush green, given the amount of leafage visible. And a farmhouse. Not large, but it had a well-kept look to it.

Her gaze shifted to the second printout, of the back of the photo. First, names—*The Green family with Prudence Willard.* Then—*Without your help, we wouldn't be here. God bless you. The Greens.*

Tess smiled. Wherever the farm was, it seemed it was home to this family—the Greens—and that either Prudence or the folks in Chester Hill had helped them get there. "Lovely."

"Very. But…" LuAnn straightened and looked at Sylvia and Stan. "Why would anyone take it from the chair? And how could they have?"

Questions that had begun to trickle into Tess's mind earlier too, but which she'd pushed aside when the phones started ringing.

Sylvia shook her head. "I really have no idea. It's just a photo—it's not as though it's something valuable. And it was definitely there yesterday afternoon." She looked at her husband. "I wasn't really paying any attention to it after I ran into Tess—I was too busy trying to set up the mystery for the professor. You were with the chair though, weren't you?"

Stan blinked at her. "When you didn't have me running around planting clues? Sure. Now and then."

Tess tapped a finger to the desktop. "Well, whoever replaced the photo with that IOU obviously had to take one out and put the other in. Did you have the chair dismantled at the museum for long?"

"Uh." Stan lifted a hand and rubbed the back of his neck. "Yeah. I didn't actually put it back together until about noon today. Didn't think I really needed to, and I was running all over town."

"Planting those clues for me." Sylvia sighed. "So it was left unattended for quite a while. From about four yesterday afternoon to about noon today. I mean, we were in and out, but..."

"And the photo was in the leg? Not on a table or anything?" LuAnn's gaze was still on the prints. "Obviously you scanned it."

"We did, right away. But it kept curling up and rolling off the desk, so I figured it was safest back in the leg." Sylvia shook her head.

"I didn't look that closely when I put the thing back together though. Just saw the white paper and assumed it was the photo." Stan dropped his hand back to his side.

"Well obviously someone came into the museum and switched it out. Do you guys have a surveillance camera or anything?" Janice asked.

Stan shifted closer to Sylvia. "Not that I know of. If there are any, Maybelline didn't show us anything about them."

"At least you thought to scan it. That was good thinking." Tess smiled at the couple. Easy as it would be to point fingers, she could hardly blame them for not taking steps to protect the original photo. Who in the world would have thought that someone would come into the museum in broad daylight and steal the thing? As they said, it was just a photo. Interesting, but not valuable. Tess wouldn't have thought to secure it either. Especially because... "Wait. Whoever took this had to know it was there. Right? No one's just going to stroll in and go looking in chair legs on the off chance there's something hidden in one. Even if the leg was off the chair, it didn't exactly scream, 'Come and look inside me!'"

"So who else knew about it?" LuAnn moved around to the back side of the desk and reached down for one of her many notebooks and a pen. "You two, obviously. And us." She wrote their names, each on a line, including everyone from the Sherlock Society. "Not that our guests could have possibly done it. We were all together the entire time since you called us about it yesterday, Sylvia. Still, I'll be thorough." She looked up. "Who else?"

Sylvia clasped her hands to her elbows. "Um. The couple who brought it in, obviously. Cheryl and...what was his name? Bobby or something?"

"No, Roberts was their last name. Or maybe Robertson. I don't know. They called Thursday night to tell us about it and then brought it over on Friday morning."

"I have no idea who else they may have told," Sylvia said. "But I haven't mentioned it to anyone but you guys. Stan?"

He shook his head. "I honestly wasn't even thinking about it, other than as the final clue I had to take care of for you. Getting it here, I mean. I didn't say anything to anyone."

"Hmm." LuAnn looked at her list. Which was empty, if one discounted all of them and the society.

Tess sighed. "I don't think we really have enough information right now to figure out who it could have been. Could you guys get in touch with the couple who brought it to you?"

From somewhere in Janice's vicinity, a chime went off. "Oh!" Janice pulled her cell phone out of her pocket and swiped the alarm off. "Not now though. Pasties are done." She looked up. "You ladies want to help me get everything out and ready?"

"Absolutely." Tess moved first toward the parlor. "Dinner will be out in just a few, guys. Any decisions on the extra night?"

"I think we're all good." Graham, stationed again at the bulletin board, nudged his glasses up higher on his nose. "Oberlin's getting slammed too, so everyone's pretty under-standing about it."

"Bud hasn't returned yet, but he often sets his own hours anyway." Uncle Harold looked over toward Matti, clearly want-ing her verification on this, but she didn't even seem to hear him. She sat in a chair in the corner of the room, a little bit removed from the circle of furniture they'd made, and her gaze was distant.

Tess smiled. "Good. Give us five to get everything out and plated, and then come on over to the café, okay?"

At her uncle's nod, she hurried toward the kitchen. But her mind lingered behind. Not on the photograph, not now. On Matti. She said another silent prayer for her as she joined her friends in the warm, fragrant space.

LuAnn greeted her with a smile. "I've assigned myself the salads, and Janice is plating the pasties. You want to handle the drinks?"

"Sure." As Tess reached into the fridge for the pitchers of water and tea, a thought fluttered into her mind and settled. It was silly, in a way, but…well, but it stuck. She grabbed the pitchers and then let the fridge shut. "Do you know if we have any peaches? Canned or frozen ones?"

Janice scooped the meat pies from baking sheets to plates like a pro. "I bet we do. Winnie keeps a lot of fruit on hand for her recipes. Why?"

"Peach tea. I was just remembering that the last time I was in Oberlin visiting Uncle Harold, we had dinner with Matti and Bud, and she'd made some. Said it was her absolute favorite drink."

Janice paused in her task long enough to smile at her. "Well, that could cheer her up. The fact that you remembered and thought of it, especially."

LuAnn was already scouring the cabinets. "Here we go. I thought there were some up there. Do you only need the canned peaches?"

"Pretty sure, yeah. I looked up the recipe after she served it, it was so good. Very simple. Just puree the peaches and add it to the tea." Tess slid the pitchers onto the counter and went for the blender. "Shouldn't take but a minute, and we can add a dollop for anyone who wants it."

"Sounds delicious." LuAnn slid the peaches over to Tess and went back to her salad-making.

By the time the chatter of the group filtered through the door from the café, they had everything ready to go. The tables were already set with glasses and silverware, and they soon served the plates.

Tess set a glass of peach tea before Matti with a smile. "Here you go, Matti. Especially for you."

Matti sent her a funny look, but she reached for the glass and sipped. And her face lit up. "Peach!" When she looked back up again, her eyes looked a bit misty. "You made this for me?"

Tess smiled and patted her shoulder. "There's enough to go around, of course—but yes. I hope it's still your favorite."

For one brief moment, Matti covered Tess's fingers with her own and squeezed. Then she reached for her glass again. "Thanks, Tess."

"My pleasure." She moved to fill other glasses, but her heart was smiling to match her lips.

Matti was digging into her meal with relish.

CHAPTER THIRTEEN

September 1858

Marietta lay far in the distance. With her wrists bound, Prudence wasn't quite sure how she was going to get back to it. Back to the farm. To Jason. Darkness had long ago fallen, and exhaustion had set in. Her husband would be frantic with worry by now. No one, absolutely no one, had any idea where she was.

Frankly, she scarcely knew. All she could have said was that she was on Charity, her wrists tied to the pommel, the horse's leads in the hands of her captor, who sat atop his own horse a step away. That Marietta lay behind them and some vague expanse of Ohio lay before. Night hid from her eyes which road they were on.

Perhaps it was just the tiredness weighing too heavily to allow for normal emotions, but she wasn't scared. She should be, by all logic. The silent man a few feet away had kidnapped her and forced her to come with him. And yet a strange peace had blanketed her when he tied her to her horse—threatening to knock her on the head and sling her up like a sack of potatoes if she didn't mount nicely on her own.

She'd mounted nicely. She'd give this man no reason to harm her.

The moon winked down at her, stars peeking through the burnished leaves whenever she looked up.

He telleth the number of the stars; he calleth them all by their names. The verse from the Psalms washed over her mind, soothing the frayed edges of her spirit. Her husband may not know where she was, but her Lord still saw her. He who fastened each star in the heavens had His hand on her as well. And though He did not keep every terrible thing man devised from taking place, He did promise to stand beside His followers even through the darkest of trials.

If she died on this journey, she would be with Him, and He would comfort Jason. If she was sold back into slavery, He would go with her into the land of captivity.

He would take her through the worst…and because of Him, she could hope for the best. Hope that the fact that this man had provided her with food and water as dusk stole through the forest meant that he intended her no real harm. He'd not touched her, other than to help her up and down from the horse. Maybe the Lord had whispered constraint and compassion into his heart.

The man angled his head up as they came out of the line of trees, most likely gauging the time. He then looked at her. "Ready to tell me yet what you were trying to do at the auction?"

She did her best to send him a withering look, though she didn't likely look very intimidating with her hands bound before her. "Was this thy plan? To wait until I was too tired to think and then interrogate me?"

Was it a trick of the moonlight, or did his lips twitch? "Mostly, miss, my plan was to keep you from getting in the way again while I do what needs to be done."

"Ma'am."

"What?"

She jerked her chin up. "I am a *ma'am*, not a *miss*. Though the Friends prefer to use full names rather than titles."

"Good for them." But he didn't ask for her name. Which was just as well, because she wouldn't have given him her real one anyway. She simply wanted him to know that she had someone waiting for her. She'd be missed. She'd be searched for.

Though she was growing rather tired of thinking of him simply as "the man" or "her captor." "What of thee? Has thee a name, or shall I continue to call thee merely 'him' in my thoughts?"

He just grunted.

Such eloquence. Prudence repositioned herself in the saddle, trying to banish all longing thoughts of her soft, warm bed. "Perhaps I will call thee Talks A Lot."

He pressed his lips together.

"Or Looks Straight Ahead."

He at least sent another dart of a glance at her. "Do I look like I'm from some Indian tribe to you?"

"No. But their naming conventions certainly make sense when one has only appearance and actions to go by."

Prudence shivered when a gust of autumn wind whipped down the road. "Perhaps Blue Jay, for the feather in thy hat."

He reached up and touched a hand to it. "Hm. Forgot that was there." But he didn't remove it. Instead, he...smiled.

Prudence sucked in a breath of the chilly air. He seemed entirely different when he smiled. Softer. "Did someone give it to thee?" Surely if he'd tucked it into the band himself, he wouldn't have forgotten about it. And the remembering wouldn't have pleased him so.

For a moment he regarded her, steady as a snake waiting for its prey. Then he looked straight ahead again. "My daughter."

She jolted. The sudden movement made her horse side-step, but Blue Jay brought it back into order with a tug on the lead and a soft click of his tongue. Her words came out quiet as river fog. "Thee has a daughter?"

He nodded and rolled his shoulders. "Lucy. She's five. Sweetest little thing ever to set foot on God's green earth." And his voice, when he spoke of her, was all warmth and love.

A man could be a monster in some ways and still love his child. She knew it—she'd seen it before. The fact that Blue Jay was clearly a doting father didn't negate the fact that he'd been hunting Shandy. Didn't mean he'd treat her, a woman not of his blood, with fairness.

But it reminded her that he wasn't only monster—he was man. And the fact that he shared that softer bit of himself so readily... Was he trying to make her aware of it? To manipulate her into trusting him, perhaps? Or at least not fighting him?

If so, it was clever of him, and it had achieved its purpose before she could stop herself from reacting. She tightened her fingers around the pommel. "Has thee a wife at home with Lucy?"

He nodded. "Josephine. Nearly as sweet as our girl. When she wants to be." He smirked, laughter in his words. "And when she doesn't—well, watch out." He looked her way again, then back to the dark road. "I imagine your husband knows exactly what I mean."

Rather than answer, she took a cue from him and looked straight ahead. "Where is home?"

"Back East." A vague answer, to be sure, but more than she'd expected from him.

The moonlight fell on a crossroads, and Blue Jay brought their mounts to a halt as they neared it. He dismounted, crouching down to examine…what? Something on the road? The road itself?

When he stood again, he pointed to the left. "This way."

Her gaze flickered to the sign at the intersection, its words just discernible in the silver light. *Chester Hill.*

Her pulse quickened. She had Friends in Chester Hill. Young Levi and his parents, not to mention other workers on the Underground Railroad that frequently accepted "packages" from her hands. If they went all the way to the town, she'd be able to find help. She'd be recognized.

At least, if there was any light to see her by. "Could we rest a while?" She needed to delay their arrival into the area until morning.

But instead of helping her down, Blue Jay swung back up. "Sorry, ma'am. We need to keep moving while the trail's fresh."

Trail? Her breath balled up in her chest. "Who are we tracking?" But she knew. Who could it be, other than Isaiah Brown and Johnmark Smith, with Shandy?

Apparently he assumed she'd figure it out, because he said nothing.

Prudence forced her breathing to regulate again, praying with every intake, every exhale. *Lord, protect them. Save them. Lead them to safety.*

Could she distract Blue Jay from his course somehow? She tried to think of a likely way to do so, but her thoughts were a jumble of exhaustion and confusion.

Why were the Friends and Shandy heading to Chester Hill? Why hadn't they stopped in Marietta to reunite the young woman with her husband? Did they realize they were being tracked and did not want to lead this man to the Underground Railroad outposts in their own town? Did they think they could lose him on the way to the next stop, then get Billy to Shandy later?

"If thee is tracking them, why does thee need me? Just let me go—"

"I intend to, ma'am. Once I've traded you to them for the girl."

No. She didn't know what the Friends would do when faced with a situation like that. They certainly couldn't resign the poor fugitive to a terrible fate—but they also wouldn't let Prudence, a member of their community, their friend, wife of their friend, suffer. "Thee assumes much, Blue Jay."

"And you don't give me enough credit, Mrs. Quaker. I saw you arrive at the auction and search for them in the crowd. I saw you making your way toward them."

"Thee has no idea for whom I was searching—"

"Yes. I do."

She huffed out a breath. There would be no convincing him that she didn't know the men who had bought Shandy. He was already convinced—and since it was the truth, she hadn't any idea how to dissuade him from it.

He was determined to find them. And clearly he meant to overtake them well before they reached Chester Hill. He would keep moving until he did so. Would her friends stop for the night somewhere, or push onward to the relative safety of the next hiding place?

"How does thee know thee is tracking whom thee means to? It is a public road—"

"One of your friends' wheels is a bit off camber. It swivels just a bit with every rotation. You can see the oddity in the track. I noticed it right away when they pulled out from the auction, when there was no mistaking whose track it was."

Prudence blinked, looked down at the road passing slowly beneath them. She could just barely make out any tracks at all in the darkness. Certainly no oddities in them. But what she did know was that Johnmark, whose carriage they'd driven to the auction, would never suffer his vehicle to be in need of repair. He was, after all, a wheelwright. "I think thee must have struck thy head. Thee is imagining this supposed swivel."

He snorted a laugh. "No. I'm not."

"It is not possible that thee—"

"Oh, but it is. It's really quite amazing what you can reason out when you pay attention."

Prudence shook her head. She knew that a good tracker could find a trail she'd never begin to see, trained as they were to notice the smallest details in the brush and dirt. Heaven help them all when a man with such skills became a slave hunter. "Perhaps I should call thee Bloodhound instead of Blue Jay," she muttered.

He sent her a lopsided smile, strangely friendly for the conversation. "I prefer the bird, if it's all the same to you. I like the reminder of my girl."

She ought to opt for the dog just to spite him, but she wouldn't. "What else does thee think thee has discovered with thy amazing powers of deduction?" If she could learn what he knew, perhaps it would be easier to misdirect him. Or escape him.

"That you're not new to this sort of thing, for starters. You're quick on your feet, capable of improvising, and always on the lookout for a way out of a situation." He looked her way, cocking his head to the side as he considered her. "But you don't take unnecessary risks either. No doubt because you have that Mr. Quaker you'd like to make it home to."

How in the world…?

His expression softened, and he faced forward again. "I certainly understand that. I've promised my wife I wouldn't take undue risks either. Gotta get home to her and the children. We've a boy, too—just three months old. We call him Brendan, after my father."

Her throat tightened. Partly at the insight he had no business having. Partly at the longing that swept over her at the thought of this man and his wife having a growing family, while she and Jason had only each other and their heartfelt yearnings.

She swallowed back the emotion. "Thee clearly has much to live for back East. Why is thee out here, tracking helpless slaves, when thee ought to be home with thy wife and children?"

He didn't pause, didn't flinch. Just said, "It's my job. I'm good at it. And I like to think I'm restoring some balance to the world."

She ought to stop her tongue. But he already knew, in general terms, who she was. What she stood for. And he didn't seem the violent type. What did she have to lose? "Thee considers returning slaves to their masters a matter of balance? Then thy definition is skewed. Returning them to *freedom* would be restoring balance. None of God's children were created for slavery."

He adjusted the brim of his hat, not looking over at her. "You assume much, Mrs. Quaker."

"It takes no assumption to know that much about God's will. If slavery were of Him, He would not have sent a Savior who spoke of freedom and equality."

"I believe He also told slaves to obey their masters—earnestly and sincerely. Colossians, isn't it?"

She huffed and tried to move her wrists a bit in the ropes. He hadn't tied her too tightly, but even so, it was uncomfortable to have them always in the same position.

"Ropes aren't rubbing, are they? I tried to keep your sleeves under them."

He had. And while her skin was grateful, her tired mind was growing as annoyed with his thoughtfulness as with his opinions. "I think I preferred thee silent and angry."

"Look, I can appreciate what you and your friends are trying to do. But all you've actually managed to achieve is keeping that girl away from her family."

Family. Every cramp of her stomach brought the word to mind. She wanted to give one to Jason. Wanted it more than anything. And yet...if the Lord said "no," if He intended instead for her and her husband to serve Him only in this way...could she accept that? Could she not just accept it but thrive?

Moisture stung her eyes, and she couldn't blame it on the breeze that blew. "She made her choice on which family she wanted to remain with. I don't know who she had left on the plantation she fled, but she wanted to be with her husband."

"Her husband?" For the first time since she knocked him over that afternoon, Blue Jay looked at her with surprise. "No one said anything about a husband. Where is he?"

Had she said too much? Probably. But for all he knew, the husband was a free black. "He is not under thy jurisdiction."

"I didn't ask if he was. I asked *where* he was."

Prudence lifted a shoulder. "How am I to know?" He could be in the room at Riverfront House still. But he could also be en route to Chester Hill to be reunited with his wife.

Blue Jay muttered something that sounded suspiciously like "Fool woman" and shook his head. He said no more.

Nor did she. She feared she'd already said far too much.

They plodded along through the night, stopping now and then for short rests to eat and to check the trail again. So far as she could tell, they had the road to themselves—most people weren't fool enough to try to travel at night. But the Friends were obviously set on getting Shandy to Chester Hill as soon as possible, and the cover of darkness was generally a runaway's friend.

Prudence eventually sagged against Charity's neck, stealing a few snatches of sleep here and there until her balance shifted, and she jerked awake again. By the time dawn brushed the horizon, she was sore and still exhausted and not at all certain that the hardtack Blue Jay had given her a couple hours before wasn't about to come up again.

"Whoa." He pulled his horse up, and hers with it.

Prudence forced herself to sit straight again, blinking against sleep to see what put that note of caution in his voice.

Up ahead, she saw the familiar outlines of the Quaker Inn Station. *Praise be to God.* And parked outside it, Johnmark Smith's buggy.

But Blue Jay wasn't looking at the quarry he'd been hunting all this night. He was craning his head around to look behind them.

It took her a moment to realize why. To note the sound of pounding hooves.

He moved quickly, as if he hadn't also been up all night. He led the horses off the road and into the cover of the forest, then tugged Prudence off her saddle and into a crouch behind a waxy-leafed rhododendron bush. "Not a word," he whispered.

She made no promises. If it was Jason on the road, or someone else she knew, she'd stand up and scream so quickly, Blue Jay wouldn't have time to react.

But as the figure took form in the dawn, emerging from the fog that had slithered its fingers over the land, her heart sank. Certainly not Jason. Not any Friend from Marietta. Could whoever it was still help her though? She was nearly ready to test it and see, when the man turned his face a bit more toward them.

Blue Jay sucked in a breath. So did Prudence. She recognized the newcomer after all—and he definitely wasn't a friend. He was a slave hunter. She'd seen him around these parts before. She held that breath she'd pulled in until he was well past, willing the horses to just keep munching on the grass they'd found, heads down.

He headed straight for the inn.

When the door closed on him, Blue Jay vaulted to his feet, tugging her up too. "Come on. We'd better hurry if we want to get to her before he does."

Prudence held her ground, too many thoughts swirling to know quite how to sort them. "Why? Because he is thy rival?"

"No, blast it all! Because he was hired to drag her back."
He seemed genuinely panicked.

That part she understood. As for why… "And thee was not?"

He reached for her wrists and started working the knots loose. "No."

"Then who is thee?"

The ropes loosened, but she didn't bolt. Not now.

He looked her squarely in the eye. "Quinn McKinnon, ma'am. One of Pinkerton's detectives. I was hired by Shandy's uncle to find her and purchase her freedom."

And she'd foiled him. Her stomach heaved, forcing her back to her knees. She really was a fool woman.

CHAPTER FOURTEEN

Tess flipped another page of her copy of Prudence Willard's journal, more skimming than really reading. Just looking for those key words—Chester Hill. Thus far she'd not seen anything, and she was nearly through the second third of the journal, which she'd been assigned. Janice was taking the first section, LuAnn the last.

They were currently lounging on their couches and chairs in their shared living room on the fourth floor so they could run things by each other in comfort as they read, without interfering with the lively Sherlock debate underway on the main floor. They'd listened to the discussion during dinner, even chiming in now and then, but as they'd cleaned up afterward, they all decided they'd rather look some more into the current Prudence mystery rather than try to remember the novel none of them had read recently.

Tess turned yet another page and sighed. "I'm not seeing any mention at all of Chester Hill or another inn there. Anyone having better luck?"

Janice shook her head. "None. I had this vague hope that maybe she'd mention having lived or worked or even visited someone there, and we just never paid attention to it before, but nothing. Clearly they knew each other, though."

"Well, if the inn was run by other Quakers, then it seems safe to assume they were aware of each other, at least." LuAnn turned another page in her copy. She'd moved to the floor and was reading even as she twisted her body into some of the complicated stretches that always made Tess ache just to watch. "Thirty miles was a bit too far away in those days to really be part of the same community, but I daresay there was some overlap."

"But if she never mentions them, then that leaves us with absolutely nothing to go on." Tess flipped another page. "She doesn't often use proper names though, I guess. More like initials. So maybe we shouldn't even be looking for 'Chester Hill.' Maybe we should be looking for '*CH*.' Or even '*QI*' or '*QIS*' for the Quaker Inn Station."

"Wait a minute." LuAnn untangled herself and sat normally, flipping quickly through her pages. "I may have seen a *QI*."

Tess and Janice both paused in their own searches and waited for her pages to settle. Smiling, LuAnn tapped a line. "Yeah, here we go. August 14, 1864. She says she visited with *L* and his parents at *QI* that day and found them all well."

"*L*." Tess met Janice's gaze. "*LL*, do you think? The person who carved out the legs of the chair?"

"Hard to say. But it's possible, right?" Janice grinned. "It would make sense. We know the chair's from Quaker Inn, and how many other things would have the initials *QI*? And if there's an *L* at *QI*, it could well be the same *L* who marked the chair."

"Does the entry say anything else about the visit?" Tess stuck a finger in her page, ready to flip to 1864 if need be.

But LuAnn shook her head. "No. Just that their work continued as much as possible, but the war had made things difficult. If she's mentioning it here, I don't think it's too big a stretch to assume it was Underground Railroad work, but that's all she says."

"Hmm." Tess smoothed out her page. "I'll try to keep an eye out for 'inn' and '*QI*' as I'm skimming."

"I'll do the same," Janice said. "I was trying to look for *farm* too, to see if she mentions meeting a family at a farm that would match the photo, but that's been drudgery. She mentions farms plenty—but I think it's pretty much always theirs."

LuAnn settled into another stretch. "Maybe we should actually read instead of just looking for key words."

"I wish I'd found the time to type this up, and then we'd be able to search the document for any key words we please." Tess shrugged. "Coulda, shoulda, woulda."

They fell silent again as they each went back to it. Tess tried to do more reading this time, not just looking for the distinctive capital *Q* or other initials of interest, but absorbing at least a few words from each sentence, each line. Enough to remind herself of what each entry was about. She'd read the whole thing enough that it just took a bit of reminding to recall generally what Prudence was talking about.

Her gaze snagged on an entry. "Here's one. In 1861. 'Today we took Moses to visit at *QI* and spent the night with the Friends there. We all enjoyed the visit, reminiscing about old times. But there was far more left unsaid, spoken of only in silent gazes, than we could ever dare put to words.'"

"Definitely sounds like fellow Underground Railroad workers." LuAnn stretched out one leg and leaned over it.

"It does." Tess turned to the next entry and realized she'd reached the end of her section. She returned to the beginning of it so that she could go back through the early entries looking for the initials.

She hadn't gone very far—just into late November of 1858—when another instance caught her eye. She read it silently first before interrupting her friends this time. "I think I found another one. Listen to this.

"'Our Friends from *QI* visited, and I was so grateful for the chance to see them again. We have planned a longer visit in the spring, and I will try to visit *S* and *B* beforehand so I can take news of them with me. But for today, it was enough to know they cared enough to check on me. Today, yet again, I sit back and consider the Friends with which the Lord saw fit to place me in my hour of need, and I am struck with awe at His goodness and mercies. For not only did He give me a family, not only did He give me companions, He prepared me to join a mighty force, fighting for His justice. I am but one of many Friends helping in this, my cause. And I am honored and humbled to be numbered among their ranks.'"

"Very interesting." LuAnn had moved into a general sprawl and rested her chin on her hands. "I wonder who *S* and *B* are."

"I don't know." Tess went backward again, looking for those initials. "There's a *B* and an *S* mentioned in September. Oh, this is cool."

"What?" Janice flipped her own pages ahead, no doubt looking for the same entry.

"She mentions a detective in the September entry and how his powers of observation astounded her." Tess chuckled. "I should show this one to Uncle Harold."

"You should." LuAnn checked her watch and pushed herself up. "Speaking of Uncle Harold, we should go check on the Sherlock Society and see if they need anything else before bed. If everyone else is as tired after that hike through the snow as I am, they'll start making their way up to their rooms soon."

Janice closed her journal copy. "I know I'm beat. We can look through these more tomorrow."

"Agreed." Tess pushed herself to her feet, though she didn't put her printout aside as the others did. She'd take it down with her. Uncle Harold always loved any mention of detectives. He'd probably be especially intrigued to realize their predecessor here at Wayfarers Inn had apparently worked with one during one of her missions. Detectives, aiding not only in crime and justice, but in the abolition movement. Who'd have thought?

That was probably quite an interesting story. Too bad Prudence didn't provide so much as an initial to tell Tess who this detective might have been.

She followed her friends down the stairs, smiling at the laughter that drifted up to greet them. It was fun having groups stay like this. Rather than individual guests going quietly about their business, there was a real community atmosphere. A family feel. She loved the idea that their inn could provide a place for that.

Once on the ground floor, Tess flipped on the porch light to marvel at the snow outside. "Whoa."

"What?" Janice looked out the other window and gasped. "Whoa indeed."

"That has to be at least a foot," LuAnn said from behind Tess. "Man, it's really been putting it down for the last few hours. Have the forecasters given this one a funny name yet?"

"Probably." Tess chuckled. "I was wrong to doubt them this time, that's for sure."

"All right." Uncle Harold's voice came from inside the parlor, punctuated by the shuffle of many feet. "Until tomorrow then, my sleuths. Sweet dreams!"

"Looks like our timing is perfect." Janice spun away from the door.

As the society exited—Stan and Sylvia among them—the Inn Crowd asked if anyone needed anything. The group, however, universally assured them that they were set and wished them a good night. A few detoured to peek out the windows at the snow. Tess had left the porch light on to illuminate it.

She snagged her uncle's arm as he brought up the rear, leaning up to kiss his cheek. "Have a good evening?"

"I've had a smashing day all round." He patted the hand she'd settled on his arm. "You have a lovely inn here, Tessie. We've all been enjoying ourselves immensely."

"Good." She lifted the printout a bit. "Have I told you about the journal we discovered when we first bought the place? Written by a Quaker woman who worked at the original hotel and used it as a stop on the Underground Railroad?"

"You have." He glanced down at it, though his eyes weren't quite as bright as she expected them to be over the mention of actual historical documents. He led her toward the stairs.

"Well, I just rediscovered an entry where she's talking about a detective she met."

There, a flare of interest. But it was quickly banked, drowned out by a yawn. He patted her hand again. "That sounds quite intriguing. But if you could show it to me in the morning, I think I'd be better able to appreciate it. This old man has pushed himself quite far enough for one day, I think."

"Oh!" He had some dark circles under his eyes, and the lines of his face seemed to have deepened a bit. It *was* getting late, and he'd had a lot of exercise. They all had—but they weren't all eighty-four. "Of course. Tomorrow's great, no rush. And you certainly don't have to take any time away from your planned activities for it. If not before, I'll show you over lunch with the family."

He lifted his brows. "I highly doubt that will happen, my girl. You've looked outside, I know."

She glanced over her shoulder at the windows as they mounted the first steps. "Oh. I guess I was figuring it would be done by then and..."

And that was a lot of snow to clear out, both off the roads and from driveways. The chances of it happening by lunch-time were slim, to say the least. She sighed. "I guess you're right."

He chuckled and bumped their shoulders together. "Chin up, lassie. Even if the others can't come, you and your favorite uncle can enjoy a nice lunch together, can't we? It'll be like old times. Do you remember our ice cream dates?"

"As if I could forget." She smiled at those golden memories. The sweet days of childhood when Uncle Harold taking her out for a treat on a summer afternoon was what she lived for. She bumped his shoulder back. "Hey, I bet we could make some snow-cream."

"I don't know. Think we could scrape enough of it together for that?"

Thinking of the mountains of snow they'd have to contend with, she laughed. "Maybe. If we really hunt for it."

They traveled a few steps in silence before a sigh worked its way out. "I'm sorry though. It's been so long since you've gotten to see them all."

"Well, there's no controlling the weather." She couldn't help but notice that he didn't express any regret over the missed opportunity.

Had he not really wanted to have lunch with them all? Had he instead been looking forward to another meal with his crew? He certainly hadn't greeted the news-that-shouldn't-have-been-news of the meal plans with great enthusiasm. Just with the insistence that she hadn't said anything to him about it.

They reached the second-floor landing, where she'd booked him into Maple and Mum so he wouldn't have so many stairs to manage. He may be spry for his age, but it just seemed reasonable to put the younger bodies on the higher floors. Especially since she knew well her uncle wouldn't consent to the elevator unless he was carrying something.

Rather than say anything more about the lunch, she simply said good night, kissed his cheek again, and watched him open his door and disappear into the room.

Her shoulders sagged a bit as she turned back to the stairs to help get the main floor ready for the night. The familiar routine did little to soothe her. Maybe her concerns of that morning were unfounded—Uncle Harold's mind was clearly as sharp as ever. But the alleviation of one particular concern didn't alter the realization it had brought.

She switched off the lamps in the parlor and then paused at the window overlooking Front Street. The porch light still shone through the night, catching on the endless snowflakes making a mad dash for the ground and on the thick blanket of them already there. It was beautiful, even if it did act as a sledgehammer to her plans.

She didn't know how long she had left with Uncle Harold. Maybe a decade. God willing, even more. But it could as easily be months or a few short years. But the older they all got, the closer the inevitable drew. She was going to lose her uncle one of these days. And she hated the thought. More, she hated that he'd be in Oberlin, where he said he belonged. And she'd be here, where she did. And when that dreaded time came, her kids wouldn't quite understand the loss she felt, because they didn't know him like she did. And her grandkids wouldn't even notice that he was gone. There would be a debate about whether Jeff Jr. and Lizzie could even take the time off work to make it to the funeral.

What morbid thoughts. She gave herself a little shake and returned to the stairs. The café was already dark, which meant the kitchen would be too. They always left a few small lights on in case anyone needed to come downstairs during the night, but otherwise, all was dim and still.

She'd left the porch light on, just so anyone on this side of the inn could look out and see the snow. And so the neighbors could look out and see the inn, shining there.

The long day in the snow had caught up with her too, and she was feeling it in her legs by the time she reached the fourth floor again. Often after they shut everything up for the night, the Inn Crowd would gather in their little kitchen over tea or ice cream or just to chat for a few more minutes. Tonight, though, LuAnn's and Janice's bedroom doors were both shut already, and only the night-light shone from their shared space. They probably hadn't seen her at the window in the parlor and thought she was already upstairs. Already preparing for bed.

Tired as she was, her mind was spinning enough that she didn't think she'd be able to sleep quite yet. So she slipped into her sitting room instead of her bedroom and settled down at her laptop. Might as well clear out any emails that had come in.

There was nothing of interest. Nothing to distract her from her melancholy thoughts. Leaning her elbow onto her desk and resting her cheek against her palm, she scrolled through the usual junk mail, deleting as she went. Read a few real ones, but they didn't need immediate replies.

She found herself scrolling down into the emails already marked as read, her eyes looking for her uncle's name. When she spotted it, she clicked it and then scrolled past his brief reply, to the message she'd sent him about lunch.

We're so excited you're coming! Our usual checkout time is eleven, but why don't you plan on staying a little longer? I'd love to host you for lunch. It's been so long! Too long.

She blinked at the screen. That was it? That's all she'd written? In her mind, as she wrote it, the "we" had been her and Jeff Jr. and Lizzie, but it read more like she meant the Inn Crowd. When she'd typed "host," she'd meant hosting him and her family because it had been too long since they'd all been together. But it could just as easily have meant that she wanted to host his club, and that she hadn't had time with him and Matti and Bud in too long.

No wonder he hadn't had a clue what she meant. Shaking her head at herself, Tess closed out of her email and shut down her computer.

Time for bed. She may not be sleepy, but she was certainly exhausted.

CHAPTER FIFTEEN

Morning hadn't dawned so much as unfurled—softly, gently, the light seeping through the clouds and over the town like a flower blossoming. Snow still fell, though not with the intensity of last night. Tess had no idea how much was out there. A lot. Definitely over a foot, but given the way it blurred all the surfaces, she couldn't quite gauge it without going outside with a yardstick. And at the moment, she had no desire whatsoever to open the door and let in the cold.

She sat in the downstairs kitchen, a stool pulled up to the counter so she could look out the window. Steam curled its way up from her mug of coffee, which she held cradled between her palms. It was early. Not quite six o'clock. But she'd come fully awake at five thirty, and when her thoughts immediately started ricocheting around, she figured it was pointless to hope for more sleep, so she'd just gotten up. Might as well get this morning's cinnamon rolls into the oven and enjoy some quiet.

The quiet seemed to have dug its way into her very bones. Occasionally, that was a pleasant feeling. It had been when Jeff was still alive. Those rare moments of solitude, when she knew he'd come padding out any minute, were crystalline and beautiful. But since he'd died, it was altogether different. So many mornings she found herself doing alone the things they used to do together, just missing him. The quiet wasn't so kind then.

The same sort of mood took possession of her now—for the first time in months. With the inn and her friends consuming her days, there'd been less time for such introspection. And certainly less quiet.

Sometimes she just wished she could pause the world. Keep the snow from falling. Keep her uncle from aging. Keep herself from expectations that led to disappointment. Her eyes flicked down to her phone. Dark and silent now, but when she'd gotten up, there had been text messages waiting for her on the screen. Lizzie, saying there was absolutely no way they'd make it for lunch, of course. She and Michael expected to be clearing snow and romping with the triplets all morning. And Jeff Jr., saying to tell Uncle Harold hello and he'd be sure to catch him next time—and asking if they needed any help with snow removal.

They were good kids. She knew they had no choice. Knew there was no reason for her to be upset by their very logical assumption that lunch couldn't happen. But she also knew they wouldn't really be distressed about the cancellation. They didn't miss Uncle Harold like she did. He hadn't been the part of their lives that he'd been of hers.

Maybe that was what made her feel melancholy. She lifted her cup and took a sip of the hot, fragrant brew.

"Do you have another one of those?"

Tess jumped, jerked, and was glad her mug hadn't been full, or she'd have worn her coffee.

Her uncle's chuckle curled into the silence like dawn in a snowstorm. Softly, gently, unlike those words that had scared the daylights out of her. "Sorry. I assumed you'd hear me coming. Those heavenly smells lifted me straight out of bed like a cartoon character."

Oh, he knew how to make her smile. Tess stood and pulled a second cup from the cupboard. "Guess I was lost in thought."

"I hope they were good ones." He came up beside her, smelling of soap and laundry detergent as he put an arm around her shoulders and gave her a squeeze.

She wasn't about to tell him otherwise, so she focused instead on coffee. "How would you like it?" He was one of the few people she knew who never drank it the same way two cups in a row.

"Hmm." He glanced out the window, smacking his lips as if tasting the coffee he'd soon be drinking. "Black for now."

"Straight up it is." She poured the cup and handed it to him as he settled onto the stool beside hers.

"Quite a storm." He looked far more at peace gazing out at the snow than she had felt.

She sat back down on her stool. "That it was."

He took a sip, savored it, and took his time in swallowing. When he did, it was with a nod. "You've built a grand thing here, my girl. A beautiful place of business that welcomes visitors like home. Good food. Good coffee." He toasted her with his mug. "And a sweet, sweet spirit. A place of ministry."

His words warmed her more than her drink ever could. Though she still wrapped her hands around the mug and felt that dreadful quiet easing away. "That's what we wanted to do. What we've prayed it can be."

"I know. That's why I knew we had to come this weekend, snow or no snow." His brows puckered a bit. "Matti needed it. Needs the kind of comfort I knew you could give."

Tess reached out and settled her hand on his. If Matti was hurting, she knew he would be too. "What's going on?"

"Not mine to say." He shook his head and met her eye. "But keep her in your prayers, my girl. If something were to happen to her—I don't know what I'd do. She's my girl, as surely as you are."

"I know she is." She gave his hand a squeeze that echoed the one in her heart. "And she's as proud to be as I am. I'm so glad you have her and Bud, Uncle Harold. So, so glad."

"Now." He straightened, puffed out his chest a bit, and gave her a stern look. "I'm glad too, as well you know. But I know you're thinking of it because you worry. You needn't."

"Of course I need to. You're my family, and you're all alone."

His smile curved up, sweet as a cinnamon roll and as unyielding as a snowfall. "I'm your family, Tessie. But I'm not all alone. How could I be, surrounded as I am by such wonderful friends?"

She sighed into her mug. "It's not the same."

"Isn't it? Are these friends of yours not your family as surely as Lizzie and Jeff?"

"They are." No hesitation necessary for that answer. "But still. I can't imagine not having my kids and grandkids. Not having had Jeff."

"Hmm." He nodded and leaned into the stool's back, his eyes on the white world outside. "It was the same for your parents. And for my parents. I always assumed it would be my lot too. But when Clarissa died..."

Tess swiveled her stool around so she could face him, knowing her eyes were wide. "Who? Who's Clarissa?"

His smile had turned a bit sad. "The woman I was supposed to marry."

"What?" She rested her palm flat against the countertop. "How do I not know about this? You were engaged?"

"Nearly. I'd bought the ring and planned the perfect proposal." His eyes slid shut. The corners of his lips twitched with secret memories. "She was the prettiest thing, my Clarissa Rose. We were young—just nineteen—but I knew. I knew she was the one for me. I wanted nothing more than to make her my wife."

Nineteen. Tess hadn't even been born yet. No wonder, then, she didn't remember Clarissa. Though why she'd never heard stories of her... "What happened?"

"A car accident." He huffed out a breath and opened his eyes. "Senseless. Pointless. The romantic in me could have accepted it more easily, I always thought, if it had been some purposeful death. Malaria contracted on a mission trip or an accident she found herself in when she was trying to save someone else. That's the kind of person she was—she *would* have sacrificed herself for another. But she just fell asleep driving home from the soda shop where she worked one night. A week before I planned to slide my ring onto her finger."

"Oh, Uncle Harold. You must have been crushed."

"They all told me it would fade, that I'd find another love, and it would be more beautiful for the pain I'd gone through." His lips twitched again. "Your father even accused me once of holding on to the memory of her out of pure stubbornness."

Tess chuckled. "Dad was not the sentimental type."

"No, practical to the bone, that one. But it wasn't stubbornness, Tessie. And it certainly wasn't that I didn't want to find someone else to love, to have a family. Especially," he added, reaching up to tweak her nose, "once you came along, and I saw what a joy it could be to raise children."

She rolled her eyes and chuckled into her coffee mug. "So your bachelorhood wasn't just a decision. Not an attempt to be like Sherlock."

"Gracious, I'm not as silly as that. No. I just really do have a story similar to LuAnn's." He glanced up at the ceiling. Or perhaps at the floors above it. "Though, teasing aside, I am glad to hear she may have found someone. I prayed for years that I would."

"But not anymore?"

He shot her an amused look. "At my age?"

"Stranger things have happened—and we serve a big God."

"That we do." He reached for her hand again. "A God so big that He could help me see there's more than one way to make a family. Instead of giving me a wife, he gave me a daughter and a son in Matti and Bud. He gave me students to pour my heart into. He led me to form the Sherlock Society, which has been more family to me than I deserve."

She nodded, because she knew it was true. Just as it had been true for LuAnn, who had plenty of kids to love over the years and plenty of people who considered her one of their own—like Tess's and Janice's families both did. "I don't mean to worry. I just think sometimes about how the members of the club come and go and..."

"They do. As members of any family do. Which is why my heart fairly burst yesterday when GG opened that door." He grinned. "Can you imagine the affirmation I felt? Seeing one of my first members, a student from so long ago, going to such trouble to make my day? I haven't seen her in decades—I didn't even know she'd gotten married. But our conversations meant something to her. So much that she still remembers them, that they've helped shape her. The Sherlock Society, even though she hasn't been a member for thirty years, is part of the fabric of her being now."

Tess hadn't paused to think about that yesterday, with all the hustle and bustle, the mysteries solved and mysteries discovered. But he was right. "That really is amazing."

"What it is, is awesome, in the truest meaning of the word. It fills me with awe. One of those moments that proves to me my life has been well spent. That this thing God has called me to do is worthwhile."

"Hmm." She let that soak in, deep down. She'd always assumed his teaching was his calling. But she'd never really paused to consider that running the Sherlock Society was too, every bit as much.

She'd thought it was just fun. But it was more than that. It was joy. Peace. The knowledge that he had touched lives. He'd achieved far more wisdom than she could ever hope to attain. A life well spent indeed. And even more, well *lived.* She held tight to his fingers. "You make me proud, Uncle Harold."

"As you do me, my girl. This place." He used his coffee cup to motion to the inn at large. "It is for you what my society has been for me. A way to minister to those the Lord brings to you."

She opened her mouth, but no words came out. She'd never really considered that his club was a ministry for him. Fun, yes. Education. Obsession, her father had always called it. But of course it was more. Because God was more, and Uncle Harold had always loved Him above all.

Slowly, she nodded. "Yeah. That's exactly what the inn is. And what your club is."

His smile gleamed all the way up into his eyes. "You have a lot of your father in you—the practicality, the business mind. But you have your mother's giving spirit. And, I like to think, a bit of me in there too. I'm so glad to know you understand."

"I don't know if I do entirely," she admitted. "But I'm beginning to. I'm trying to."

"You do. If you didn't, you wouldn't be here, in this place, doing what you do. You wouldn't have the friends you have. You wouldn't be bringing the story alive."

Sometimes he and LuAnn really did sound like carbon copies of each other. "The story?"

What she and her cousins had always called the "Professor Look" came over him. "It's the most powerful motivator humanity has. Not guns or tanks, not laws or edicts. Stories. They have the ability to sink into our hearts and become a part of us. To transform us. This is why Jesus told so many parables, and why it was so important that the Gospel writers wrote down *His* story for us to read centuries later. This is why I've spent so many years teaching literature and why God called me to begin the Sherlock Society. Because through story, we can change lives. Change the whole world."

She didn't interrupt. Just trailed a finger around the edge of her cup and smiled.

All the encouragement he needed to continue. "Some people doubt me when I say such things. But it's true. There are the ways easily spotted—the fact that Doyle's fictional character truly helped pioneer the field of criminology; the fact that the inventions Asimov described in his science fiction inspired scientists to create them in reality. But it's the deeper ways that matter most. That Tolkien and Lewis helped reignite faith in the world after a war that had stripped a generation of it." He leaned forward and tapped a finger to the counter. "This inn is part of the story, Tessie. A place where so many stories were born and lived out, so many chapters written as people sought freedom. People come here looking for that, whether they recognize it or not. They come looking for a story, and while you serve it to them, you also show them the greatest Story. The story of our Lord."

Tears blurred her eyes. But they were good tears. Happy tears. Healing tears. "You should write this stuff down."

"Oh, I have. You can sort through it all once I've gone home and decide what's worth keeping." He winked and drained the last of his coffee.

The last bit of hers had gone cold in her cup. But that was okay. Just like, somehow, it was okay right now to hear him talk about dying. Somehow, he made the inevitable sound like just one more part of the story. "God's been good to us, hasn't He?"

"So good, Tessie. He's given us friends, family, careers we love, ways to give back, to reach others for Him. But"— he nudged her with his elbow, winking again—"He blessed me more. He gave me a sleuth for a niece. Nothing could have made this old man happier."

She laughed and stood, reaching for his mug. "More coffee?"

"More coffee. And show me that journal you were talking about last night."

The quiet hadn't been peaceful. But the words certainly were. "You got it."

CHAPTER SIXTEEN

Janice looked from Tess to Uncle Harold with raised brows. "You're sure? You don't mind giving up some of your society time?" Janice seemed eager to say yes, given the way she'd perked up at his suggestion, but never wanting to impose upon their guests.

With a wink for Tess, Uncle Harold nodded. "My original plan was to finish up the Sherlock stuff this morning and catch my church's evening service when we got back to Oberlin. But as our plans have changed, we must adapt. So if you don't mind being our musician..."

"I'd be delighted." In proof, Janice scampered around the furniture that had been moved this way and that, sidestepping whiteboards and corkboards until she arrived at her piano bench. A few moments later, a hymnal was opened in front of her, and her fingers were working their magic on the ivories. LuAnn passed around a few other hymnals Janice had lying around for the guests to share if they wanted to sing along.

Tess drew in a deep breath, savoring the old familiar song like sweet spring air. "I love hearing her play."

"She has a real gift." Her uncle shifted back into the lobby and called out toward the café, "In here, everyone. Janice is blessing us with her talent, and CC is going to share a short piece she wrote this morning."

The piece was a devotional, inspired by the falling snow. Tess had already read it over breakfast, which was what had inspired the impromptu church service. They may not be able to get out, but who ever said one needed to be in a church to have church?

She hadn't known how the Sherlock Society would feel about the idea, but her uncle hadn't apparently deemed it a matter for a vote. One of the benefits of being the professor, she supposed. Occasionally, he simply got to lay down the law, and his students would file into the parlor with smiles on their faces.

At least half of them were regular church goers, she knew. Some of the others she wasn't sure about. And Sylvia and Stan she was pretty sure weren't. But if anyone found they didn't want to stick around, no one would stop them from slipping back to the café or up to their rooms. It would be clear pretty quickly what the nature of this gathering was.

Rather than take one of the seats, which were in short supply, Tess simply leaned against the wall and closed her eyes so she could immerse herself in the music Janice was teasing from the piano. It never failed to amaze her how her friend could turn those little black dots on the page into something so beautiful and alive.

Once the commotion had settled, Janice joined her voice to the mix. Within a few notes, Tess and LuAnn had both joined in, in harmony. Through the first verse of "Be Thou My Vision," no one else joined them, but on the second, Harold took up the tenor line, and one of the other men the bass. Tess wasn't sure which of them and didn't want to open her eyes to find out.

When they'd finished the song, a few people actually applauded. Tess finally blinked her eyes open. She was facing the chair Matti had been in last night—in which she sat again. And Tess looked just in time to see her wiping her cheeks.

A nudge on her spirit had her pushing off the wall. She caught Janice's gaze and gave her a quick hand signal to keep playing. The rousing opening bars of "There Is Power in the Blood" met Tess's ears as she crouched down beside Matti.

She'd swiped a tissue from a box on her way over and pressed it into her friend's hand. "There you go."

Instead of just dabbing at her eyes, Matti balled up the tissue, held it to her face, and dissolved. Her shoulders shook with sobs.

Tess perched on the arm of the chair and slid her arm around Matti's shoulders. She didn't say anything. She didn't know what words to offer, and the Lord didn't whisper any into her spirit. But she hoped it was enough to sit there as the voices around them rose to glorify God and to let Matti know that, whatever it was, she wasn't alone.

"I'm sorry," Matti gasped somewhere in the third verse. "I didn't mean to lose it."

"You don't need to apologize." Tess handed over the second tissue she'd grabbed along with the first and tucked into her pocket.

This one Matti used to wipe her cheeks. "I just...I had a lumpectomy last week." Her nostrils flared, and her lips quivered. "I'm supposed to get results back tomorrow, though I have no idea if that will be postponed now."

"Oh, Matti." Tess reached for her hand.

Matti clung to it. "I'm scared, Tess. I'm so scared. My mom died from breast cancer, and so did my aunt." She squeezed her eyes shut, and more tears dripped out. "I don't want to die. Not yet. Not like this. I'm so scared."

"Oh, sweetie. Of course you're scared!" Tess pulled Matti close to her side. "We all would be."

Matti shook her head. "My mom—she was this p-pillar of faith, you know?" Her breath had gone ragged with the sobs, her chest heaving. "She never doubted that God had her. That He could heal her if He wanted to—and that if she didn't receive it here on earth, she'd get it for sure in h-heaven." A keen filled her throat, though she swallowed it back before anyone but Tess would have heard it over the music.

Tess just rubbed a hand over her arm.

"But I watched her die. I saw the p-pain she was in. How s-sick the chemo made her. I . . . I d-don't want to do that, Tess."

"I know." Tess squeezed her friend's fingers even more tightly.

"Then I th-think, 'My faith must not be strong enough. I shouldn't be so . . . so scared.'"

"Don't let that voice rule you, Matti." Tess leaned down until she could touch her forehead to Matti's head and whisper the words into her ear. "Even Jesus was tormented by the thought of facing death. It isn't just normal to fear—it's healthy. And it's human. That doesn't mean you don't trust Him. It just

means that something else is louder right now. And God under-
stands that. He watched His own Son go through it."

Matti sniffled and sucked in a breath.

Tess gave her shoulders a squeeze. "Can I pray with you?"
At Matti's quick nod, she did. She prayed for peace. She prayed
for Matti to be aware of God's presence, of His grace wrapping
around her like an embrace. She prayed for health and good
results and healing. And then she thanked the Lord for bringing Matti here this weekend, so this time of uncertainty could
be passed with those who loved her best.

Matti echoed her amen and kept on clinging to her hand.
"I didn't want to come. I didn't. But Bud and Harold were right.
This was where I needed to be."

"Of course it is. With your family."

"Yeah." Matti pulled in a deep breath, held it for a second,
then let it ease out again. "Thank you. For the note on my pillow. For the tea. For the music. Thank you for listening. I
think...I think I needed to get that out."

"That's what I'm here for."

Janice launched into another hymn, a slower one this time.
Tess kept holding Matti's hand, just listening to the familiar
words and praying silently. At some point she felt a light touch
on her shoulder and lifted her head.

Bud stood a step behind her. He held out some fresh tissues. And looked like he needed one himself. He mouthed
thank you and then backed away again.

Tess smiled and handed the tissues to Matti. Ultimately,
Bud was the one who would support her the most if the

diagnosis was bad. The one who would celebrate with her if it was good. He and Uncle Harold. But sometimes, you just needed to talk to someone a step removed. Sometimes, your fears were so loud that they drowned out the rest of your story.

As if Janice heard her thoughts, she transitioned into "I Love to Tell the Story." Tess drew in a slow breath to fill her lungs and let her gaze wander around the room. She didn't look at the people, not really, just soaked in the presence of the Lord and the family filling her home now. Harold's family, and hers. So many stories, as her uncle would say, momentarily entwined. Real and fictional. Present and past.

Her gaze settled on the corkboard. On the scanned photograph of Prudence that Tom had insisted on tacking up that morning before breakfast, when the Inn Crowd had shown it to everyone. "Part of the mystery," he'd said, grinning.

Part of the story. Prudence's story, and that of the smiling family with whom she stood.

Janice's fingers stilled on the keys, and LuAnn stepped forward with a smile that most of the group probably wouldn't recognize as a little bit nervous. It was different, getting up and sharing her own writing. Different from just talking about and teaching about someone else's. But she lifted her chin and raised the notebook she'd written her thoughts down in that morning.

Matti's fingers relaxed a bit in Tess's.

LuAnn cleared her throat. "This morning, not surprisingly, I was thinking about snow. I was thinking about how the blood of the Lamb makes us as white and pure as those drifts outside. But as I studied our world, I realized it was a lot more than that. Look out the window."

Those in the group craned their necks to obey.

LuAnn nodded toward the transformed world. "It isn't just white. Snow covers things. It hides them, just as we are hidden in the wings of our Lord. Snow rounds the edges, just as our God will round ours, if we let Him. Snow has this remarkable ability to become all we see, just as our Savior fills our vision."

Tess's lips pulled up. Janice hadn't had the chance to read LuAnn's musings this morning, but somehow she'd known exactly what hymns to select.

"Snow can be a powerful, driving force. But one flake—" LuAnn paused and lowered her notebook. "One flake is nothing, in one sense. It has no power on its own. But it has infinite beauty. When we look at a snowflake, we see the laws that the Creator put into effect, we see the patterns He set in motion. And we, my friends, are the same. We are the possessors of infinite beauty. We are made, each one of us, in His image…yet each one, like a crystal of snow, is different. Because He is infinite, while we are finite. He is the atmosphere to our single flake.

"But one of the most amazing things He did for us was to set us with other snowflakes. We see what effect a snowstorm, a blizzard, can have. And the same is true of His children. Alone, we may be so small that sometimes we think we go unseen. But we're part of something. Part of a driving force. And together, we can work miracles. We can turn a plain into a mountain." She motioned to the street, where snowbanks had made hills out of nothing. "We have only to play out our role in His story."

Tess still had one tissue in her hand, which was a good thing. She needed it to dab at her own eyes just now.

Janice began to play again, softly. LuAnn closed her eyes and lifted a hand. "Dear Lord, thank You for filling our home today, when we can't get out to worship You. Thank You for filling our hearts every day that we let You in. Thank You for giving us this fellowship of friends. Of family. Bless each one here, Father, and draw us all closer to You. Soothe hurting hearts and speak truth to our spirits. Fill our conversations through the rest of the day. Amen."

"Amen." Tess gave Matti's hand one last squeeze and then gave in to the demands of a tingling foot and stood. "How about a cup of tea, Matti?"

The breath her friend drew in sounded...renewed. "That would be wonderful."

"Coming right up." She slipped out and over to the café, savoring now the solitude that felt so heavy this morning. She hummed along with the music still coming from the piano, fixed two cups of tea, and eased back into the parlor a few minutes later with the sure knowledge that God had moved here today. Moved hearts. Moved minds. Moved mountains.

Matti had moved too—from her chair to the couch, beside Bud. Good. Tess handed her the teacup with a smile and then drifted over to the corkboard. She started out just looking at the photograph of Prudence, but as the music came to a halt and soft conversation filled the room, her attention shifted to the other items tacked into place from Sylvia's game. The letter that was taped to the door. The measurements of the tires that they'd written down. The Polaroid snapshots Hiram took.

She'd seen him scrawl something onto the bottom of each one, but she hadn't looked at what they were until now. Timestamps. Locations. Like a thorough detective should, she supposed. She followed the trail of them backward, back to the beginning, to their arrival at the museum Friday night. When the world was just beginning to whiten enough to be a hazard to drivers.

Like that one car that had been idling outside the museum, whose driver had been gripping the wheel in a panic as she puttered away. At, apparently, 4:32 p.m.

She took a step forward as she read the time, though she quickly recoiled when she felt something under her shoe. "Well, what do you know?" Bending down, she scooped up a bright red thumbtack from where it was half-hidden under the edge of the rug. "Number one hundred."

When she straightened again, something about that photo of the car snagged her attention. Her gaze flicked from that one to the one directly before it, before they'd crossed the street. Before she'd even looked up at the museum, apparently, because she didn't remember seeing anyone walking away from the building.

"Wait a minute," she mumbled, squinting at the tiny image. Though it was too small to make out details, she could clearly see a figure, probably a woman. Hunched over a bit, as if she were hurrying. Aimed directly at the car that even in that photo had a plume of exhaust coming from the back.

"Guys? Guys!" She spun, searching for LuAnn and Janice. Or, frankly, anyone who was near enough to hear her. "Did anyone actually try the museum door on Friday night? Was it locked?"

The other conversations buzzing in the room came to an abrupt halt. Within seconds, a crowd of amateur detectives—her best friends and her uncle's crew—had gathered around her. She asked her question again.

Harold looked to Bud. "You took the note off the door. Did you test the knob?"

Bud nodded. "It was locked."

"Sylvia? Stan?" Tess turned lifted brows their way. "Were you really gone by then? Did you lock the door behind you, or could someone have gotten in after you left and before we arrived?"

Sylvia squinted at the photo—until someone passed her a magnifying glass. She laughed but put it use. "Is this the time you guys came by? We were already gone by then. We left right around four, on our way to Cara and Ronan's. Did you lock the door, babe?"

Stan's arms were crossed over his chest, but he didn't look forbidding. Just thoughtful. "I . . . thought so. But all I can honestly remember doing is putting up the letter." He scrubbed a hand over his bristly jaw. "You know, when I came by the next morning to do the tire tracks, I went through the back and to the front door to make sure the note was gone. I didn't have to unlock the deadbolt, just the door handle. I remember thinking I must have been more distracted than I'd thought. We always lock the deadbolt on the front door as well as the knob from the inside, then exit through the back."

"I assume the handle is the kind that can be locked from inside, then you just shut the door behind you?" LuAnn asked.

At their nods, a grin began to form on Tess's lips. "I think we're finally onto something. Allow me to set up a scenario. You guys left at four, forgetting to lock the door behind you. The person in the photo, who is clearly coming away from the museum, went in and took the photo from the chair. They went in through the front and out the same way—locking the knob's lock behind them." She pointed to the Polaroid with the figure.

"Whoa." Hiram leaned close. "I didn't even notice her. I was just taking photos of the building, I thought. B-roll sort of stuff. She kinda blends in with the background, doesn't she?"

"And we weren't looking for anyone coming from the museum at that point. Excellent observational skills, my girl." Uncle Harold gave her shoulder a squeeze.

"I have no idea why she locked up behind her, but she must have, for it to have been locked when Bud tried the door." Tess tapped the next photo. "This is where she seemed to be heading. The car was still there when we came up, then pulled out before we crossed the street. Our culprit must have gotten into this car."

"I *knew* the car was a clue!" Hiram shot a grin at Harold.

Her uncle chuckled. "You were correct. Not in the mystery I had us solving, but in the one none of us knew was playing out. So, those of you with better eyes than I have, what details can we tell about the car?"

Sylvia moved the magnifying glass over the photo, to more chuckling. Even so, the Polaroid image just wasn't all that clear. They all stared at it for a minute before Tom said, "This is stupid. I took all the same shots on my phone, more or less—let me check those and toss them onto a computer screen, and we can look at it zoomed in."

Graham reached under his glasses to rub his eyes. "That sounds like a fantastic idea."

Everyone scurried to make room, fetch a laptop, and then get the pictures displayed. It took a few minutes, but at last Tom pulled one up with the car—he hadn't caught the figure moving toward it, but he had gotten a good shot of the vehicle itself.

LuAnn wrinkled her nose. "Remember what I was saying about snow obscuring things? I can't even tell the make and model."

"But it's green. A bright green, not a dark one. There's no question about that," Ollie said.

"What's this?" Kim circled a finger over part of the screen. "On the door of the car?"

"Looks like one of those decal things." Tom clicked the mouse and zoomed in a bit more. "There's snow on part of it, but we can probably figure out what it says, if it's for a local business. *G-R-E*, something-something, snow, *M-B*."

"And those look like leaves, don't they?" Ollie indicated the bottom part of the logo.

They did look like leaves. Sort of. Though they were in an odd position. Almost like...fingers?

"Greene Thumb!" Janice said on a squeal, turning to Tess and LuAnn with wide eyes. "That's the nursery a few miles out of town where we sourced the plants for our garden!"

"Of course!" Now Tess could see it clearly. The leaves forming a fist with a thumbs-up. The flower blossoming from the thumb was totally obscured behind the snow, along with half the letters that arched over the top. But it couldn't be anything else.

"Greene? With an *E*?" Stan looked from them to Sylvia. "Like, a last name?"

Tess sifted through her mental files, trying to remember what she'd no doubt seen on invoices and receipts. "I think so. Isn't it run by a Greene family? I remember thinking it was one of those perfect last names for a profession."

"Could that be...?" LuAnn wandered back over to the board and tapped the scan of the back of the photo. "Maybe it's just a coincidence. This Green family doesn't have an *E* on the end."

"That doesn't necessarily mean anything. Surnames have been known to mutate over the years." Sylvia moved over to stand beside LuAnn. "Especially before the normalizing of spelling with the advent of Webster's Dictionary, and when it wasn't often written down."

"True," LuAnn agreed. "And if the people in that photograph were freed slaves, the sad truth is that they might not have even known how to read or write, at least not for a while. A later generation could have decided on the spelling. For all we know, the writing on the back of the photograph could have been done by the photographer, not one of them."

Tess caught Tom's eye. "Do a search on that nursery, would you? Pull up their phone number. Might at least be worth a call to see if they came to the museum for any particular reason. We won't accuse them outright of stealing the photo, of course."

"Sure." Tom tabbed away from his photo viewer and pulled up a web browser, though rather than a search engine, it just displayed a pixelated dinosaur and an error message. "Uh. Maybe I don't have the wi-fi on?"

"Or..." Having a feeling she knew what she'd discover, Tess turned on the inn's cordless handset they'd brought in with them. Nothing. "Lines are down. I bet the internet is too. Hold on." A few steps and she was at the front desk computer, jiggling the mouse to bring it back to life. She pulled up her browser with the same result. "Yep."

Tom had followed her out, with Kim and Ollie. "Guess that isn't too surprising. I could look it up on my cell, though. There's still data."

"Oh, you don't need to do that. I thought it would save us a minute, but I do have their info stored in our files. Just a sec." A few clicks and a bit of typing was all it took to pull up the invoice. "Yep, here we go. Greene Thumb Nursery and Garden Center. Contact, Shandy Greene. And the number..." She pulled a little square notepad and pen forward and jotted it down. Calling from the inn clearly wouldn't work, but cell phones seemed to be operating just fine.

LuAnn appeared at her side, her phone already out. "Want me to do the honors?"

"Go for it."

She called the number and put it on Speaker, which meant they all heard the three-tone chime and then "We're sorry. Your call cannot be completed as dialed. Please hang up and try again."

"Whoa, that takes me back." Ollie grinned. "I haven't heard one of those messages in years."

"Probably because we don't really know anyone with a landline anymore." Kim turned her frown toward the door. "Guess that nursery must still have one though."

"Not surprising." Tom had apparently looked them up on his phone after all. "Looks like they've been in business since 1956, and their last three digits are zero-zero-zero. Those are prized numbers, aren't they? Easy to remember. They've no doubt kept it all these years. Which would mean keeping the landline."

"Well, huh." Tess leaned onto the front desk. "Guess we've hit another wall."

"Just a minor setback, that's all." LuAnn offered a bright smile. "I think we're finally getting somewhere though. We just needed to put our collective brains together."

Tom chuckled and put his phone back into his pocket. "Snowflake power."

CHAPTER SEVENTEEN

September 1858

"I do not understand." Prudence spoke in the barest whisper as she darted across the road behind Quinn McKinnon. The horses were still tethered in the woods, where they were happily grazing and resting. "How could her uncle hire a Pinkerton detective?"

"Because he's made a success of himself since he purchased his freedom twenty years ago, that's how." McKinnon flattened himself against the wide trunk of a tree, motioning for her to follow suit. "Enough of one, at least, that he's been able to save up to purchase his family's freedom too."

"Shandy?"

"Well." McKinnon peered around the tree, inch by inch. "He thought he was saving up for his brother's freedom. Only, as it turns out, his brother—Shandy's father—died four years ago. Shandy's the only family he has left now."

"What grief he must have felt, to learn such a thing." Prudence peeked out on her side too. The only thing she saw was the hunter's horse tied up outside the inn, beside

Johnmark's buggy. No people were stirring, either outside or at the windows.

"Mitigated by learning that Shandy was still on the same plantation, though, and doing well. He contacted the owner, and he agreed to the price, so I went on the uncle's behalf to deliver the money and escort Shandy to his farm. But when I got there, it was to learn that she'd run away just a couple of days before."

Prudence winced and settled back against the tree trunk. If only the young woman had waited—but she had no way of knowing that legal freedom was just around the bend. And even if she had, her husband still would have been enslaved. "So thee set out to find her?"

McKinnon's face hardened. Funny how it instilled confidence in her now, rather than either annoyance or fear. "I was hired to deliver her to her uncle. Not to return empty-handed, while she's sold off again."

She motioned toward the inn. "This hunter?"

"Her master was none too happy with her for running off—he hired this fellow to bring her back and informed me that there wasn't enough money in all Ohio to buy her freedom now."

Prudence spread her fingers against the rough bark of the tree. "What is thy plan, Quinn McKinnon?"

His jaw ticked. "I'm going to get her safely to her uncle. And then I'm going to go back to the plantation and pray her owner's calmed down enough to value cash in hand above one slave girl who's been missing for weeks already. I hadn't taken into account the husband though. Is he from the same place?"

She shook her head. "A neighboring plantation. But that is not what I meant. I meant what is thy plan *now*? For getting her safely out of here?"

He glanced around the tree again, seeing who knew what in the fog between here and the side of the inn. "Well, my original plan was to wait until we were all in one place, explain the situation to you and your friends—" Here he paused to shoot her a look. "They are actually your friends, right?"

She nodded.

"Good. I was going to explain it all and ask for your friends' help in getting her to her uncle while I led this fellow away. But he must have been moving faster than we were last night."

Prudence sighed. "If thee had just told me—"

"As if you'd have believed me?"

He had a point. Frankly, she only believed him now because she recognized the newcomer. And, in part, because of the blue jay feather in the band of his hat. "Granted. But now what do we do?"

"Well, I'm guessing if those Quaker gents brought her here, it's friendly."

"Did thee see the sign?"

"Hmm?" He edged out a little more and breathed a little laugh. "Quaker Inn Station. More friends of yours, then?"

"With a capital *F*."

"Good. Hopefully she's already somewhere safe, out of sight. So…all right." He slid back into his original position, turning his head to face her. "How about if you go around to the kitchen entrance? Greet the folks in there. See where Parker is. Shouldn't look suspicious for a Quaker woman to be visiting her neighbors. When it's safe to talk, tell them what's going on. If they agree to help, then I'll need to give the men instructions for getting to her uncle's farm."

"All right." Prudence pointed to the woodshed behind the inn. "In the meantime, hide thyself in there. If this Parker would recognize thee as quickly as thee did him—"

"Oh, he will. We've already tangled once, about a week ago."

"Then it is important he does not see thee." She didn't think he would recognize her though. And if he did, it would only be as a Riverfront House employee. And as McKinnon said, no one would think it odd for one Quaker to visit another. "Stay out of sight at all costs. I will come fetch thee as soon as it's safe."

For one brief moment, she considered instead just leaving him hidden there. Finding the Friends, verifying Shandy was safely hidden, and taking off again for home. Jason. Billy, who would be so anxious for news of his wife.

But that was foolish. She couldn't do this on her own, not with Parker there. And not when all she had to offer the two escapees was more running, more hiding, more possible captures.

Quinn McKinnon was offering real freedom. Bought and paid for. She could only help them. He, thanks to Shandy's uncle, could save them. Redeem them.

Perhaps he read her fleeting doubts in her face. He reached up, slid the feather out of his hat, and held it out to her. "Here. I think Lucy would want you to have this now. She said it was for family—she was excited when I told her I was off to help put one back together. Seems you're helping with that now too."

Family. Prudence took the feather, ran her fingers up the quill with a smile, and then tucked it into her pocket. "I thank thee. When this is all over, I will send thee with a few white goose quills for Lucy. I have a pet goose—Patience."

His lips quirked up. "She's been after us to get her a goose."

"Then she will treasure them as I will this. When this is over."

"When we've put a family back together." He held out a hand, and she clasped it. "Go with God, Mrs. Quaker."

"My name is Prudence." She smiled and stepped out from behind the tree. One deep breath to school her features—off with the last hectic day, with the worries, with the doubts, with the fears—and then she strolled through the yard as if she had every right to do so. Just another neighbor, coming to pay a call at the inn.

The kitchen door opened before she could even raise a hand to knock, and young Levi stood there, his eyes wide. "Prudence Willard! What is thee doing here?"

Prudence smiled, but she also touched a finger to her lips to encourage him to keep his exclamations quiet. "I thought it high time I visit thy parents, Levi Liller."

"But…" His brows drew together, but he stepped aside and motioned her in. His voice was now only a whisper. "I barely made it home before dark last night. Where did thee stay? Thee could not have left this morning and made it here already."

"Levi? Who is it?" A woman came into view as Prudence stepped fully into the kitchen, her hands busy stirring a wooden spoon through whatever was in the bowl she held at her waist. Though her eyes widened at spotting her, Elsie Liller simply said, "Good morning, Prudence Willard!" at a normal volume.

This was a woman who knew that revealing her surprise could endanger lives.

Prudence inclined her head. "Good morning, Elsie Liller. I was out for a morning stroll and thought I saw the carriage of Johnmark Smith tied to thy hitching post."

"Thee did indeed. He regaled us with fine stories last night and promised us more over breakfast." Elsie darted a quick glance toward the kitchen door, which no doubt opened directly to the dining room. Likely where both the Friends and the slave hunter sat. "He is no doubt entertaining our other guests even now, if thee wishes to join him. We have a few others who have stopped in for breakfast and news as well." Her gaze was pointed. "One who just arrived from Marietta way. Though he said he'd been traveling all night, and that he will likely need a bed after a meal."

Prudence nodded her thanks for the information. "Did Isaiah Brown travel with Johnmark this time?"

"No. I believe he had business to attend elsewhere, though he has promised to visit us soon."

Prudence let out a little breath. He must have gone back to Marietta to fetch Billy, then, while Johnmark continued to Chester Hill with Shandy. Perhaps they deemed it less of a risk to keep the two separated for now, until they were well away from the auction and the man who had found their cave to begin with.

"I don't wish to interrupt his stories," she said. "Perhaps I can lend thee a hand in here for now?"

"I wouldn't turn down the help. Levi"—his mother pointed toward a plate of biscuits and gravy sitting on the table and then at the floor—"go upstairs and tell thy sister to come and help too, please."

"Yes, ma'am." Levi flashed a smile and took off at a run, the plate in hand.

"Here. If thee would scramble the eggs, I would be much obliged." Elsie nudged forward a basket of fresh brown eggs and a bowl.

Prudence pumped some water into the sink so she could wash the horse and forest off her hands and then began cracking the eggs into the bowl.

Once she was at work, Elsie slid to her side and whispered, "Does thee need Johnmark Smith or our unrecorded guest?" She glanced down.

"Both. But not with the newcomer here. It is she he seeks."

Elsie nodded and kept mixing the batter in her bowl. A cake, from the looks of its consistency. She'd whisked it to a creamy, light color and would no doubt soon be pouring it into the pan sitting ready by the stove. "He is weary," she murmured. "We will feed him well and send him to the room farthest from the door. For his own rest and peace, of course."

"Of course." Prudence smiled. And kept working. A few minutes later a girl of about eight meandered into the kitchen and was promptly given a task to accomplish while her mother poured the batter into a cake pan and slid it into the oven. Levi didn't return, but Prudence hadn't expected him to. He'd be making his way to where Shandy was hidden to deliver that plate of food, she'd guess.

For the next half hour, she simply did the tasks that her hands knew so well, praying along with each one. Much as part of her wanted to hurry it all along, the wise part knew that to do so would be to take unnecessary risk. She served up plates, handed them to Elsie to deliver to the dining room, and then began washing the dishes—first the pots and pans, and then, as she was finishing those, the plates and cups now emptied of their contents.

"Here." A steaming plate appeared under her nose. "Thee must eat as well. Thee looks fit to collapse, Prudence Willard."

Her stomach growled in anticipation. She took it but paused before even picking up a fork. Her head swiveled toward the exit to the outside. The woodshed. It was hardly fair that she got to enjoy a hot meal while McKinnon hunched against the cold among the firewood, with nothing but stale hardtack in his sack.

Elsie followed her gaze, and apparently its meaning. "Perhaps I'd better ask Levi to bring in some more wood. Of course, knowing him, he'll want to eat out there."

The little girl sent her mother a questioning look. "But Mama, Levi already ate."

Elsie winked and said, "Growing boys, though, can always use a second helping, it seems."

Prudence nodded and mouthed her thanks, not daring to speak it out loud. The sweet little girl—Phoebe, was it?—would probably ask what she was thanking her mother for.

At last, Levi returned and was given his next assignment, and Elsie swung through the door to the dining room again to show the newcomer to a room. Phoebe scampered off to go and play, and Prudence settled into a chair with her food.

She was through half of her biscuit when the hairs on the back of her neck prickled up. Footsteps were coming toward the door, and they were too heavy to be Elsie's or Levi's. Prudence stood. It was probably just Elsie's husband. Or even Johnmark Smith.

Yet somehow she wasn't surprised when Parker pushed into the kitchen, his eyes settling immediately on her.

He didn't know who she was, not really. She mustn't panic. With that litany running through her mind, she forced a smile to her lips. "Good morning. May I help thee?"

A moment later, she was staring down the barrel of a pistol. "Oh, you certainly can, sweetheart. Come right out here with the rest of your friends. Then you can tell me what you've done with the girl."

CHAPTER EIGHTEEN

Tess stood in front of the wide front windows, arms wrapped around herself and her cup of tea—reheated—in hand. She still couldn't quite believe the mountains of snow out there. It would take the plows all day to clear it from the city's streets. And the mounds they'd make probably wouldn't melt until well into spring.

"I hate that there's nothing we can do to pursue these clues." Hiram kept turning from the window to the corkboard, antsy. "Can't call, don't have a number to text, can't go out in this."

"I emailed." Tess had used her cell to do it, only hoping that Shandy Greene would check her email on her cell phone, but it was something. Maybe. Or maybe the woman would just delete it and ignore them altogether.

"Yeah, but..." Hiram paused midsentence and tilted his head toward the window. "Are those...bells?"

Tess's eyes widened, and she turned to peer down the street. "It *is* bells! Genuine jingle bells." With a laugh, she leaned closer to the glass as a horse-drawn sleigh came gliding down the road. "It's Clint!"

"What?" LuAnn slid up on one side, Janice on the other. "Well, look at that. Never let it be said that Clint Lowery lets a little snow get in his way of a good time."

"He's slowing. Oh, he must be stopping in to say hello." Janice lifted her brows. "He's in the same business the Greenes are—I wonder if he knows anything about Greene Thumb."

"Worth asking." Tess spun away from the window, toward the front door.

She pulled it open just in time to hear Clint's "Whoa" to his horses. He looked her way, and she lifted an arm in greeting.

"Halloo the inn!" he shouted, laughter in his voice. He reached down then came up with a tall, slender thermos. "Thought I'd stop in for a refill, and to see how you all fared in the storm."

"Come on in." She pulled the door shut most of the way behind her, huddling into her sweater, while she waited for him to set the brake and climb down. She kept her toes on the welcome mat, since beyond that snow had drifted. "We're all fine—though the phone and internet lines are down. How are things on your farm?"

"Cozy." He was bundled up from tip to toe, smiling as he waded through the eight inches that had re-covered the sidewalks after Thorn shoveled yesterday. "Thought I'd take the sleigh out for a run and check on everyone."

As he neared, she nudged the door open again and stepped inside ahead of him. He paused on the porch to stomp off the snow, sending her an arched look. "Want me to go around to the back and come in the mudroom? Or I could even just hand you my thermos and bat my eyes and ask you to refill it for me, if you don't want me dragging snow in."

"Oh, it's fine. From the windows it looked like those sidewalks drifted over quite a bit, so this is the best way."

"Besides," said Janice from behind her, "we have an interrogation planned for you."

Tess laughed.

Clint made a mock gasp of horror. "Uh-oh. What have I done now that I've brought the questions of the Inn Crowd down on my head?"

"You know what you've done." Janice put on a glare for a moment, then gave up and laughed. "Actually, we're just hoping you know something about someone else who's grabbed our attention."

"Let the man get in the door first." Tess waited for him to step gingerly onto the rug and then shut the door behind him. He made no move to budge from his two square feet. "Clint, you can come in, really. Just take your boots off and—"

"No, that's okay. I don't want to interrupt anything." He nodded toward the parlor, where the Sherlock Society milled around.

She had a feeling arguing with him wouldn't accomplish much, given the horses and sleigh outside. "All right. Let me refill your coffee for you. Janice can start the interrogation."

"Not without us, you don't!" LuAnn's laughing exclamation came from the parlor. As Tess strode into the café, she saw her friend and Uncle Harold both emerging into the lobby area.

It only took her a minute to top off Clint's thermos. She got back just in time to hear Janice finishing her first question about the Greenes and see Clint's nod.

"I've met them several times—really nice family. My farm's on the opposite side of town, of course, and we focus on different things, so I wouldn't call them rivals or anything. We tend to refer customers to each other more than we compete for them, I think."

"Do you know much about the family itself? Or just the nursery?" LuAnn asked. She had her notebook out and pen poised. There would no doubt be mystery notes below the devotional she'd written that morning.

"More about the business, I daresay." He accepted the thermos Tess held out to him with a smile. "But the Greenes are good people. I've dealt mostly with Shandy—the young woman who runs most of the business side of things these days. Her dad's still the genius behind the greenhouses and other plants, and her mom handles a lot of the marketing, I think. Her grandmother still lives on-site too. No…" His brow puckered in thought. "It's her great-grandmother. Not sure where her grandmother is, but I remember Lee—Shandy's dad—calling her Gram. Apparently she once had quite the reputation for her preserves—they gave me one of the jars from her last batch when I bought my farm and went over to introduce myself. I don't think she's been healthy enough for canning for a while though."

Certainly not the sort of family that sounded like they'd go around stealing historic artifacts. But then…they *might* be the type to leave an IOU for something they felt the need to take.

"Can't really think of anything else to tell you about them." Clint frowned in thought for a moment, then shrugged. "As I said, I don't know them really well."

"Well, that's more than we knew five minutes ago." LuAnn finished writing something, punctuating it with a period and then closing the notebook. "Thanks."

"Sure. And thanks for the coffee. What do I owe you?" He tugged off a glove.

"Oh, heavens, Clint, don't worry about it," Tess said. "It's just black coffee. Our treat."

He paused and flashed that charming smile of his again. "All right, then you need to let me take you lovely ladies for a sleigh ride in payment. What do you say?"

"Oh." Tess looked to her friends, seeing in their eyes the same idea that immediately sparked to life in her mind. "How long a ride is one thermos full of coffee worth?"

Clint looked from one of them to another, taking in the grinning Uncle Harold too, with amusement in his eyes. "Where do you have in mind?"

LuAnn slid her mini notebook back into her pocket. "Are you going as far as Greene Thumb? And would you have time to let us talk to them there and then bring us home?"

Clint chuckled. "I could...but it might cost you a cinnamon roll."

Tess was already hurrying away. "Deal!"

The snow had finally stopped completely, and the sky had brightened to a crisp, light gray with a few cracks of blue breaking through. Tess snuggled down under the blanket and closer to her uncle's side. They'd taken the first of the two seats, and LuAnn and Janice sat behind them. Clint was perched on the driver's seat in front of them all, his matching bay horses jingling their way through the countryside.

The Greene farm was only a few miles outside of town, but the horses didn't exactly pull the sleigh at highway speeds; they'd already been out for about half an hour. Frankly, Tess was amazed at how easily they navigated the sleigh through this much snow. But then, she supposed that was what sleighs had been designed for.

"This is an unexpected delight." Uncle Harold had his scarf up over his mouth, and she could just make his words out through it.

She smiled. "It is, isn't it?" She'd been a bit surprised when he announced that he wanted to come along rather than return to the parlor to moderate the resuming Sherlock conversation. But she certainly hadn't argued. A sleigh ride through the countryside wasn't a family lunch—but it was just as fun, in a different way.

And as much as she'd hoped her kids and grandkids would get to see him today, she had to admit, this was nice. Some time with just the two of them.

If one discounted LuAnn and Janice behind them. Which was easy to do in the sleigh, where the bells and sound of the runners cutting into the snow and the wind whistling through the trees made it difficult to hear between the seats anyway.

The landscape looked truly transformed with the snow. Signs were covered, turns impossible to differentiate. She was none too convinced that they'd actually be able to find Greene Thumb. But apparently Clint and his horses had a better sense of such things than she did, because a minute later he was urging them through what might have been a lane between the trees. There was a hump of snow that could have been a sign, maybe. Or a shrub. Or just a drift. She really couldn't be sure.

The lane wound through the forest for a few minutes, and Tess had the sensation of crossing into another world. She almost expected to see the Nutcracker standing guard—or perhaps chasing an enchanted mouse through the woods. But when they emerged from the trees again, a farm rolled out in front of them. Covered in white, but even so, she could make out the even rows of short trees, the varying heights between rows probably denoting different types. There were fields, greenhouses, a massive building that bore the Greene Thumb sign on the side under the awning, and through whose giant doors one would probably stroll in the summer to browse their selection of plants.

Tess's eyes tracked past the impressive commercial enterprises, following what she assumed was the driveway, toward the farmhouse in the distance. It was a sprawling thing, its white siding nearly blending in with the snow. "Charming." She breathed into her own scarf, trying to memorize the way the snow looked on the peaked roof, on the shrubs and trees that surrounded it, on the carport off to the side.

Carport. Under it, she could make out a car with bright green paint alongside a matching truck. Both had some snow on them from where it had blown in, but the truck's roof was bare. The car's however, was not. It had a few inches on top.

Janice's head popped up on Tess's side. "Looks like the car from the photo."

"Not a surprise." LuAnn had scooted close too. "Given that it had their logo on the side."

"Well sure, but that didn't mean this was where it had gone, necessarily. Or that she was still here." Janice rested her arms on the back of Tess's seat.

"I still can't think why she'd come into the museum and take the photo," Tess said.

"Don't you?" Harold must be smiling behind his scarf—his cheeks had moved up to his eyes. "Look closer, Tessie."

She followed his nod back toward the farmhouse. It had rather typical Victorian architecture—gingerbread under the eaves, a wide front porch that looked to bend around at least part of the sides too. The central portion looked fairly small, but it sprawled out on the right and left. Original, or additions?

Additions. Her breath caught. As was the gingerbread. But the central part, that was original house. And it was a match to the house behind the Green family in the photograph, as were the hills and trees that rolled into the distance behind it. If she imagined lush leaves instead of snow... "This is the place. From the photo."

"This is the family." Harold's gloved hand gripped hers. "The family your Prudence Willard was with."

The farm could easily have changed hands since the 1860s—it would be remarkable if it hadn't. But what were the chances, really, that it went from the Greens to the Greenes and *wasn't* the same family? "Maybe so."

"I think it is. Why else would they be interested in that photograph?"

She granted her uncle's point with a nod.

Clint pulled the horses to a halt and secured the reins, hopped down, and then reached up to help them down too. "Here we go, folks. End of the line."

Tess smiled as she put her hand in his and climbed out. "Thanks, Clint. We appreciate the ride."

"My pleasure."

She stepped out of the way so the others could climb down too and looked at the house again. And smiled. This was probably right about where Prudence and the Greens had been standing when that photo had been taken.

Once they were all back on the ground, they began wading toward the house. Much like at the inn, there was a bit of a path where the snow had been shoveled before, but it was covered with at least eight inches. As they drew closer, though, Tess could hear the familiar sound of a shovel digging into snow, then the thud of a heavy clump landing somewhere else.

"Do we see who's outside or go to the house?" she asked her friends.

LuAnn pointed around the side of the house, where a newly shoveled path led from a side door. "I say we find who's out here."

They headed that way, though well before they reached the shoveled section, a man rounded the corner. He lifted a hand in greeting. "Morning! I thought I heard sleigh bells. Clint, isn't it?"

Clint, who had been in the rear of their group, slipped through to the front and met the man with a smile and a hand extended. "Good to see you again, Lee. Hope you don't mind a visit."

"Not at all." Lee Greene sounded like he could be somewhere in his fifties, though it was kind of hard to tell such things through the hat, scarf, coat, and sunglasses that hid all but a narrow strip of his face. "Quite a surprise though. I can't say as I expected to see anybody coming up that lane for a couple of days, at best." He swiped his sunglasses off after he shook Clint's hand.

His eyes looked...tired. Sad. Worried. "I was just clearing a path to the garage, though, so I could get the snowblower out." He shook his head. "I'm not sure Gram's going to make it more than another day or two. We're going to need the road clear."

"Aw, man. I'm so sorry to hear that." Sincerity saturated Clint's tone. "She's quite a lady."

"That she is. But as she keeps reminding us, she's ninety-eight years old and ready to go home." Lee sighed then looked to the rest of them. "Forgive me. You ladies look familiar, but..."

LuAnn stepped forward first, her hand held out for a shake too. "LuAnn Sherrill, Janice Eastman, and Tess Wallace. We own Wayfarers Inn in Marietta. Friends of Clint's."

"That's it. Wayfarers." Lee planted his shovel into the snow and leaned on it. "I read a few of the articles about you three buying and renovating the old place. It was a hotel during the Civil War, wasn't it?"

"That's right," Tess said.

He nodded. "And a stop on the Underground Railroad."

"It was." Janice smiled. "There's so much history there. We've had a blast discovering bits and pieces of it. When we first bought the place, we even found a journal, written by one of the UR conductors in Marietta. A Quaker woman named—"

"Prudence Willard." Lee's lips turned up, though his smile looked as sad as his eyes. "Yep. I remember that too."

He must have a better memory for names than Tess did— she couldn't usually pluck one out of her mind when she'd read about it in an article months ago.

He straightened again and half-turned back the way he'd come from. "Follow me around this way. You can take your snow things off on our enclosed porch and then get warmed up inside with Nikki and Shandy and Gram. I've got these walks pretty much cleared."

"Thanks," LuAnn said. "We won't impose long."

"Isn't an imposition at all. Gram loves company. We've got her set up in the living room—she'll probably think you came just to see her."

Tess exchanged a glance with her friends. She wasn't exactly sure how they were going to go about sharing their real reasons for coming—but this certainly wasn't the situation she'd expected to be walking into.

September 1858

Prudence's wrists were bound again, and Parker hadn't been nearly so conscientious about it as McKinnon had been. The rope dug into her skin, and he'd wrenched her arms behind her at an uncomfortable angle. She'd been shoved to the floor in the parlor along with the others.

"This is utter foolishness." Elias Liller's face was red with fury. "Thee has no right to come into our home and act this way. We run a respectable—"

"You run a place that welcomes Negroes who've run away from their rightful owners, and I aim to shut you down for good." Parker leveled a finger at Elias's nose, his scowl darker than a storm cloud. "Now, I'd rather take the girl back to her master alive. But if you don't want to cooperate, then I'll not lose any sleep over burning this place down over all of you, her included. She in a hidden room somewhere? A basement?"

Elsie's chin came up, fire sparking in her eyes. "I have no idea of whom thee speaks. The only people at this inn are the ones thee sees before thee now."

The Lillers—three of them, anyway. Prudence. Johnmark Smith. And one other man she didn't recognize, but who wore plain garb indicating that he too was a Quaker.

Little Phoebe had nestled herself to her mother's side. Even her wrists were bound. But she didn't cry or whimper. She just glared at Parker along with the rest of them.

Levi, at least, was still free. She said a prayer that he stayed out in the shed with McKinnon, that he didn't come back inside in the next few minutes, oblivious to the danger he'd be walking into. She prayed that Shandy and any other runaways hidden on the property stayed silent. Prayed that the Lord would deliver them somehow.

"I'm going to give y'all five minutes." Parker swung his pistol around the room, pausing on each of them. "Five minutes to tell me what I want to know. Because I know well you have her. I saw you leave the auction with her." He pointed the gun at Johnmark.

She hadn't noticed the slave hunter at the auction. But then, she hadn't been looking. She'd been focused only on finding the Friends, and then on McKinnon.

Johnmark lifted his brows. "If you saw me at the auction," he said, his words carefully scrubbed, "then you know I bought a slave fairly and legally—"

"Hardly legally, when she already belongs to someone else. Buying stolen property doesn't make it yours," Parker snarled. "I already settled that with the auctioneer, before he could pay those no-good, lousy thieves that meant to profit off her. When I gave him proof she was already owned, he had little choice but to give the purchase price to me." He patted his pocket. "If I have to burn the girl along with the rest of you, Mr. Marsh will at least be getting her cost. And if I can deliver her alive, I guess that money will just be my bonus."

"Now, see here. If you mean to take the girl back, then you'll be returning the money to *me*." Johnmark did a wonderful job of looking outraged for purely monetary reasons.

But the slave hunter's face lit with pure malevolence. "What's the point of that? You'll be dead by then, I suspect. Unless you decide right now to tell me where she is. But given that we both know you're one of *them*"—he motioned toward the Lillers with his gun—"I have me a feeling you'll hold your tongue. And that's all right too. Maybe…" He made a show of measuring them all, tilting his head back and forth, pursing his lips.

Then he knelt down before Elsie and Phoebe and touched the tip of the pistol's barrel to the bottom of the girl's chin. "Maybe *this* one will talk."

"Leave the child alone." Prudence pressed her shoulders to the wall and used the leverage to push back to her feet. She didn't know if she'd ever carry a child of her own. But there was a child here already. A little girl with parents watching on, with a brother somewhere nearby. Johnmark and his wife had a brood of six that needed him. Even McKinnon, out in the shed, had a daughter who would be waiting for him to come home, an infant son who needed to know his father.

She lifted her chin. Better to take his attention herself. If it all went wrong, if she died today, Jason would mourn her—but he'd know she died saving others. He'd be proud. And they both knew the risks before they got involved in such work. "I will show thee where she is."

The man's smirk was one of the ugliest things she'd ever seen. "That's more like it." He stood again. "Come on, then."

Sending the Lillers a look that promised she'd protect them, Prudence skirted the armchair between herself and Parker. "She is not in the house. There is a cave nearby." If she could draw him away, then McKinnon and Levi could come in and free the others, get help. She'd lead him in the direction away from the shed, into the woods. He clearly didn't realize she wasn't from Chester Hill and didn't actually know the area that well. She just had to *look* like she did.

Before she could move another step, something flew through the open parlor door. A blur of black coat and too-long hair and a hat absent its blue jay feather. McKinnon crashed into Parker with enough force that the two fell to the floor in a tangle of limbs and deep-throated screams, knocking the armchair over in the process. She couldn't make sense of all the movement and shouts, but her gaze had no trouble tracking the pistol as it swung wildly this way and that. Parker struggling to get off a shot. McKinnon trying to wrestle it from his hand.

Now Phoebe cried, and Prudence certainly couldn't blame her. The girl had pushed to her feet, helped by her mother, who was shouting, "Run outside, Phoebe! Run! Find Levi!"

After a moment's hesitation, Phoebe spun for the door.

She couldn't have seen the gun take aim for her. But Prudence did. "No!" The scream erupted from the deepest pit of her stomach. With her wrists bound, she couldn't grab the girl. She could only run into her, shoving her out of the way, down to the floor behind the dubious cover of the overturned chair.

A bullet shattered the room. Screams followed in its wake.

Prudence huddled there, overtop the sobbing Phoebe. Waiting. Waiting to feel the pain, or to hear another bullet. For the next tragedy to strike.

Instead, all she heard was a grunt from the other side of the room. And then McKinnon's voice. "I'll untie you all in a minute. Let me get him secured first. Prudence? You all right?"

Her breath came back to her lungs in a whoosh. She eased off poor Phoebe. "I am well. What of thee, Phoebe? Did I hurt thee?"

The little girl shook her head.

"Looks like the chair's the only thing injured." Even as he spoke, McKinnon was employing some of the same rope Parker had used on them to tie him up. Not gently either, she noted.

Parker lay unconscious on the floor, blood trickling out of his nose.

"Where's Levi?" Elsie asked, pushing to her knees.

McKinnon smiled. "I sent him for the sheriff. This fellow's about to be arrested for attempted murder, I should think."

Prudence, settling to a seat on the floor, shook her head. "How did thee know there was trouble inside, Quinn McKinnon?"

He chuckled and came her way, a knife out to cut the ropes. "I told you, Mrs. Quaker. You notice all sorts of things when you're paying attention." He sliced through her bonds. "I'll explain it all later. For now, I believe we have a family to reunite—I spotted the other one of your friends coming up the road with a young man while Levi was running for the sheriff."

Isaiah with Billy. Excellent. Prudence sagged against the chair in relief.

As the adrenaline ebbed, exhaustion swept over her like a flooding river. Her eyes slid shut for a moment, her ears buzzing with the sounds of the Lillers' chatter, Levi entering with the sheriff, that man's eagerness to take Parker into custody—he was a friend of the freedom movement too, she knew.

And then she must have drifted off for a moment, sagging there against the chair. Because she dreamed she heard Jason's voice saying her name. Felt his strong hands on her shoulders.

"Come, my beloved." She could even smell him, the dream was so vivid. Fresh air and soap and the lingering scent of hay. "Thee needs to rest."

She forced her eyes open, marveling when the dream held firm. He was really there, cradling her in his arms, lifting her, despite his bad leg. She ought to get down. Insist upon it. She didn't want to cause him pain. But the only thing she could convince her body to do was to whisper, "I thought it was Billy with Isaiah."

Her husband smiled. "He was too." He nodded to the left.

There, just inside the door, stood Billy—Shandy in his arms.

With a smile on her lips, Prudence rested her head on Jason's shoulder and let the exhaustion win.

Chapter Nineteen

The Greene family home was an eclectic mash of old and new, mixed and matched into undeniable charm. An old wooden rocker that looked to have seen the better part of a century beside a sleek metallic sculpture of a tree still shiny and new. An oil painting realistically done of the farm hanging over the fireplace, and an abstract print on the wall opposite.

A young woman who couldn't be more than twenty-five clasped the hand of one whose skin looked thin and papery with age. Gram, Tess would bet, who was ninety-eight. She had an oxygen tube positioned under her nose and was stretched out in a hospital bed situated by the front windows.

The young woman must be Shandy. She looked over when they entered, her eyes every bit as tired and weary as her father's had been.

A middle-aged woman stepped forward to greet them, smiling and introducing herself as Nikki, Lee's wife. Shandy's mom. She didn't seem to question who they were or how they got there—though the sleigh was clearly visible from the big front windows, so that part probably wasn't very mysterious.

"So nice of you to come out in all this," Nikki said, waving a hand at the snow. "The community's been so good to us these last few weeks. People dropping by with meals or just to spend a few hours, to read or sing to her. There's nothing Gram likes better than company."

Tess's smile felt a bit stiff on her lips. Guilty. They hadn't come to help—they'd come to question. But she knew the others wouldn't push for answers any more than she intended to do now. They were here, where their curiosity had led them. Now they would see what the Lord might have in store.

"Are you all from Calvary Church? We've missed so many Sundays this last year, running Gram to dialysis, that I'm afraid I haven't met many new people."

Janice shook her head, reached out, and took Nikki's hand. "We attend Christ Fellowship. My husband was actually the pastor there until his death a few years ago."

A bit of a light went on in Nikki's eyes. "Oh, Pastor Eastman! Of course. I knew you looked familiar."

Janice smiled. "We purchased some plants from you all when we did the gardens at the inn—we own Wayfarers, on Front Street. But you mostly dealt with our contractor, Thorn."

"That's right." Nikki smiled at Janice and then motioned with her head toward the kitchen. "I was just about to put together some lunch. Why don't you all make yourselves comfortable? It's just sandwiches, but there's plenty. Someone brought over a tray of them on Friday."

They moved farther into the living room, Tess trying to take it all in. There was a lot of life crammed into this room. Generations of it. Hand-stitched sampler pillows, quilts that looked to be genuine patchwork, furniture so beautiful it must have been handmade. It went beyond being lovely or charming. It was…well, it was a *home*. The kind that welcomed you the moment you stepped inside.

The woman on the bed shifted a bit, though her eyes were still closed. An expression of pain flittered onto her face, then off it again.

When she relaxed, Shandy let out a breath. And turned a bit on her chair to face them more fully. "Did you say Wayfarers Inn? That's the place that used to be Riverfront House, isn't it?"

"That's right." LuAnn took a seat on the sofa, and Janice settled beside her.

Tess moved toward a chair, but as she spun to sit, she halted instead. On the folding TV table pulled up beside the hospital bed, a picture frame stood, beside a glass of water, a box of tissues, and a stack of books. A picture frame displaying a black-and-white photo of a family of four in front of a farmhouse. With Prudence Willard at their side, a gosling in hand.

Shandy followed her gaze. Looked back to Tess. And deflated. "Do you recognize her, or the photo itself?"

Tess took a step closer to the bed instead of sitting, making sure to keep her face friendly. "Both, actually. Prudence Willard has strong ties to the inn. So when the folks at the museum saw that photo, they called us about it."

Tears filled Shandy's eyes. "I didn't mean to *take it*, take it. I just wanted to make a copy of it. For Gram—I didn't know if she'd make it another day, to wait and ask permission. Then the snow started, and she got so much worse, and… I just haven't gotten it back yet. But I will."

"It's all right, Shandy." Tess eased up beside her chair and touched the young woman's wrist. "I think mostly we were just all curious why the photo vanished."

"Gram always talked about it. When she was a girl, that photo—well, another print of it, I guess—sat right there, on the mantel. It always intrigued her so much, given the story *her* gram told about it." She twisted in her chair and nodded to a little alcove Tess hadn't noticed, where a painting hung on the wall.

Five people in front of a farmhouse. A background of lush green. A yellow-gray gosling in one woman's hands. The style was abstract, the faces not looking much like the photograph, but it had clearly been inspired by it.

Tess sucked in a breath. Her friends and uncle, having also turned to see what Shandy indicated, sounded equally surprised.

Tess recovered first and turned back to Shandy. "Do you know the story? We'd love to hear it."

Though the young woman nodded, her smile was lopsided. "No one tells it like Gram, though. I should probably let her do the honors. You feel up to it, Gram?"

Tess glanced down, a bit surprised to find that Gram's eyes had opened. Though they seemed hazy and confused. She blinked slowly a few times. "What story, Shan?"

"The story your gram told you when you were little. About how her parents found their way home."

Gram's lips quavered their way into a smile. "That's a good story. Our family's story." Her gaze sharpened and settled on

Tess. "We've been here on this land over a hundred and seventy years now, you know. It's our land. Always been our land, since the first Green bought it, right and legally, after he bought his own freedom."

Tess smiled, shifting a bit to make room for her uncle when she felt him come up alongside her. "We would love to hear your family's story. It seems they knew Prudence—and we've been learning a lot about her since we bought Wayfarers Inn."

Gram nodded against the pillow. "Prudence Willard—that was a name my family spoke of as if it belonged to a saint. I think she probably was." Her eyes slid shut for a moment, then swung back open. "Her and Quinn McKinnon. They're the ones who helped the first Shandy—my great-great-grandmother—find her uncle. And this place—his farm."

"Quinn McKinnon?" Tess looked over to Janice and LuAnn, where they sat beside Clint. "I don't recognize that name. Do you?"

They both shook their heads.

"He was a detective. A Pinkerton." Gram chuckled—a dry, raspy sound, but still it spoke of joy.

"The detective!" Tess aimed a grin at her uncle. "Must be that entry I showed you."

He grinned right back. "He was tied to all this too? Now that must be a good story."

"Oh, it is. You see, Abraham Green had saved enough to buy his freedom in the 1830s. He was a big, strong fella, as you can see in the picture. But more than that, he was clever. Soon earned himself enough to buy this beautiful farm in Ohio.

Found himself a pretty wife, and they settled down here and built this very house."

As she spoke, Gram's voice seemed to grow stronger. Steadier. Fell into a rhythm. "But Abraham never forgot his family that he'd left behind on the plantation. He had a little brother there, and they'd always been close. He warned his brother not to run away—said he'd get him out right, soon as he could. So he saved and he saved. But his brother, he was even bigger and stronger. He was worth as much as this land." Gram shook her head. "Abraham kept making offers over the years, but his old master, Mr. Marsh, kept refusing him. 'He's worth more than that,' he'd say. Even though Abraham's brother was getting older. Weaker. If he'd sold him, he'd not have fetched the amount Abraham had offered. Still, Marsh refused."

When Gram paused, coughing, Shandy slipped an arm under her shoulders to raise her up a bit and reached for the water glass. She fit the straw easily between Gram's lips.

The old woman smiled up at her great-granddaughter and patted her on the cheek after her breathing eased. "Finally, after a lot of years of putting aside what they could while they worked to get the farm running, he had the price Marsh demanded. Abraham wrote to him again, asking to buy his brother's freedom, only to be informed that his brother had died four years before of malaria."

Tess leaned back a bit, into Uncle Harold. "That's so sad."

Gram nodded. "It was. But the steward who wrote this reply to Abraham, he'd known him and liked him. He told him that he had a niece—all grown up now—with no family left on the plantation after her father died. So Abraham and his wife, who'd never had any kids of their own, decided to purchase her freedom instead. Now, she wasn't worth as much as her father had been, in monetary terms. They came to an agreement right quick. But Shandy didn't know any of this. And while her uncle was hiring Quinn McKinnon to pay Mr. Marsh and escort her here to Ohio, she was running off—with the man she'd married in secret from a neighboring place."

LuAnn grinned. "I bet his name started with a *B*."

"Billy." Shandy nodded to the painting again. "That's them in the picture. Shandy and Billy are the young ones. Abraham and his wife, Eugenia, the older two."

Gram picked up her story again, telling them about how Prudence had been the one to meet Billy after Shandy had been captured, how she and other area Friends had gone out of their way to get her back. How Quinn McKinnon had been about the same task, and they'd ended up working together just in the nick of time to save them all when a slave hunter caught up to them at their next stop in Chester Hill.

At that, Janice clapped her hands. "At the Quaker Inn Station! Where that photo was rolled up in the leg of a chair."

Gram smiled. "I don't know about that. But they delivered Shandy and Billy to Abraham's farm—right here outside Marietta. They'd actually run across a corner of his land when they were in hiding, and they didn't even know it. So Quinn McKinnon took the money Abraham had given him and what the Quakers had raised to buy her freedom, and he convinced

Mr. Marsh to give her her papers—then he walked right over to the neighboring farm and convinced Billy's owner to do the same. He came back the next spring and handed them their freedom. Legal and right. No more running required. Prudence and her husband came out to see him while he was here, and that's when they took that picture."

LuAnn studied the painting. "Quinn McKinnon must have been the one to take the picture, since he's not in it."

Shandy sighed. "They must have made a few prints of the photo. The one my Gram remembers was destroyed in a fire in the 1930s."

"I cried and cried," Gram rasped. "I was just a girl. Nine years old when it happened."

"She loved that photo—loved the stories her family had told her about it."

Gram nodded. "So my mama..." She trailed off into another cough.

"Her mother painted it instead, in her style."

"It's beautiful." Janice wiped her cheeks. "The whole story's beautiful."

"It is." Tess lifted her brows at Shandy. "And I daresay no one begrudges you bringing the photograph here to show to your grandmother again. But how did you know it was at the museum?"

A squeak drew everyone's attention to the doorway, where Nikki was entering with an old-fashioned wheeled tray, an enormous stack of sandwiches on top.

Shandy got up to help her get it into position. "Some folks emailed me, saying they found it in an old chair, and they were wondering if we were related to the Green family in the photo. They said they recognized the farmhouse from when they were out here buying peach trees last year. But I wasn't checking my email regularly then, and by the time I saw it and replied, they'd already donated it to the museum."

"I told her the folks at the museum would probably be happy to let us borrow it for a few days." Nikki smiled warmly. "For Gram's sake."

"That was Friday. I headed straight to the museum, and it was unlocked, but no one was there. And there was a note on the door saying something about heading home—I figured the note wasn't for me, so I just left it. But then I saw the chair. And the photo was right there in the leg, so..." She shrugged. "I really meant to bring it back the next morning, but this snowstorm had other ideas."

Harold chuckled. "At least you locked up as you left."

Shandy gnawed on her lip. "Well you never know what crazy person might just stroll in off the street and take something. I didn't want anyone *else* to do that."

Their laughter all joined with hers, not fading totally away until Nikki held up a stack of plates. "All right, everyone. You've had your story. Now some lunch."

Chapter Twenty

April 1859

The wagon creaked along, steady and slow as the April sunshine filtered down on them through the trees. Prudence tilted her face up to welcome its kiss, smiling at the way the light made jewels of the leaves. She loved the first green of spring. Bright and vibrant and so very alive. The kind of life that sprang forth after the dormant season.

She spread a hand over the enormous round of her stomach, where the babe within kicked yet again. She wasn't sure how she'd fit through the farmhouse door if she really had a month to go. "How much longer, does thee think?"

"Just a few minutes." Jason angled a grin at her. "Does thee not recognize the path in the daylight?"

She rolled her eyes and repositioned herself on the seat. She'd brought a cushion to sit on, but even so, it wasn't exactly comfortable. She was ready to get down and stretch her legs. "It has been a while since I've made the trip in a wagon instead of on horseback, that's all."

Her husband shook his head. "I told thee it was too long a trip in thy condition."

"Nonsense." Her back would probably be sore for a few days after the bumpy ride, but who knew when she'd be able to make the journey again? "I am happy to be out of the house for a few days. And I have been looking forward to visiting the Lillers again."

"I know." Which was why Jason hadn't actually put up a fuss at the idea of traveling the thirty miles to Chester Hill. The weather was fair and, when one didn't have a slave hunter on one's trail and traveled during daylight hours, the road wasn't difficult. "They will be glad for an update on the Greens too, I suspect."

"It is not often that we know what comes of those we help. To have a family able to settle so nearby—it's a true gift of God."

"He is good to us. No question." Jason covered the hand she had on her stomach and leaned over to steal a kiss.

And then they were out of the cover of the trees, into the unmitigated sunlight of the open road. There was the inn, situated at the edge of town, just as it had been six months ago. Only now, instead of a foggy morning, she saw it in the light of a spring afternoon. And there would be no detective hiding in the woodshed.

Probably.

He never had explained how he knew they needed help— or if he had, she'd slept through it. She'd asked him when they met at the Greens' farm last month, but he'd just shaken his head, a shimmer of laughter in his eyes. "When next you're there, Prudence Willard," he'd said, "open your eyes and really look around. You'll figure it out."

She'd huffed her opinion of that. And handed him the gosling she'd been saving for his Lucy. And perhaps took a bit too much delight at the look of panic in his eyes.

"How am I supposed to travel all the way back to Chicago with *this*?"

"Thee is a clever fellow. Thee will find a way to manage," she'd said.

Jason had come up then and put a hand on her shoulder. "If thy daughter is so fond of farm animals, Quinn McKinnon, perhaps thee should consider moving somewhere with a bit more space. There is land yet to be had here in Ohio."

She'd thought McKinnon's laugh was a dismissal, she truly had. But the letter tucked into her apron pocket said otherwise. He'd told his wife about the places he'd seen in his travels, and he and his Josephine had decided they'd rather raise their little ones away from the city. They were coming to Ohio, sometime in the next year. They'd asked Jason to keep his eye out for any farmland to be had for a reasonable price.

McKinnon had grown up on a farm, and he was ready to go back to one.

A shout returned her to the present, and to the yard where Phoebe and Levi raced toward them, calling their names.

Prudence couldn't have held back her smile had she wanted to. Sometimes, given the secrecy of their work, it felt as though she was alone on this path. Though she knew there were others, they rarely met in person. When they did, they hardly dared to speak of the risks they took and the number of people they hid beneath floors, in tunnels, in secret rooms.

But then there were the times like last September, when she was keenly aware of the community to which she belonged and the lengths they would go to for each other and anyone else who needed their help.

She was proud to be counted among such Friends. And excited to spend a weekend with a few of them now.

Jason pulled the wagon to a halt at the hitching post and helped Prudence down. When she turned, the Liller children were both there, faces lit by joy as they clamored for her attention.

"Come see the sampler I'm working on," Phoebe said, tugging on her hand. "Mama says the stitches are as fine as any she's seen."

"Aw, Prudence Willard doesn't care about stitches." Levi flashed a smile. "Wait until thee sees the carving I've done."

She put an arm around each and hugged them to her, laughing when the babe kicked a greeting too. "I will see stitches and carving both."

Jason grinned at her. "I will see to the horses and bring in our things. Thee had better go ahead in with these rascals before they pull thy arms off."

They were already tugging her toward the door. She found it a bit amusing that Levi, who was nearly as tall as she now, pulled with just as much excitement as his little sister.

He'd proven himself capable of great responsibility, this lad—but clearly there was still some boy left in him, and it did her heart good.

How strange to think she'd barely recognized him when he showed up in the kitchen of the Riverfront House. It seemed that now these two precious faces would be etched forever onto her heart. And Phoebe, who hadn't even known who Prudence was when she showed up in the inn's kitchen, had apparently taken to naming every doll and kitten and pup she saw after her. *It seems all one needs to do to become her best friend*, Elsie wrote in her last letter, *is save her from a bullet.*

The smell of cinnamon wafted out to greet them as the children led her inside. Chatter reached her from the parlor, but the children pulled her straight past the door. She glanced into the room as she went past though. She didn't know any of the guests gathered there. But if she closed her eyes, she could still picture Johnmark and the Lillers on the floor, and see the blur of Quinn McKinnon as he raced in to save the day.

Phoebe and Levi pulled her into the kitchen, where Elsie was peeking into the oven, and an unfamiliar girl stirred something on the stove.

"They are here, Mama!" Phoebe bounced on her toes. "May I show her my sampler now?"

Elsie straightened with a smile. "Of course thee may. Run upstairs to fetch it, and bring it down to her. I daresay she is tired after a full day on the road."

"Not compared to my last trip here," Prudence said with a grin.

Levi tugged her another step before he let go of her hand. "Let me show thee what I have done, Prudence Willard. Does thee recognize this?" He scampered around the worktable, to a chair that looked rather out of place here in the kitchen. It was more for comfort than utility. It would look far more at home in a parlor than…

She gasped. "The chair! The chair that saved thy sister's life!"

"And thine." Levi grinned and tipped it carefully over onto its back. "Come and see."

She stepped closer, one hand supporting her stomach by rote as much as need, and crouched down. There, on the part of the frame that was thickest, was a hole. Wood still splintered around it, light scars against the dark stain.

Prudence reached out, running a finger gently over the broken pieces. Then she let it dip inside, until she felt the cold circle of metal. A shudder coursed through her, followed quickly on its heels by a wave of gratitude. Had Parker aimed another inch lower, the bullet would have pierced the thin wooden bottom, passed straight through the spring and batting, and found a home in either her body or Phoebe's.

One inch lower, and their families would have been mourning together instead of rejoicing.

How good the Lord was to them that day.

"Watch." From his pocket, Levi extracted a screwdriver and leaned over the base of the chair. Prudence watched, bemused, as he took off one of the legs and handed it to her.

She nearly opened her mouth to ask what she ought to be seeing. But then she saw that the leg, curved and decorative, had been partly hollowed out. And inside was something white and curled.

Darting a curious look at him, she reached into the hole and pulled out the thick paper. A laugh burst out. "I see thee received the photo we sent."

Elsie knelt down beside her. "We did. But we decided we oughtn't to display it. Some of our guests would think it odd if we were to showcase a photograph of a Negro family. And if they start asking questions, then we can do less good."

"So I came up with this." Levi was working now on the other leg. "It seemed a fitting place to hide such a thing. And we've room, now, for other items as well." He eased the second leg off and showed her that compartment too.

She took it, ran her fingers over the smooth carving, and smiled her approval. "Thee did an excellent job on this, Levi. I am impressed." Her smile grew when she spotted the *LL* inside it. "And I see thee signed thy work."

Levi's fair cheeks flushed. "Father said it is not a matter of pride to sign one's work; it is a matter of accepting responsibility for it. If it fails, then everyone knows who to blame. And if it does its job as it should, then they know who to come to for more work."

"Thy father is a wise man." Prudence handed the empty leg back to him and looked down at the photograph again.

"Thee has a print of it too, does thee not?"

"I do. As we haven't the guests coming through our doors that thee has, we put it on our mantel. In the same place the

Greens put theirs." A symbol of the friendship they were all determined to grow.

"I wish we could do the same." Elsie sighed and pushed to her feet, reaching a hand out to help Prudence up too. "But at least we know it is there. And every time we sit in this chair, we will remember."

Prudence put her hand in her friend's and accepted the assistance. Then she glanced out the kitchen door, to the woodshed visible beyond it. "Does thee mind if I slip out for just a moment? Tell Phoebe I will be back inside as soon as I take care of a few things."

"Of course."

She probably thought Prudence was going in search of the privy—which wasn't a bad idea. But first, she had to satisfy the question that had been niggling for months. What had Quinn McKinnon noticed from his position outside that had made him send Levi for the sheriff and sneak inside the house?

The evening sunshine welcomed her back outside, and she breathed in the fresh air as she strode across the yard. The air carried the bite of woodsmoke from the cookstove. And a hint, too, of the same cinnamon smell she'd noticed when she went inside. In fact, the closer she drew to the shed, the more she could smell it. At its front, she turned around to face the inn again. The breeze, gentle as it was today—as it had been that morning—wafted the smoke directly toward her.

Her brows drew together. What would he have been smelling that morning? Breakfast had been done. The scents of eggs and meat and biscuits may have tormented him at first, but not by the time Parker captured everyone. There was nothing else being served.

The bowl. The batter. Cake—Elsie had put a cake in the oven. It should have needed only a half-hour or so to bake, but it had surely been longer than that. Had it begun to burn? Had the smell of it reached McKinnon out here?

She searched her memory, but she couldn't honestly recall any particular smells while they were in the parlor. But then, she'd been focused on other things.

It could have been the smell of the cake, at least in part. But she could still be missing some greater clue. She spun back to face the shed, walled on three sides and roofed, but open on this one. There was a path into it, though, so the menfolk could come in to move the stacks around, add more to them, and take what they needed. To warm the inn in cold weather and keep the kitchen stove burning, they'd have to be constantly maintaining this place.

She slid between the stacks of wood, noting that now, above smoke and cinnamon, she smelled the wood itself. There was more room in here than she'd expected—enough for a man to move around.

"Is thee lost? Or just curious about where Quinn McKinnon spent that morning?"

She poked her head back out into the aisle, smiling at Levi. "Curious. I am still not certain how he knew we needed help. But thee was with him, Levi. Perhaps thee can tell me. Thus far, my only guess is that perhaps he smelled a cake burning."

Levi grinned. "Likely. I did too. And Mother never lets her cakes burn, so that was alarming."

"But was that all it took?"

Levi shook his head. And pointed at the ground.

Prudence arched her brows. "There is some clue on the ground?"

"No," he laughed. "Under it. Here, I will show thee." He edged around her, back into the same opening she'd been in before. Only, instead of standing as she'd done, he crouched down and slid one of the stacks of wood to the side.

Her mouth fell open. Only now, with it moved, could she see the wheels attached to a pallet that held the wood. And below it, a trap door. "Clever."

"He felt the cooler air from the cellar coming up and out. I never would have thought he could have, given how cool it was that morning, but apparently he did. He was just moving this aside when I found him to give him his breakfast." Levi tugged the door up. "I knew that if he had shown up with thee, he was trustworthy. Even so, my first thought was to distract him."

"It would have been mine as well."

He nodded. "But it was irrelevant. The moment he opened the door, Shandy sprang out and told him of the situation in the house."

At this, Prudence frowned. "But did thee not take her breakfast to her earlier? From the house, though. Had thee gone out here, thee would have met Quinn McKinnon already."

"The cellar has several exits and tunnels connecting it to different trap doors all over the property. She was in the part below the main house—which was how she heard what was going on inside. She'd been feeling her way along the tunnels, trying to find another way out so she could help."

"Ah." It had been a foolish thing to do—Shandy had to have known she'd be putting herself straight back into the jaws of danger. But it was also a good thing to do, ultimately. "Was thee surprised to see her?"

Levi chuckled. "*I* was. But the detective wasn't. He said he had heard the shuffling and felt a draft, which was why he began searching for an opening."

"So he smelled the burning cake, heard Shandy moving below the woodshed, and felt the air." Prudence shook her head. "And here I'd assumed he'd *seen* something."

Levi closed the door again and moved the wood back atop it. "He did, once Shandy told what she had heard. She couldn't be sure where in the house the slave hunter had everyone—she had gotten understandably turned around. But Quinn McKinnon edged around and noticed that the curtains in the parlor were closed, while every other set on the ground floor was open. He figured Parker had closed them so anyone coming by wouldn't see him in there, waving a gun at everyone."

Prudence smiled. Quinn McKinnon had been right. All the pieces had been there…she just had to look for them.

CHAPTER TWENTY-ONE

Tess sat on the loveseat near the end of Gram's hospital bed, her sandwich plate empty and her cup of iced tea just refilled. Had someone asked on Friday what she'd be doing on Sunday, she never would have guessed that she'd be sitting in the living room of a family she barely knew, laughing with them, while their matriarch lay in a hospital bed, likely with only hours or days remaining.

But she was. And she was glad.

She leaned into her uncle's side. "See there. I told you we'd have a family lunch."

He chuckled and leaned right back. "Not the family you'd intended—but I think this is exactly where the Lord wanted us to be today."

"I think you're right." She couldn't help but smile as she looked around the living room.

The Greenes certainly hadn't been expecting company today, but it seemed to have buoyed them. Lee had taken a break before he got the snowblower out—probably because Nikki had called out for him to get himself in here like a good host and have lunch with them—and some of the shadows had left his eyes as he watched his grandmother laugh. Nikki seemed to take real joy from bringing out those plates of sandwiches and cookies and cakes that neighbors had been bringing by all week and sharing them with someone. And Shandy had admitted she felt a whole lot better now that she had official permission from the museum curators—they'd texted Sylvia and Stan—to keep the photo right there on Gram's bedside table until the end.

"Now." Janice scooted forward onto the edge of her cushion. "You said neighbors have been coming by to talk, read, and sing." She sent a pointed gaze to Tess and then LuAnn. "We can do that too. What do you say, ladies? A reprise of 'Be Thou My Vision'?"

As if they could refuse, given the happy little gasp that came from Gram's parched lips. "My favorite. Help me sit up a bit more, Shandy."

As Shandy adjusted the hospital bed, Tess set her cup down and crossed the room to join her friends. Clint gave them an encouraging thumbs-up from his chair, and Uncle Harold made a show of rising and moving to stand between Clint and the bed "so he'd be able to see the angels sing too."

Janice gave them their note, and they launched into the first verse, still fresh in Tess's mind after singing it that morning. But it was the second verse that stirred her heart as the words came from her lips.

Be Thou my Wisdom, and Thou my true Word;
I ever with Thee and Thou with me, Lord;
Thou my great Father, and I Thy true son;
Thou in me dwelling, and I with Thee one.

He was the Word—the true story, the one they must share with as many as they could. The one worth risking everything for. The one—the only One—in whom they could ever find a true home.

They finished out the song, bowed to the applause, and may have launched into another hymn if they hadn't all noticed the way Uncle Harold's gaze had fixed on Gram's bedside table. He stepped nearer, a smile on his lips, and picked up the book on the top of the stack.

"Is this what you've been reading, my dear?"

The old woman blinked up at him. "Well, it's what they've been reading to me. My favorite."

His smile grew. "May I have the honor of reading you a chapter or two?"

In answer, Shandy sprang from the chair. "Of course you can. Here you go, Professor Westerfield." Poor girl—she was probably ready for a bit of a break and yet so afraid to leave her great-grandmother's side. But it would be easier to do for a few minutes, knowing Gram would enjoy it too.

Uncle Harold settled into the chair and opened the book with a flourish. "*The Valley of Fear*, by Sir Arthur Conan Doyle. Chapter five."

Chuckling under her breath, Tess settled onto the couch with LuAnn and Janice this time. Her uncle, it seemed, was home—he had a book in his hand, a ready audience, and a family ready to receive the special way of ministering that he knew so well how to impart.

Dear Reader,

When a series is on book twenty, it isn't always easy to come up with a fresh idea. For this book, a lot of different bits and pieces combined. At the heart of it all was a pair of socks. Yep—socks. It was the Christmas season when I was brainstorming what I wanted this book to be about, and my best friend sent me some fun socks as a gift—including a pair with the iconic Sherlock silhouettes. (Yes, the very ones I describe Harold having sent to Tess for Christmas.) I was wearing them one day as I was trying to come up with a concept, and my daughter said, "Write a Sherlock book." I laughed...and then I thought about it. And thought some more. And realized that I absolutely loved the idea.

Of course, that was more an overarching theme than a story. But at this same time, my last great-uncle passed away—Harold McDonald. While I didn't know him super well, I was incredibly moved by the way this loss hit my mom. He was the last of her father's generation, the last of a collection of brothers. She'd already lost her father, years ago, and her other uncles. Losing this one hit hard. Especially because Harold was such a character—he loved big, he laughed big. I watched my mom brush the tears from her cheeks as she said, "He was a special one," and I knew that this pain—the pain we all have or will know—is as beautiful as it is difficult. We hate losing those we love. And yet, when we can look back on their lives and see how the Lord worked in and through them, we can rejoice in a life well lived.

My mom has also been after me ever since I signed on for this series to "use the chair!" "The chair" is a family heirloom currently sitting in her house, its pretty new upholstery covering the rather grim story that goes along with it. It, much like the chair in this story, had a bullet rip through it. But unlike my fictional chair, our family's chair didn't save a life. In fact, a life ended there in that chair, from an accidental firing of a gun being cleaned on the first floor while an unfortunate person sat directly above them on the second. I decided a happier purpose ought to be served, so while I used the *idea* of a chair and a bullet, I decided to make a hero of it. Other details about Quaker Inn Station, which no longer stands, I fictionalized for my purposes.

I hope, as you read this story that touched on themes of loss and love, home and family, that you were moved, as I was in the writing of it, to marvel at the great lengths to which our Lord went to call us His own and give us an eternal home. May He bless you and yours in all you do.

Cheers,

Roseanna

ABOUT THE AUTHOR

Roseanna M. White is a best-selling, Christy Award nominated author who has long claimed that words are the air she breathes. When not writing fiction, she's homeschooling her two kids, editing, designing book covers, and pretending her house will clean itself. Roseanna is the author of a slew of historical novels that span several continents and thousands of years. Spies and war and mayhem always seem to find their way into her books...to offset her real life, which is blessedly ordinary. You can learn more about her and her stories and sign up for her newsletter at roseannamwhite.com

THE QUAKER INN STATION

One of Washington County, Ohio's historical stops on the Underground Railroad is, unfortunately, lost to time. No building now remains of the inn located in Chester Hill, around thirty miles outside of Marietta, but the stories of its history are still remembered. The inn was owned by Quakers, and yet was public—which means that people of all types and persuasions rented a room for a night or two under its roof. Like many Quakers, the ones who ran this inn were fervent abolitionists, and they actively hid runaway slaves. There were times when they hosted the very people who were hunting for the fugitives the inn employees were hiding in their homes. The actual station master of this stop on the Underground Railroad was Elias Bundy. As in many Quaker communities, this stop was managed with the full support and assistance of the elders of the Quaker church. Though the building no longer stands, their legacy remains, and countless people searching for freedom were helped along their journey by these Friends.

Cornish Pasties

8 servings

FOR THE CRUST:

3 cups all-purpose flour

4 pinches salt

1 cup (2 sticks) cold butter, cut into small pieces

1 cup orange juice

FOR THE FILLING:

½ lb stewing beef/chuck roast, cut into small pieces

1 medium potato, diced

1 turnip, diced

1 onion, diced

Salt and pepper

Butter

Combine flour and salt in the bowl of a stand mixer or a large bowl. Add butter and combine until it forms a crumbly mixture. Slowly add in the orange juice and mix just until combined. Pat into a disc and wrap in plastic; refrigerate at least 6 hours or overnight.

When ready to assemble, preheat the oven to 350 degrees. Divide dough into 8 equal sections and roll each out on a lightly floured surface into a circle.

Combine the meat, vegetables, and salt and pepper in a bowl, stirring to evenly distribute the ingredients. Place a scoop of the mixture into the center of the dough round. Add a few dabs of butter. Fold the pastry dough over and crimp the edges to seal. Arrange on greased or parchement paper-lined baking sheets.

Whisk an egg with a tablespoon of water and brush over the pasties for a glaze. Bake 30 to 45 minutes, until golden brown.

Read on for a sneak peek of another exciting book
in the Secrets of Wayfarers Inn series!

A Place to Belong
by Beth Adams

Why do you torture yourself like that?"

Janice Eastman looked up and saw that Tess was standing behind her holding a brown earthenware mug. Tiny wisps of steam curled up over the rim.

"Was I doing it again?"

Tess nodded, and gestured at the jigsaw puzzle Janice was working on. "You know, they make puzzles that show kittens and things. You don't have to do one that makes you sad."

Janice looked down at the puzzle box lid, which showed a beautiful watercolor picture of a seaside, wrapped in climbing roses and flanked by hydrangeas and black-eyed-susans. In the background, colorful sailboats bobbed in the water under a clear blue sky. "This doesn't make me sad. It makes me happy to think of summer."

"That's why you keep sighing?" LuAnn looked up from her book, smiling. She was wrapped up in a soft wool blanket and cradling a cup of tea on the couch with Tom purring beside her. Oh dear. Janice must have sighed pretty loudly if it had distracted LuAnn from her book.

"I guess it does seem pretty far away on a day like today." Janice pointed toward the window, where a sleet-gray sky hung low and heavy. A fire roared in the hearth, the heat was cranked up, and the apartment the friends shared on the top floor of Wayfarers Inn was warm and cozy. But the frigid wind whistled outside, and the temperatures had dropped into the single digits. It wasn't unusual weather for February, but it did make it seem like summer would never come back. Janice slid an edge piece into place and looked up. "Looking at a summer scene reminds me that warmer days are ahead."

"Well, they can't really get colder now, can they?" Tess laughed, then reached down and picked up a piece of puzzle with a flash of red on it. She held it up to the picture on the box top. It was a part of one of the sails, Janice knew. Beneath the table, Huck, their stray-dog-turned-pet stirred, resettling with his head closer to the baseboard heater.

"Tomorrow is supposed to be the coldest. It should warm up after that." LuAnn readjusted the blanket around herself as an engine revved outside the window. "And at least we're not outside."

"Those poor guys." Tess slipped the piece into the right spot and then walked over to the window and peered out toward the yard, where two men in heavy jackets and hard hats were using a backhoe to dig up the yard. "I can't imagine a worse time of year to be doing that. The ground has to be frozen solid."

"I can imagine a worse time," LuAnn said. "When we have an inn full of guests. Let's be thankful it happened in the slow period."

"I suppose if you have to have your sewer pipe give out, it's better to do it when there aren't many people around," Tess said.

Janice knew she was right, although it was the freezing temperatures that had frozen the pipe that ran under the yard to the city sewer line in the first place. Thankfully, it was only the basement that had been affected, and no guest rooms felt the effects. Their guests, Steve and Beatrice Walton, who were here celebrating their thirtieth anniversary, had been very understanding. But it was still disruptive to have heavy machinery digging outside what was supposed to be a restful retreat at an inn. When Janice had looked out earlier, it had seemed like the plumbing crew had torn up half the yard trying to get to the burst pipe.

Janice's cell phone buzzed on the counter, and she pushed herself up and retrieved it. *Stacy.* Janice unplugged the phone and picked it up. Her daughter didn't often call. She hoped there wasn't something wrong with Larry. Stacy didn't always know what to do when he spiked a fever or developed a rash, and now that Janice lived at the inn, she wasn't always there to help.

"Hi, Stacy." Janice tried to keep her voice level. Stacy had made it clear that she thought Janice worried too much, so she tried to keep her anxieties to herself. Of course she worried about her only daughter and only grandchild. "How is everything?"

"Hi, Mom. Things are good. How are you?"

Janice heard the theme song to *The Magic School Bus* on the other end of the phone.

"Cold. But aside from that, we're fine." No need to go into the sewer problems right now. "What's going on?" And then, a beat later, she added, "Is everything okay with Larry?"

"Larry is fine, Mom." Stacy made a noise that Janice couldn't interpret. "He had a good day at school. His teacher said he spent most of the day dressed as a firefighter and trying to save the other students."

Janice chuckled, picturing it. He was such a tender-hearted little boy.

"He just finished lunch and is watching some TV."

Before Janice could say anything, Stacy added, "Don't worry. I won't let him watch too much. I just needed something to distract him while I work on some of my online classes."

"I wasn't going to say a thing," Janice said. "You do what you have to do." Truthfully, Janice did think Stacy relied on television to be a babysitter more than she should, but she knew that was typical these days, and Stacy had it tough being a single mom. And Janice's relationship with her daughter could be prickly at times. The last thing Janice wanted to do was upset her over something small.

"Well anyway, I was calling to see if you had any plans tonight."

"Tonight? No, there's nothing on the calendar tonight. Do you need me to babysit?" LuAnn thought Stacy sometimes took advantage of how willing Janice was to watch Larry, but Janice was always glad for an opportunity to spend time with the little guy. And if it helped Stacy out, so much the better. On a cold night like this, they could do movie night and make up a big bowl of popcorn and cuddle under a blanket. She'd been wanting to show Larry *Peter Pan*. It had been Stuart's favorite movie when he was this age.

"Actually, no. I wondered if you might want to come over for dinner."

"For dinner?" Janice wasn't sure she'd heard her right.

"Yep. Dinner. That meal after lunch and before bed?" Stacy laughed, but there was something raw in her voice. Something almost vulnerable. What was going on?

"Sure." Janice swallowed. "I'd love to." And then, a moment later, she added, "What can I bring?"

"No need to bring anything," Stacy said. "Just yourself. There's—" Her voice broke off, and Janice's pulse sped up. *What* was going on? Was Stacy sick, and needed to tell her in person?

"There's someone I'd like you to meet."

"Oh." It took a moment for Janice's mouth to catch up with her mind. "A special someone?"

"Yeah," Stacy said. "I guess you could say that. And I thought, well, he's coming over for dinner, and I thought maybe this would be a good time for you to meet him."

"Of course. I would love to."

"Okay. Great. How about six thirty. Would that work?"

"That sounds perfect," Janice said. "I'm looking forward to it."

"See you then." Stacy ended the call, and Janice stood still, looking down at her phone for a moment. A special someone.

Janice knew Stacy had been out on dates over the years. It was natural; of course she didn't want to be single forever. But she usually kept that part of her life hidden from Janice. Probably, she had to admit, in part because of the way Janice had reacted when she'd found out Stacy was pregnant with Larry. If she was honest, Janice could have handled that better. She'd been so shocked, so hurt, so sad for the future she'd imagined for her daughter that had just vanished forever. And then there was the fact that Lawrence had been the pastor of their small church. She'd known it was a stereotype that pastor's kids often got into trouble, but she'd still been floored when it had actually happened in her family.

"Everything okay?" Tess asked. She still stood by the window, her hands wrapped around the mug of tea.

"Stacy just invited me for dinner," she said.

"That sounds like good news," LuAnn said from the couch.

"Yes. I guess it is." She set the phone back down on the counter and plugged it in. "She wants me to meet someone. A guy."

"Well that *is* good news," Tess said. "We'll want a full report."

Janice nodded. It *was* good news—both that Stacy had met someone and that she wanted to introduce him to her. Janice had never even met Larry's father, whose presence in Stacy's life had lasted for only a few weeks, so meeting this man was a step in the right direction. So why did she feel so confused?

She looked up when a loud ringing sound filled the apartment. It took her a moment to realize it was the doorbell they'd installed at the back door, where they received deliveries. She met Tess's and LuAnn's eyes, but both seemed surprised too.

They weren't expecting any deliveries today. Winnie, who worked in the café on the first floor, had already gone home, or else she would have been down there to receive the visitor.

"I'll get it." Tess was already walking toward the stairs.

When Tess's footsteps had vanished down the wooden stairs, LuAnn turned to Janice.

"Are you sure you're all right?"

"Yes." Janice sighed and sat back down at the card table. "Just surprised. But I know it's a good thing." She ran her hand through a pile of dark blue puzzle pieces. It was amazing how many different shades of dark blue there were, navy and indigo and midnight blue, and how they all blended together to make it nearly impossible to tell one piece from another.

LuAnn continued to watch her for a minute longer, and then she turned back to her book. Janice continued to sort the pieces, fitting a few into the right spaces in the mass of ocean behind the sailboats. Janice knew she should go downstairs and work on the laundry, or run a duster around the library, or any one of the hundreds of tasks that always needed to be done around the inn, but it was so peaceful in here. Which, she now realized, meant the machines working outside had stopped. Hopefully they'd gotten the patch of yard they needed uncovered and could start to fix the plumbing problem.

Another few moments went by, and both of their cell phones buzzed. Janice pulled her phone out and saw a message from Tess.

You guys should come down to the kitchen and check out what they found in the yard.

Janice glanced at LuAnn, who was already pushing herself up. *We'll be right down,* Janice texted back.

"What in the world?" LuAnn asked, but Janice just headed for the stairs. It could be anything. Maybe it was another tunnel, like the one in the basement that had been used to smuggle runaway slaves to freedom. Or maybe it was—ugh, she hoped it wasn't bones or anything horrible like that.

Tess was in the kitchen looking down at something on the table. Two men in work boots and heavy coats stood on the far side. These were the workers the plumber Tom Davis had hired to expose the pipes so he could fix the sewer line. They both looked up as LuAnn and Janice came into the kitchen.

"You poor things. You must be frozen," Janice said, at the same time that LuAnn said, "What is it?"

They all laughed, and one of the men, the taller of the two, said, "We're all right. The cab is heated. But it does feel nice to come in here for a bit."

"We wanted to show you this right away," the shorter, stockier man said, gesturing at what looked like a metal cash box or something similar. Tess had laid newspaper on the table underneath it, and it was about a foot long, maybe eight inches high, and about that wide. Judging by the corrosion of the metal and the rust spots, it had been in the ground for a while.

"This was in the yard?" Janice asked. The sewer line ran away from the river, behind the inn, toward the main line that sat under the street.

"The machine hit it, so we stopped and dug it out," the taller man said. "We didn't find anything else around it, but we'll let you know if we uncover anything else." It sounded like an exit line, but both men stayed, looking at the box, and Janice realized they were as curious as she was to find out what was inside.

"Thank you," Tess said, lifting up a metal padlock that held the box shut. It was rusted in spots and covered in a layer of dirt. The keyhole at the bottom was caked with grime and moss. "This thing seems solid."

"I don't suppose there was a key buried anywhere near it?" LuAnn asked. Janice knew she was joking, but the taller man responded as if she was serious.

"I'm afraid we didn't find anything."

Janice ran her finger along the top of the box. The metal was cold, and her finger came up caked in grime.

"We could get it open," the stockier workman volunteered. "It would destroy the lock, but it would get you inside."

Janice looked at Tess and then LuAnn, and realized right away that they were all on the same page. "Please."

The men went outside and returned a few minutes later with a sledgehammer. "Better stand back," the shorter one said, and set the box on the floor. Tess, Janice, and LuAnn all backed up, and he swung the hammer, hitting the lock. Janice flinched, but the lock held, and he swung the hammer again, and once more before the lock gave with a snapping sound.

"There you go." He reached out and pulled the lock off the metal hook it was threaded through. He set it on the newspaper and hoisted the box onto the table. "Give it a try now."

Tess was the closest, so she reached out and grasped the edge of the metal lid with both hands. She tugged, and Janice held her breath. A part of her was afraid of what they would find, and she prayed it wasn't something scary or gruesome. But mostly, she was intrigued.

Tess had to tug a couple times, but then, with a scrape of metal on metal, the lid lifted on its rusty hinges. The smell of must and something sour was the first thing that hit Janice.

She leaned over so she could see inside. What was—was it possible—

"Oh my," LuAnn said, her eyes wide.

All Janice could do was stare.

If you'd like to read the rest of this exciting story, *A Place to Belong* by Beth Adams, visit: shopguideposts.org to sign up for the series or to purchase the individual book.